Out
of the
Running

ROBIN TIMMERMAN

Order this book online at www.trafford.com
or email orders@trafford.com

Most Trafford titles are also available at major online book retailers.

Print information available on the last page.

ISBN: 978-1-4907-9068-8 (sc)
ISBN: 978-1-4907-9069-5 (hc)
ISBN: 978-1-4907-9073-2 (e)

Library of Congress Control Number: 2018910352

Trafford rev. 09/07/2018

www.trafford.com
North America & international
toll-free: 1 888 232 4444 (USA & Canada)
fax: 812 355 4082

J une, sweet June !
On Middle Island, the ditches glow with spreading stands of orange
daylilies.
The roadsides are exploding with pink and purple phlox, rivaling the
best works of the Impressionists.
Even the gravelled road edges produce the color and scent of pink
clover, the gossamer puffs of hairy goatsbeard and the exquisite weave
of queen anne's lace.

In the swamp, a tall blue heron fishes, green frogs rest on lily pads.
Incandescent dragon and damsel flies dart, jewelled wings reflecting
the sunlight.
And rising from the juicy green water, there is the curve of a large,
olive-coloured shell
Small eyes and a heavy snout
A female snapping turtle, about to pull herself up on a moss-
encrusted log.

But at the sound of approaching, thudding footsteps, she hesitates.
The heron grows still, the frogs dive beneath the lilypads.

*The other, larger beings move quickly on the path, breathing hard as
they pass.*
The big snapper slides back into the water.

The runners continue, paying no heed.
They will spare no time to savour summer's beauty
There is ground to cover and a stopwatch clicking in a pocket.
They disappear around a curve in the path.

*The morning is quiet again, the water creatures return to their various
pursuits.*
*The snapper scrambles with her scaly claws and pulls herself up on the
log. She weighs nearly twenty pounds, it's a big effort.*
*But the disturbance is gone, at least for the moment. And the sun feels
so good.*

*   *   *

The first thing they noticed was the shoes, good quality
running shoes sticking out of the grassy verge that bordered the
track. The man-made rubber and leather footwear made a jarring
note against the backdrop of softly nodding pink and purple phlox
flowers and the slender stems of delicate buttercups.

Chief Halstead had given out only terse details.

"A couple of women found the guy, near the kilometer 8 post.
His feet were sticking out of the bushes onto the road."

"Dead?"

"Seems to be. The caller just said that the man wasn't moving
and he looked dead. They were out on a practice run."

Officer Pete Jakes winced. "Lucky they had their cell phones
with them."

Halstead snorted. "Doesn't everybody nowadays?"

"You have to admit they come in handy sometimes, chief."

Pete slowed at the Benson crossroad turn and pulled off onto
the grass. He drew up beside a red Honda, the only car there.
Luckily this was a section of the upcoming Marathon route where

the runners would be travelling right on the actual road, making easy access for the ambulance. Other sections were a gravelled or dirt track that ran past picturesque farm fields and woodlots and made a big curve around the swamp.

A woman was slumped on the roadside, she looked ill. Her friend was tending to her, offering a water bottle. She looked up as the officers arrived.

"Oh thank goodness, you're here," she said fervently, standing up. "I think my friend here is in shock."

Halstead introduced himself as Pete moved quickly across the road. He assured her that an ambulance was coming.

She took a breath. She seemed a sensible woman and not unduly overcome, like her friend.

"Ginny was running on that side and she noticed the colour of his shirt, she thought it was a clump of bright flowers I guess. I had run on ahead but I heard her cry out, so I stopped. She was pointing into the ditch and her face was white as a sheet. When I pushed the weeds aside a bit, I could see the blue and white marathon shirt … on a man," she added.

"Did you touch him?" Halstead asked. "Could he speak?"

"I work at the admitting desk of a city hospital," she said. "I'm not a nurse but I know enough to check for vital signs, to see if he was alive."

That explained her relative calm, Halstead thought.

"He was face down and there was blood under his head," she went on. "I told Ginny to call 911 right away. Then I came to wait with her over here. I went to check on the man a couple of times but there was no change and I couldn't find a pulse. I didn't try to turn him over."

"Chief," Pete called. "Can you come here a minute?"

Halstead excused himself. "Wrap a sweater around your friend," he told the woman. Keep her warm."

Pete was crouched in the roadside weeds, looking down at the victim.

A man, as she had said. Face down in the dirt. He wore running sweats, the Marathon blue t-shirt, and the tell-tale sneakers. The matching marathon cap had flown off and lay in the weeds some distance away.

Pete indicated the awkwardly sprawled legs, the arms thrown out in a desperate attempt to break the fall. Stated the obvious.

"He's been hit by a vehicle."

Halstead nodded, his expression grim.

"Damn." He stood and scowled at the mute trees that lined this bit of the road.

"I knew this Marathon business was going to be bad news."

2

THREE WEEKS EARLIER.

"This way, lads." Bert Jardine greeted the two policemen. "Glad you could come out so quick, it's the darnedest thing."

The Jardine farm was a typically well-kept Island operation. Two hundred acres of mixed grain and soy crops surrounding a century old, three-story red brick home and neatly-painted outbuildings. Six generations of Jardines had lived and farmed on the property, and the blue and white Ontario heritage sign proudly displayed on a post by the mailbox, confirmed this.

Bert Jardine was a big man but showing his sixty-odd years and Pete thought that he would soon be passing on the running of the farm to the next generation, his three sons. A handsome golden retriever, with the affability of the breed, enthusiastically followed his master and the two policemen to a large metal sided garage at the side of the house. The hooped roof and oversized entrance doors showed that the building was used to store farm machinery and equipment.

A crudely smashed lock and dented metal siding definitely looked out of place in such an orderly set-up. Pete nodded to his partner, Jory Stutke to take a picture.

Jardine grimaced. "That's a mess isn't it? Going to cost me a few bucks to fix it too. At least the devils didn't get much for all their work."

He patted the big dog's head. "Thanks to Sammy here, waking us up."

"This was around ten last night?" Pete asked.

The farmer nodded.

"You were all in the house asleep?"

"Yup"

This time of year most farmers were in bed by nine. Then up at 5:00 a.m. to do chores. The thieves could have driven into the lane by the garage and not be seen from the bedroom windows at the back of the house. They could have taken off with a lot more if the dog hadn't woken the family.

"You said they got a chain saw though?"

Bert scowled. "A good one too, cost me near a thousand bucks. Only bought the damn thing this winter. The old one broke when the lads were working down in the swamp."

Pete sighed, already knowing the answer. "I don't suppose you know the serial number or any other identifying mark."

Jardine shrugged, "Never needed to to before this. Ted White, my neighbour has been sharing equipment with me for years. If my chain saw or seeder wasn't here, it was up at his place. Nobody had to break into nowhere. And who wants to steal a chainsaw unless they want to work?"

Unless you can get a few quick bucks for selling the thing.

Pete could see that Jory had the same unsaid thought.

Jardine scowled. "But I guess things are different nowadays."

Yes they are, Bert. As we keep telling you and the other farmers on the Island.

As at last fall's crime prevention workshop. Held in November so the farmers couldn't use the excuse that they had to be out on the land and couldn't spare the time for a thorough discussion of safety measures.

Measures such as checking door and window locks, keeping outside areas well lit, and maintaining fences in good repair. Such as posting No Trespassing signs, using timers and motion sensors, reporting anything suspicious to the police.

And Number One on the list: recording ID numbers on equipment and tools and keeping an up to date inventory.

"The insurance people are going to want that information too," he said.

Jardine snorted. "Good luck trying to get money out of that bunch."

He shifted impatiently. "Seems like a lot of bother to me. In the old days your neighbours kept a lookout." He looked at Sammy, "Or a dog was all you needed."

"True," Pete agreed, "but times are different now. A lot of the younger farmers now have jobs in town, and do their farming part-time in the evenings and on weekends. And all you old folks are going south for longer winter holidays. There were four reported break-ins on this road in February alone."

He wrote out the meagre details of the robbery in his notebook and snapped it shut.

"We get a weekly provincial list of recovered stolen items at the station, and we'll check that out for your chainsaw, Bert. But I can't hold out much hope. Most of this stuff is spirited away pretty quickly."

Jardine pushed his ruined door shut, then moodily accompanied the two policemen back to the cruiser.

"Now there's going to be this blamed marathon and a hundred strangers coming right past our door. Could be thieves or god knows what in the bunch. Who thought up that bright idea?"

"I think that most of the participants will be interested in running rather than stealing," Pete said mildly. He wasn't about to volunteer the information that his wife Ali had been working for the past year with the Marathon organizing committee.

But Jardine wasn't done. "Time was this was a farming community, not a playground for some runners. But nobody wants to do any real work any more. In my own family, the one son is studying computers at college. The other wants to go to work for one of them oil companies in the middle east. And Bobby – well you know about Bobby, he's no help at all. I'll be bringing in the hay myself."

Everyone knew about Bobby Jardine. At thirty, he was still a shambling, child-like fellow big enough to do farmwork but more apt to wander into town and hang around the Village Grill. Semi-autistic some said. His father wasn't sympathetic though, had no truck with labels and thought his son was just plain lazy.

He looked out to a distant hedgerow, a soft blue line in the morning.

"The boys will likely sell the place anyway," he said bitterly. "No respect for what their grandparents and Marg and I made here."

No love either, Pete bet he meant, but was too crusty to say it.

"Old grouch," Jory said as they drove away. ""Wouldn't allow any changes on the Island if he had his way. The Marathon is a great idea."

They covered part of the planned route now, on their way back to town. The event was a charity run, to help raise money for new scanning equipment at the nearby Bonville and District hospital. There would actually be two runs. A half-marathon loop of 21 kms and a shorter 10 km loop for the less hardy.

Participants would hardly qualify for the Boston or similar big city Marathons, but the run had attracted a fair bit of attention. There were the locals of course from the Island and Bonville, the city across the causeway, but thanks to a social media campaign from the Marathon committee, others were coming as well.

Apparently there was a growing tourist industry for people who sought out places to run. The Island, where most of the run would be on gravel or dirt paths, past rolling rural scenery was a big draw.

Jory drummed excitedly on the dashboard. "The Island needs some livening up. It will be fun."

"You just want that medal," Pete laughed. There were no cash prizes as the race was a fundraiser but there would be various medals, ribbons and awards.

"You know it, Jakes. I'm in it for the glory and you're going to eat my dust, old man." Both officers would be making the longer run.

"You wish." *Old man? Thirty-four wasn't old, was it?*

He supposed from fresh-faced Stutke's point of view, the nearly ten years difference in their ages seemed like an eon. Otherwise they were fairly well matched. Both were sturdily built rather than lanky. Both in good shape. Both had blond hair, though Pete's was cut a bit shorter than even regulation required.

Jory sighed. "Of course this isn't a qualifying event. Then we'd get some real runners coming. Like those Kenyans who win at Boston every year. One guy almost cracked the two hour record."

"You never know," Pete said, "There might be a future champion marathoner right here on the Island."

"Here I am," Jory said.

Pete laughed. "It's supposed to be for a personal best anyway, not a contest."

"Ah go on, " Jory. "It's a race alright."

Pete thought of what Bert Jardine had said about change. How he was resisting it.

He guessed that was another downside of aging and made a resolve to resist the process himself.

*   *   *

This time of year, the Jakes ate their supper out on the screened back porch, overlooking their one-acre back yard. Nothing as grand as the Jardine farm of course but they loved every blade of grass, day lily and Manitoba maple in it. They'd met in war-torn, dusty Afghanistan where Pete was serving with the Canadian army and Ali was on a United Nations teaching project and it was still a treat to enjoy Ontario's peaceful country greenery.

Pete was the cook tonight and had assembled chicken tacos and a salad for the al fresco meal. Ali had placed an enormous vase of tall purple iris on the table, next to the salsa and salad dressing.

"We'll have to peek at each other, the flowers are so tall," she laughed. "But they're so beautiful."

So are you. Pretty as the flowers.

He thought he would never get tired of the sight of his wife. As elegant as a dark-haired Turkish princess, she could make even a summer outfit of tank top and shorts look exotic.

She brought two glasses of wine to the table. A police officer and a teacher, they liked to linger over a glass and discuss their respective days. But first they heard from Nevra, their four-year old daughter and the big news from junior kindergarten. The butterflies were hatching.

Kedi the cat's news followed. The big orange stray had infiltrated the Jakes household through a concerted campaign on Nevra's part. Now she interpreted his meowing remarks, which were chiefly concerned with whether any chicken bits were going to come his way.

"You go next," Ali said to Pete. "We had a Marathon Committee meeting after school and I can't bear to go over it all again."

Pete was sympathetic. The preparations had been going on for months.

He passed her the salad bowl. "Jory and I checked out a robbery at Bert Jardine's place."

She scooped out a generous forkful of greens.

"A robbery – at this time of year?" Winter was the more active season for thefts, when folks had left their homes and cottages vacant while they fled to sunnier climes. But now the summer cottages were being opened up, and the homes along the lake were populated once again. A riskier time for thieves.

"What did they take?" she asked.

"Just a chain saw this time. There was other good stuff there but the dog woke up the family."

"One of the regular perps?" she asked.

"Nobody immediately comes to mind. Things have been a lot quieter since we sent the Calder boys off on extended leave in March."

Pete used the local euphemism to refer to the fact that the youths of that particular family were spending several months as the guests of the Bonville District detention centre.

He added a dollop of sauce to his taco. "Of course there's always someone new coming along," he teased. "Some sly young lad in your grade eight class for instance, will be the thief of tomorrow."

"Bite your tongue," she said. "My kids are all stalwart, upstanding citizens."

"Ah the eternal optismism of teachers," Pete laughed.

Ali groaned. "Otherwise how could we do it?"

SLOW. MEN WORKING.

Obediently, Halstead slowed the truck. He might be nearly sixty years old and chief of his police detachment, but like most of his fellow citizens, he accepted the maxim that Canada has two seasons, winter and construction. The first spring robin barely appeared before the road equipment was dusted off and roaring out of the shed. And this was true even for his own small municipality of Middle Island, dangling as it did into Lake Ontario, at the southernmost tip of the country.

At the sign announcing the village, pop. 645, he stopped to talk with the flagman, a burly fellow wearing a safety vest marked with a big fluorescent X.

"How's it going, Steve?"

"Pretty good, Bud. We've still got this section by the causeway to finish. Hoping to get out your way before the big Marathon."

"That'd be good," Halstead said drily, imagining the chaos if the organizers had to arrange a last-minute detour. That wouldn't be a pretty sight. Middle Island was only technically an island and the half-mile long causeway was a vital link to the city of Bonville on the mainland. There was lots of open water on the other three sides, however, all the way to the United States. Any kind of traffic disruption on the causeway caused major headaches. Not too long ago, traffic had been cut down to one lane for nearly two months while crews worked to shore up the road shoulders. The memory was fresh in Islander minds.

The Middle Island police station was a functional building whose bunker-type outline was softened by the office manager's pots of red geraniums. Halstead parked the truck beside her little green Honda and noted that both cruisers were in, which meant that Pete Jakes was already here too. A most dutiful officer, that lad. He and his wife Ali were welcome additions to Island life.

'Lo chief," Jane Carrell said cheerily. She had staffed the front desk for a decade, they didn't stand much on formality.

"Amazing I got here without killing anyone," he grumbled. "It's not safe to drive into work these days, between the hydro crew's trucks and and all those crazy runners on the road."

"All good exercise," Jane soothed.

Several members of her extended family were participating or volunteering in the Marathon event. Numerous teenage nieces and nephews and even a small grandchild. Always a jaunty dresser, Jane was demonstrating an access of public spirit this morning. She tipped the brim of the brand new souvenir marathon cap at him and batted her eyes.

"Suits me, don't you think?"

The cap was cream coloured, with a circular blue crest of Middle Island on the front. He noticed then her blue blazer and cream staight skirt.

He scowled. "Bit over the top,that's what I think."

She pirouetted. "All for the hospital, chief. There's a complimentary cap for you, on your desk."

Halstead plowed on into his office. Passing the coffee room, he grunted a hello to Jakes. Pete filled two cups and followed.

Halstead sank gratefully into the chair that he had carefully adjusted over the years to accommodate his lanky length and aging back. The office was at the back of the station and looked out over a field, this time of year a soothing vista of two foot high greening corn stalks. He woudn't be buttering a nice juicy cob for another month or more.

"Thanks," he reached for the coffee. "I need this, navigating the Island roads these days is like driving an obstacle course. Runners everywhere, and they act as if they own the road. Now I'm under siege in my own office. And this is just the beginning ! I can't wait till the damn Marathon is over and we get our Island back."

Pete raised his cup. "Only twenty more days."

"I'll never make it !" Halstead shifted frustratedly, not even his chair was co-operating today.

"I suppose we should be grateful we're not hosting a professional marathon," he grumbled on. "The competition can get pretty rough in those events. Look at the fuss over the Tour de France the past couple of years. Half the athletes were all pumped up with steroids. What kind of sport is that?"

Pete grinned. "This run is for charity chief. Just a bunch of amateurs out for some fun and exercise."

"And cluttering up the roadways." He drained his coffee dregs, making a face. "But like you said, only twenty more days to go and I'll be counting every one. Enough of that nonsense though, tell me what you found at the Jardine place."

"Not much. The thieves only got away with a chain saw before the dog woke Jardine up."

Halstead nodded. "God bless pooches. Or at least home owners should."

"So I gave him the security speech again."

"Maybe he'll listen this time."

"Told him we'd keep an eye on the OPP list for his saw, but not much hope there."

Halstead nodded agreement. "Pretty hard to track those smaller items." He sighed. "A local job I suppose."

"Likely." It happened every few years. A string of thefts. Cars broken into. Maybe taken for a joyride before being abandoned, hopefully undamaged, on a back road. The perpetrators would be a couple of wild boys, who either were arrested or eventually grew up.

They did sometimes get thieves from Bonville, the city across the causeway, but that bunch usually nabbed more easily accessible items that could be hurriedly tossed into a vehicle. Like the lawn furniture spree last summer, where in one instance they'd actually dismantled and taken an entire gazebo tent.

"The Calder boys are on extended leave at the moment. Who does that leave?"

Pete shrugged. "Whoever lifted the saw, I doubt that Bert will ever see it again."

This was the reality in a rural area, where it would be easy to hide the booty in any of dozens of falling down sheds or abandoned barns.

"We'll just have to keep an ear to the ground."

A course that was often the most useful and practical line of investigation in such cases. The ground, the grapevine, the gossip. Who's got a new chain saw? Sooner or later someone would notice either the seller or the purchaser, who didn't ask where such a great bargain came from.

"Remember the guy who was selling laptops from his van?" Pete said. "He sold five before somebody reported him to us."

Halstead shook his head. "Buyers Beware" - if only they would. We wouldn't have thieves without their markets."

"You got that right," Pete stood. "I'll write up the report."

"How are you coming with the route plan for security on Marathon Day?"

Pete was the reluctant liaison with the Committee. Halstead had decided early on to stick Jakes with the job. One of the perks of being boss.

"You're a natural mediator," he'd told his second in command. "That dutiful, soldier boy face, your steady unbribeable manner."

Now the soldier boy looked frustrated. "It would be a piece of cake, if the committee would just leave it to us and the OPP. All the discussion just gets in the way. But it's coming."

Halstead offered no sympathy. "At least you don't get Marathon morning, noon and night at home. And Steph's guests haven't even arrived yet."

Pete knew that the chief's wife Steph, like all the Island business owners were looking forward to the influx of visitors. Her guest cottages at 'The Retreat' were booked solid for Marathon weekend.

"Rosie's Runners, no less," Halstead groaned. "A team of eight women runners from Merrickville. As if the place isn't full enough of women already."

"Livy's staying for awhile then?" Pete asked. Steph's twenty-year old daughter had returned from a year as an ESL teacher in Japan.

Halstead nodded. "She seems to have broken up with that fellow she was seeing over there. I don't know why and I don't really want to know. Glad to leave that stuff for the mother-daughter talks."

Pete laughed. "I hear you."

* * *

"Vern alert," came Jane's voice.

From her post at the front desk, she could see the arrival of the town mayor and give a useful heads up. Thin to the point of gauntness with sparse greying hair, the mayor always reminded Halstead of the blue heron who returned every year to spear unwitting fingerlings beside the causeway. Although the heron looked more cheerful.

This morning though, in addition to the new cream and blue marathon cap, Vern wore a navy striped tie to brighten up his suit and a beaming smile on his usually dour features. In fact he'd been pretty happy lately. Often left fuming in the David and Goliath relationship between the Middle Island population of 4000 and the ten times larger city of Bonville across the causeway, he was now gloriously triumphant. The big marathon was being held on the Island, and the Bonville mayor and council were green with envy. According to Vern at any rate.

Vern was a reluctant mayor, who maintained that he would be content to simply run his gas station on the west end of the village. Last fall though, when nobody else stepped up to replace him as head of the four person Island Council – Halstead was among the decliners -- it was decided there was no reason to waste money on an election.

The honour hadn't gone to the man's head. Though a fuss-budget, or because of that, he was a credible administrator of the Island budget and there were no major complaints against the council who with the help of the police, supervised the affairs of Middle Island. Other than the usual naysayers of course, who never seemed to understand that if there were no taxes, there would be no roads, clinics, schools, or police presence.

Halstead mustered up a greeting.

"Morning Vern, what brings you out so early?"

The mayor folded himself into a seat. "I've been at the office for hours already," he said pointedly. "These are busy days you know."

"For me too," Halstead said. "That robbery out at the Jardine's. Finishing up the May reports ...." Vern didn't take the hint. The Marathon was all that mattered to him at the moment.

"I was hoping you'd have the Marathon security arrangements ready for me."

"I gave you the draft on Monday."

"I meant the *final* security arrangements."

"There's still nearly three weeks to go, Vern. Pete's second session with the sixty volunteers is on Thursday. Everything is going well. What about you?" Halstead joked. "Going to get out your sneakers and running shorts on the big day?"

"Not me. I'll be up on the platform giving out the medals and ribbons to the runners."

And grinning for the cameras and television reporters, no doubt.

After ten more minutes of reassurances, the mayor finally rose to go.

Halstead grinned to himself as Vern left. What the hell, he was glad the guy was having a good time. Must make a change from municipal budget discussions.

Still he would be glad when Island life could get back to normal summer routine which was busy enough. The Marathon was shaping up to be one huge organizational headache, getting in the way of real work. At least these last preparations should keep the locals busy and out of trouble for a few more weeks. The theft at the Jardine place was likely a one-off smash and grab and wouldn't be repeated or at least not too soon.

The Marathon cap still sat accusingly on the corner of his desk. He picked it up and perched it above his own long, lined face. Bet he looked like an old bloodhound, and the cap was too small by half. He tossed it to the window sill.

Missed. He smirked as it landed in the waste basket.

Gotcha.

Across the polished table of the Bonville city hall committee room, Ali Jakes caught her friend Miranda's glance and rolled her eyes. Miranda, a crisply-spoken septuagenarian, returned the look.

Neither woman was fond of committee meetings and the joint Middle Island- Bonvillle Marathon Committee meetings had begun nearly eight months ago, back when there was snow on the ground and the prospect of a June run had seemed a distant dream.

Then the Friends of the Bonville Hospital came up with the idea of a marathon and the Island seemed a perfect location. Less traffic, easier to block off a route for the day.

But here they were and the dream was actually going to happen. Already in pledges and registration fees, they were nearing their goal of raising $50,000 towards the purchase of new scanning equipment for the hospital.

Though inevitably the committee members had squabbled along the way, Ali thought they all deserved a pat on the back for having got this far without actually murdering each other. Any lingering differences would have to be dropped now for this final push, if the marathon was to be pulled off smoothly. Charlene

Bond, co-ordinator of the committee, irritating though she could be at times, was the right person to get them through that challenge.

Short and sturdy, with large glasses and curly grey hair, Charlene's day job was to supervise a program that allowed people to perform community service rather than serve jail time. Miranda privately referred to Charlene as the 'chain gang' boss, but in fact she had a reputation for being a sympathetic if rather demanding taskmaster.

Now she clapped her hands to indicate chit chat was over and the meeting had begun. Crisply, she asked for reports from the various members.

"Only twenty days to go, committee members. I trust everyone is up-to-date. Barry?"

Barry Beam, was responsible for planning the key part of the entire project, the mapping and design of the Marathon Route. An engineer in the city planning department, he was donating his time as were all the other Committee members, to the project. An easy-going man, he had a quietly humourous way of deflecting Charlene's bossiness.

"Right-o captain," he saluted. "Sunday afternoon I reviewed the entire finalized course with Pete Jakes. We think we've chosen an interesting and attractive run, that includes about half paved roads, and the rest a mix of gravelled sections and dirt trails."

"Not to mention about a third of the way alongside our lovely swamp," someone said drily.

"And it *is* lovely," Barry said cheerfully. "The trail is comfortably high above the water this time of year and there's lots of nice shade for the runners."

Originally there had been some discussion of including lakeside views but that brought other difficulties of distance.

"You needn't worry about a lakeside view," Charlene scoffed. "From what I've read, runners don't look at scenery. At least not the serious ones. – that might shave a second off their time."

Barry continued. "The completed map, with markings for both the half marathon run of 21 kms and the shorter run of 10 kms, will be ready for printing by next Monday. It will also be available on the website."

"Our volunteer crew have planted posts at one kilometer intervals along the entire route. Key points are easily accessible by Island crossroads, for ease of transporting the tables and water jugs etc. for our volunteer way stations. Entrants will never be farther than 1 km from a station or an emergency exit. There will be signs up on any of the road sections to alert traffic of the oncoming runners. Also volunteers in fluorescent vests."

He looked at his notes. "Regarding timing and scoring the runners, we looked into the chip timing option, where each entrant receives a race chip they strap to their leg. But the price was about $2 per entrant. So unless the runners buy their own – and some of them will be doing that-- we'll be timing them manually using stop watches."

Charlene tutted. "That will do just fine. We're supposed to be raising money for the hospital here, not spending it on silly gadgets."

Barry nodded. "Each runner will be wearing a bib with a clear race number. Volunteers will have printing stopwatches - You press the start button and each time someone crosses the finish line,you press the lap button which prints out the finisher's time. There will be a video too, not that I'm imagining any disputes in a friendly run."

"And what are the average times?" Joyce asked. "When can we expect that people will begin to show up at the finish line."

Barry had obviously done his research. "Olympic athletes can complete a full marathon run of 42 kilometers in about two hours. Or the half marathon of 21 kilometers in one hour. That's about twelve miles an hour for our American friends."

There were gasps around the table.

Charlene sighed impatiently. "I doubt that there will be any Olympic athletes participating here. I'm sure that Barry has some more realistic statistics for us."

Barry smiled. "There are lots of exhaustively researched statistics available, broken down by gender, age, etc. but most come up with an average timing of a little over two hours to run the half marathon."

He looked down at his notes. "93% of all participants finish the run in under two and a half hours. 31% in under one hour and forty-five minutes and a speedy 7% complete it in under one hour and 30 minutes. All figures for males and females."

Charlene pursed her lips, as if that was quite exhaustive enough. However Barry enthusiastically added. "40% of most participants in marathons are 29-39."

A collective look around the table. Ali Jakes was the youngest by far, in fact at thirty, the only person in the category.

She laughed. "I won't be breaking any running records, folks. I'll be on my bicycle, supervising my Grade Eight relay team."

"How did seniors fare?" Miranda asked caustically, being a seventy-five year old member of that group herself. "Other than that famous ninety year old Swedish fellow of course."

"I don't have any stats for that group," Barry said gallantly. "But I've heard they do pretty well, even if they run half the route and walk the other half."

Charlene granted a stingy nod of approval for the report and moved on. "Debra?"

Debra Kovak was a former model but there was nothing passe about her looks. In her forties, she was as tall, willowy and coolly blonde as ever. Publicity person for the local United Appeal, she had graciously donated her strong marketing talents to the hospital fundraising event. Early on, she had dazzled the other members by immediately setting up a Website and Face Book connections for the Marathon. She had also signed up plenty of local businesses as sponsors of the run.

She turned to smile at Barry, "As soon as the map is ready, we'll send it out to all our Facebook friends. We're excited that students from the college journalism course will be making a professional video of the run as a term project. Copies will be available for sale later and the money will go to the hospital fund. Though most of the registrants will be taking their own photos on smart phones, I'm certain that they'll also want the video as a souvenir of the run."

Next under Charlene's expectant stare were Joyce Mouton and Carol Potts, who had perhaps the toughest task of all -- organizing the more than sixty volunteers,who would be deployed at the event. Joyce was a retired teacher who joked often that she had never worked harder in her life. Blessed with a still youthful energy and enthusiasm, she successfully ran a mixed crew of other retirees, highschool students and anyone else who wanted to help. Her co-worker Carol was a counsellor at a local youth centre.

"We're up and running." Joyce said gleefully.

Charlene winced - Joyce found her own jokes newly-minted at every use. However, she was invaluable as an organizer, no doubt of that.

"We've been setting up a comprehensive duty roster,' Carol said. "Everything from manning the hydration and first aid stations at the kilometer posts, to setting up the stage and finish gate. After the race, the Island women's institute and Benny's chip truck are going to host a chili supper for all the volunteers."

Charlene looked down the table.

"Ali and Stephanie?"

Stephanie Bind, like Ali, was an Island resident. A vibrant, attractive businesswoman, she had anticipated a growing trend in opening The Retreat, a lake-side lodge where city businesswoman could relax and recharge their batteries.

"It's so much fun already," Stephanie enthused. "We see runners everywhere – entire families. The route has barely been officially marked out yet, but some folks have been practising every weekend for the last month. I've got one team of guests coming early, to have a chance to check out the course."

Steph described the runner's kits she and Ali would be assembling. In each kit there was a copy of the map, a bib with a marathon number, a commemorative t-shirt and cap. There was also an environmentally approved plastic water bottle.

"A hundred and fifty runners have signed up, but we've made twenty-five extras for late arrivals. Runners include both locals from the Island and Bonville and the rest are from away."

"Water and aid stations?" Charlene asked.

"Each station will have an emergency first aid kit and be staffed with a volunteer who has a cell phone to call for assistance. Also a cooler with water available."

Steph laughed. "Though we've read that professional runners in a real marathon wouldn't scorn to give up precious seconds to fill up containers. You should see the water container gadgets advertised in the runner's magazines. Some runners won't even pause to gulp. They carry gels that they can swallow while they run. Or there's a thing like a horse bit that you can wear around your neck."

More disbelief and head-shaking.

"I wonder if the gels come in flavours," Joyce asked.

"Nevertheless," Charlene said. "Our less professional runners - not to mention the children – will need the water stations. And speaking of water and other liquids, have we ordered the portable comfort stations?"

Ali nodded. "There will be four units, positioned at intervals along the route."

Charlene turned to Miranda Paris. "Madame Treasurer – current expenses?"

Miranda consulted her notebook. "The quote for the printing of the maps is $3000. Other expenses include rental of the comfort stations for the day. Another $100 for ribbons and awards. But any necessary equipment and labour for setting up the stage in the park is all being donated. As is all the food and preparation. There's a charge of $250 for the ambulance which will be standing by the day of the run."

Charlene thanked Miranda, and moved on. "Security?"

Joyce nodded. "Officer Jakes will be addressing the volunteers next week to advise them of their various duties along the route." She smiled. "He's going to make a special point of talking about our local turtles."

"Turtles?" Charlene said dubiously, suspecting another joke.

"Yes," said Ali. "Pete wants to alert all the participants. This is the time of year the female turtles will be crossing local roads and trails to find gravelly or sandy spots to lay their eggs. They will probably try to stay out of the way of runners but they don't move quickly. It's important to tell people not to touch the turtles, to leave them alone. Especially the big snapping turtles. They mean no harm, but might retaliate if they feel threatened."

"Right," Charlene said wryly. "We don't want to upset the little mothers. Any further business?"

"There's always the weather," Miranda said. "Who's looking after the weather?"

There were startled looks around the table.

Charlene wasn't pleased. She said dismissively. "The forecast says it will be lovely. We have anticipated every difficulty. What can go wrong?"

"There's been another break-in," Halstead announced. "Not a farm, this time at the hydro equipment yard."

"What did they take?" Pete asked.

"A portable generator from the equipment shack. When the job boss got there this morning, he saw the sensor lights were on. He thought it was some kind of malfunction but when he had a look around, he found someone had been messing with the fence at the back."

The work yard was surrounded by a formidable square of chain link fence. Pete drove in through the open front gate and parked before the big trailer that served as the site office. Bill Baird, the boss on the project came down the trailer steps to greet him.

He was a big, capable looking fellow. Pretty unflappable. Had to be, considering the nature of the work, which often involved sending crews out to repair power lines in the midst of snow and ice storms. A mere break-in would hardly register as a crisis.

"They worked a hole in the fence," Baird said, leading the way around to the back. "Then the sensor lights must have come on and they took off with what they could get."

Pete eyed the spot in the link fence, where a foot or so of the metal had been twisted apart.

"Not the smartest cards in the deck," Baird said. "there's not a lot here except the backhoe and the bucket truck. Could hardly drive away with that."

He indicated the big hydro truck that was equipped with a cherry picker bucket for wire repairs.

"What else was in the equipment shack?" Pete asked.

Baird opened the door. "Some rolls of wire, road cones and flares. A post-hole digger, weed zappers. Warning signs, that sort of stuff. Oh yeah, some fuel too."

"What's the generator worth?"

"About $3500 new. But it wasn't new."

Pete nodded. "Still worth a few bucks to thieves though."

Baird shut the shack door. "There must be easier ways to steal a generator. Lots of folks around here don't even bother to lock up at night."

"I know," Pete said resignedly. "So much for safety workshops! They might better smarten up though if there's thieves around."

He told Baird about the robbery at the Jardine's last week.

"Now this break-in here. You could use something more than the light sensors. Maybe a noisy alarm system too."

"I'll run it by head office for sure," Baird said.

"Could any of your employees be involved?" he asked Baird, as they walked back to the trailer.

The project boss shrugged. "The company is thorough with background checks. And I know all the guys on this crew pretty well. I can show you the roster and time charts for the week though."

The unadorned trailer made a rough workplace but Baird's desk and records were neatly filed and up to date. Pete noted too that unlike the local farmers, Baird had accurate and up to date records of all his equipment – year, manufacturer, model, serial numbers, photos, lists of key holders. There might at least be a fighting chance to track down the generator.

There were eighteen names on the employee list. Baird thumbed quickly down the sheet. "These are the older guys," he said, marking off the first dozen. "They live around here and I've known most of them for years."

"The background checks would be years old too then," Pete pointed out. "Anyone can run into a money crisis. Gambling for instance."

Baird looked doubtful. "The guys get a pretty good paycheck. The younger ones even more. They move around a lot, from project to project. Might spend six months up north for instance, or go to work in a a disaster zone, like Haiti after the earthquake. They like the change, new places and the extra money - hardship pay."

He shook his head. "But I can't see him any of them thieving. Those kids get enough of an adrenalin boost from the dangerous work they do legitimately."

The time sheets weren't any more helpful. Tuesday had been a regular work day and all the crew had gone home by six. Local men to their homes and the other fellows to hotel accommodation in Bonville, arranged by the Ontario hydro corporation.

"I locked up and set the sensors myself," Baird said.

Pete said they'd be in touch and Baird thanked them for coming by.

*   *   *

"Learn anything?" Halstead asked.

Pete filled him in. "I tend to agree with Baird. Doesn't look as if any of his crew are involved. But I'll follow it up."

"Think they could be the same thieves who broke into Bert Jardine's shed?"

"Hard to say."

Halstead pushed back his chair. "How about some lunch? See what the Grill gossips have to say about these going-ons."

The village main street was eight blocks long. In honour of the coming event, a bright banner saying '*Welcome Marathoners*' hung over the street. Halstead had seen the shops and their wares change over the years, but the Municipal Hall, the library and the post office in the back of the drugstore were constants. Although most Island folk bought groceries at the superstores in Bonville, there was also a small grocery store, a couple of convenience stores, and a barber/hairdresser. In recent years, a sprinkling of chi-chi souvenir shops had sprung up for the tourist trade. These were only gradually re-opening after the winter.

The real summer trade came from the water. Boaters stopped regularly at the Island marinas for gas and pop or to stay for a week at a cottage or one of the fishing camps. Stephanie Bind's Retreat for professional women seeking a holiday, was a fancier upgrade. But the farms still predominated the landscape.

The Island Grill, located at the Island end of the causeway, was a fixture. A place to catch up on gossip while filling up on a burger or owner Gus Jones' chicken and chips. The décor which had remained unchanged for years, was dim and cave-like, relieved only by a wall-sized picture window overlooking the four motel rooms at the back.

In a city, the Grill might have been exclusively a man's preserve but on the Island women had little respect for such a restriction and cheerfully met at the Grill as well. They generally sat at the front, away from the bar where a wall-mounted television was permanently set at the sports channel.

A few years back, one of these ladies had suggested that Gus put in an outdoor patio at the side of the building to view the Bay. He had responded to the suggestion by plunking a couple of stained resin chairs on the back porch.

The two policemen were greeted by Gus on arrival. The proprietor was an old hippie whose laid-back manner hadn't precluded running a successful business. He was a hands-on man, usually found behind the counter by his vintage cash register. These days there was a a sign-up sheet on the counter for pledges for the marathon runners.

"Your young Stutke is up to two hundred bucks a klik now," Gus pointed to the sheet. "He's the front runner."

Halstead raised a thumb. The Grill had been the first sponsor to sign up on Jory's sheet. Many other Island and Bonville businesses were sponsoring runners as well.

Halstead led the way to a table at the back, nodding to acquaintances. The TV was on, it was time for the news. The sound was low but someone called out excitedly,

"Hey, turn it up - it's about us, about the Marathon. Look, there we are!"

A cheer went up in the Grill as the screen showed an aerial view of the island. The angle became lower, as the pilot cruised along the pretty shoreline.

The scene shifted back to the newswoman at the city television station.

"Marathon Mania is rapidly building on Middle Island. Long a favorite destination for local boaters, the Island is hosting a first Marathon run on June 22nd. In partnership with organizers from neighbouring Bonville, their goal is to raise $50,000 towards purchasing new scanning equipment for the Bonville and District hospital."

"The run is open to all area residents and in fact anyone else who wants to participate. Runners can find registration and sponsorship details on the Island Marathon website."

"To add to the excitement, two well-known local personalities are organizing rival teams in a challenge to raise the biggest contribution to the hospital fund. Our news team held interviews with the two men today."

"Hey," said Gus, as a burly silver-haired man appeared on the screen. "There's Andy Kovak."

A retired hocky player, Kovak was a popular local man who was a part-owner in a summer hockey camp in Oshawa. The interview seemed to have taken place at his home along the shore near Bonville. A big man in his late forties, but still in good shape, he posed in running shorts and the Marathon t-shirt and cap, mugging cheerfully for the camera.

"We've got a great team revving up in daily practises. We're ready for the challenge." He raised his arms above his head in a Rocky victory salute. "Yeah, Kovaks' Krushers !"

The next interview began with an outside shot of CKAS, the Bonville radio station. The camera moved inside to the lobby where the interviewer spoke with Don Rusher the manager of the station, again a well-known presence in the city. In his forties as well, but the thin, wiry Rusher looked more the part of a Marathon runner.

The man could certainly run off at the mouth, in fact was famous for it. A bundle of raucous energy, that he exhibited daily on his morning phone-in show. Talking a mile a minute, arguing vigorously with callers, spewing corny jokes.

Today he too wore the marathon gear of t-shirt and cap. In typical mode, he trash-talked the rival team.

"Rusher's Runners are gonna bury you, Kovak. Better warm up your car-washing arm."

In addition to the money they were raising, the interviewer explained, the men had agreed to a forfeit for the loser to pay. Personally washing and waxing the winner's car in a segment for the television news. The item ended with a shot of the two rivals, posing with Vern and the Bonville Mayor.

"Good for them," the waitress said. "That should pull in a few more bucks for the hospital."

Gary Plug, who ran one of the local marinas, grunted sceptically. "Rusher is likely glad of a chance to beat Kovak."

He waited for someone to ask why.

The waitress obliged. "OK why?"

"Kovak stole Rusher's wife."

"No kidding?"

"Well she wasn't his wife yet, but they were practically at the altar. The church booked, the invitations sent out. Then Kovak came to Bonville to play for a season with the Bonville Bears and that was that. The lady chose the new guy."

Halstead had a distaste for gossip. "Her privilege. That was nearly fifteen years ago and they stayed married all this time. That must be pretty old water under a pretty old bridge."

Gary shrugged. "Old feuds die hard."

*　　*　　*

Ali saw the replay of the Kovak/Rusher story on the six o'clock news. There was a bit more to the clip, some film footage of the Kovaks.

The newsanchor explained, "Mr. Kovak's wife is the former Debra Toller, model and now chairwoman of the Eastern Ontario United Appeal fund."

The film showed Debra Toller smiling beside her husband. Her upswept blond hair perfectly coiffed, she wore a smartly cut navy suit with a red silk scarf. Some enterprising junior at the TV station had even dug up some still shots from Debra's modelling days.

Pete whistled, "I can see what all the fuss was about. She's still a good-looking woman."

Ali nodded. "I've met her, she's on the Marathon Committee."

The clip ended, moving on into commercial and Pete pressed the mute button.

"What's she like?" Pete asked.

"Why do you want to know?" Ali teased. "Are you smitten?"

He waited.

She shrugged. "Debra's alright, hard-working. Some of the committee members find her a bit full of herself at times but she's been getting great publicity for the run. She handles all the social media work, started and maintains the Facebook page."

"She and Kovak have been married awhile, have kids?"

"I don't think so, she never mentions them anyway."

"What about the radio guy, Rusher?"

Ali shook her head. "I don't know anything about the man, except that he hosts a morning radio talk show and has a very irritating manner."

She pulled up her knees on the couch and frowned at him. "Now you've got *me* curious, darn it. Why all the questions?"

"I've got gossip," he teased back.

"So, give."

"It's pretty old gossip," he admitted. "When the news played at the Grill today there was a bit of talk. Seems the beautiful model

Debra used to date irritating radio guy back in the day. Till a certain hockey player stick-handled into town and into her heart."

Ali made a face. "I'm shocked – not so much at the gossip but at your pitiful analogy."

And she tossed a pillow into his chest.

The women ran smoothly in tandem, well into the second kilometer of their morning run. They wore light clothing, silk shorts and sleeveless tops and had caught their hair up in tight topknots. Above their heads, the sky and treetops unrolled in a frieze of bright blue and green. They were both teachers at the Bonville High School who had taken advantage of the freer hours of exam week to work in a run on the marathon route before classes. One woman wore an earbud and was listening to a Beethoven symphony. The other, the gym teacher, preferred to go with her own running vibe. Occasionally they looked at each other and gave a little nod or wave.

But rounding a curve in the track, the gym teacher exclaimed as she skidded off balance. She put put out a hand to stop her running mate.

What the heck is that?

Ugh !

Her friend took out the earbud and held her nose.

7

Halstead and Steph were early risers, enjoying the morning peace with each other on their private patio overlooking the lake. Soon the guest cottages would be occupied but today the view belonged only to themselves and a family of mallard ducks. By long-standing agreement, they didn't turn on the television or radio till seven a.m. Of course Halstead couldn't turn off his phone, he was the chief of police, entrusted with the safety of his Island flock. But this morning it was thankfully quiet.

"Livy still asleep?" He asked, reaching for more juice. Steph always made everything so appealing. The orange juice sparkled in a tall glass pitcher, the cloth was laid even for two, outside the open window, poppies and iris bordered the flagstone pathways.

It had been three years now, since after a decade of widowhood and solitary coffee breakfasts, he had been blessed by marrying Steph. He could still hardly believe his good fortune. Newly fifty, Steph glowed with life, from her trim body to her barely grey-streaked black hair. Vivacious didn't begin - she was the whole thesaurus entry. *Lively, spirited, bubbly, sparkling, dynamic.*

She nodded. "Livy's still dealing with a bit of jet lag I guess. She mentioned getting her bike out this afternoon though."

"A nice day for a ride," Halstead said and bit into a perfect croissant. He knew better than to offer any more comment, such as,

A week seems a bit long for jet lag. It will do the girl good to get out riding and stop moping over the boyfriend break-up.

But Steph caught the unspoken thought anyway.

"Livy will be fine," she assured, though she looked a teeny bit anxiously toward the house. "She's got that job interview in Ottawa coming up and in the meantime she can help with the Marathon. We need all the volunteers we can get."

That resolved, she turned happily to her day book which was crammed with details respecting the Retreat preparations for guests.

Halstead smiled. Lucky Steph. Happy in her work.

He was too, he guessed. At least at quiet times like this.

*   *   *

Jane looked up from the counter at the entrance of the two women in running gear, made a quick assessment and called back to the office.

"Hey Pete, can you come out to the front desk please."

He came quickly, "What's up?"

Jane wrinkled up her face and pointed, "Some people to see you."

He'd caught the smell already, winced.

"Hi Corrine," he greeted the woman holding up a pair of sneakers at arms length.

He knew the Bonville high school gym teacher well. They both coached student sports teams, girls' basketball and boys' hockey respectively.

"Hi Pete," she grimaced. "Got a present for you." She dropped the sneakers on the counter.

"A run in – literally with some dead fish – sorry Jane, I used the bag for the rest of my outfit. It's in the washer at the Island Wash and Go."

Jane shuddered. The laundromat patrons were going to love that.

Corinne turned on Pete, "And don't you dare laugh. There was a big pile of fish guts in a little dip on the trail, by the K3 post. No way I could stop, I skidded and fell right into the mess."

Pete held out his hand to ward her off, sputtered. "I can't help it. If I don't laugh, I'll puke."

It was infectious. Corrinne's friend was laughing, and Jane too. Corrine waited resignedly.

"O.K." she said finally. "What are you going to do about it mister upholder of the law?"

"Probably just some kids getting up to mischief," he protested.

"I thought that too," she agreed. "But you have to clean up that mess. Somebody could get hurt. *I'm* hurt, I'm going to have a heck of a bruise on my butt tomorrow."

Pete nodded. "O.K. we'll get on it. Thanks for coming in."

"The marathon committee aren't going to be happy about this," he said to Jane. "Could be a real headache if the kids have any more tricks up their sleeve."

"Should I call Steph or Ali to arrange a volunteer to do cleanup?"

"No that would take too long. I've got just the fellow in mind, he just drove up."

Stutke wasn't pleased. "Why me? Call some kids."

"It's an investigation of a misdemeanor. Calls for police work. Don't forget to take a shovel," he called to Jory's retreating back.

*　　*　　*

"Ugh." Jory lifted the last shovelful of messed-up fish glop and hefted the load to a spot about ten feet from the trail.

As he was walking back to the cruiser, carrying his wiped but still odorous shovel, he spotted a girl on the trail, kneeling by her bicycle. He recognized Livy Bind, Stephanie's daughter.

He nodded as he came up to her but didn't expect much of a conversation.

They were never in the same crowd at high school. Actually Livy wasn't with any crowd, not even the artsy fartsies. She'd always been sort of spacy, off on a cloud of her own.

He saw that the chain had slipped off and stopped politely, to ask if he could help. The White Knight. She was managing quite handily though, and had almost got it. Then it slipped off again.

"Darn!" she muttered. She looked up at him, "I've tried a few times but I guess it's shot."

"You hold the bike steady," he said. "I'll pull the chain on."

He could see the problem though, the chain had some badly twisted links.

"What the heck did you do to it?" he laughed.

"It's been in the garage for a year," she said ruefully. "I should have checked it before setting out."

Jory set the chain back on the grass. "It'll have to go to Win's shop. He'll fix you up with a new chain and look the rest of the bike over."

He looked around, at the isolated bit of trail. "I could give you a ride back to town."

"That's O.K.," she said. "I've already phoned my Mom and she's bringing the van."

He stood there a bit awkwardly, it seemed rude to just leave Livy on the roadside alone.

'So you were in Japan right?" he ventured. "What was that like?'

She shrugged. "Interesting. I met some nice people."

A shadow flitted across her face. He remembered some Island talk that there had been a boyfriend over there, a Japanese guy.

She swiped at a drifting bit of poplar fluff, caught it in her fingers and gave a little smile. "It's nice to be back home though."

"You look good," he said. "Different."

Downright cute in her shorts and tank top.

He knew enough never to tell a woman she'd gained weight. But in this case, it was all to the good.

"I like your hair that way." Smooth and bouncy. Not so much wild witchy woman.

She smiled. "Thanks. I see you joined the Island police force. I thought you might have gone to the city."

His turn to shrug. "I figured what would they do without me?"

"I'm sure they're glad to have you. Bud is always saying it's tough to get officers to come to the Island."

Livy called the chief Bud, since he married her mother three years ago to the approval of all concerned. It was good to hear that the chief might be pleased to have Jory on the force. He just wished that he'd been on a more dazzling police assignment than shovelling dead fish. So maybe he just wouldn't mention it.

She turned at the sound of a car motor and he saw the van coming along the road, raising up small clouds of dust round the wheels.

Damn.

Steph stopped the van and opened the back. "Mom to the rescue!"

Jory helped the ladies load the bike, though they'd have been fine on their own.

"So you're running in the marathon, Jory," Steph said. "That's a pretty impressive pledge amount you've raised."

"Thanks." At least that was better press than being a dead fish shoveller.

"See you around," he waved them off.

Wonder if Livy would ever come out for a beer.

Should have thought of that before.

Double damn.

In the van, Livy looked suspiciously at her mother. "What's that look for?"

"What look?" Steph asked innocently. "I was just thinking that it was good of Jory Stutke to give us a hand."

"He's a policeman," Livy said. "He's supposed to help people."

"Of course he is, dear." Steph slowed, while a mourning dove took her time to rise off the road.

They drove silently for a bit.

"What's Jory doing these days anyway?" Livy asked absently, looking out the window.

"He's a policeman." Steph said.

"I meant who does he hang around with?"

Steph thought. "He was seeing Gayle Palmer for quite awhile – going steady is what we used to say, what do you kids call that now? But I think they've broken up. Why?"

Shrug. "No reason."

A *lovely June night.*
Herons coming in from their evening fishing to roost in the high old snags at the swamp.

Folks sitting on their porches, not even talking, just listening to the music of the frogs who will sing for hours yet.

Young lovers sitting in pick-up trucks in the gloaming, looking out at the lake.

A peaceful night.

But elsewhere there is skulking movement.

The thieves had upped their game. This time they'd been successful.

Pete drove into the parking lot of Barry Tripp's ATV dealership. Tripp was a mechanic and operated a garage but as a sideline, sold the all terrain vehicles. There were often a half-dozen of the machines on the lot.

Barry was coming out of the shop, wiping his oil-streaked hands on a dirty rag. He was an amiable, well-liked fellow despite often having to deliver news of expensive car repairs to his clients.

'Lo Barry.'

'Lo boys. Thanks for coming out so quick. I didn't even notice that the vehicle was gone till a half-hour ago."

The two policemen followed him around to the side of the building where the remaining five vehicles were parked. The black and gold metal flanks gleamed in the morning sun.

"Nice," Jory whistled. "You've got the new Yamahas."

"Yeah and the thieves knew what they were doing. Took the one deluxe model. A $10,000 dollar machine with all the bells and whistles. 421 cc, liquid-cooled, single cylinder engine. A beauty, sweetest machine on the lot."

"So what time was this, do you figure?" Pete asked.

"It wouldn't matter," Barry said ruefully. "We were all away yesterday at my niece's wedding in Hamilton. Stayed overnight. But everything was locked, the machines chained up, like usual."

"Alarm system?" Pete asked.

Barry sighed. "Under repair. The guy from Lok-Tite was coming back with it today."

"Who would know all this?" Pete asked. "That you were away and that the alarm system was off."

Barry looked sheepish. "Almost anybody who came by or into the shop lately. I guess I might have been grouching the way you do about how long it takes to get things fixed these days. But like I said, the gate was locked at the back, the machines were chained up."

Pete looked over at Jory. Both knew it was the work of a few minutes to cut through the chain links. The trick was to have an alarm system to alert an owner re the damage. It wasn't rocket science but it was amazing how many folks refused to take the system seriously. Sometimes he felt like asking robbery victims if they actually knew what the words 'alarm system' meant. But there was no point in adding to Barry's troubles right now.

"It's a nice machine," Barry said. "I sure hope if someone just took it for a joyride, they didn't roll it in some ditch on the crossroads."

"Hasn't turned up yet," Pete said, though he didn't sound too optimistic.

"Nobody could ride it publicly around the Island," Barry said. "Far as I know no one else has bought one of those models yet."

"Dumb kids might not think of that," Pete said. "But if the machine is that noticeable, somebody will report it. You think they just drove it away?

Barry shrugged. "That would be the easiest way. Why bother trying to haul it?"

Pete walked over to the other machines. "Who would have had a key to start the thing?"

"Just me and the wife and we lock the keys in the safe at night." He grimaced. "Trouble is there's not a lot of different keys out there. And the wife found four different sites on the internet last night to tell you how to start a machine without a key. Whole videos about how to do it."

"Any suspicion who they might be? Locals I guess."

Barry looked at Jory. "You'd likely know the current crop of young joy-riders better than me these days."

Jory grinned. "I'll be asking around."

Barry sighed. "I hate to think what this is going to do to my insurance rates. They're already sky high."

"Have you checked with the neighbours – they see or hear anything?"

"There's only the Hutchins, Morley and Moira. Morley goes to bed about eight o'clock every night and I hate to upset Moira with any news about thieves. She's a nervous old biddy already."

"Any ideas?" Pete asked Jory, as they drove away.

"There's Barry's own son, Scott," Jory said diffidently. "I didn't want to say anything there, but Scott is a bit of a hot rodder."

"Barry said they were all away at this wedding."

Jory shrugged. "Scott's got buddies."

Pete frowned. "That would be kind of nasty. But if so, at least the vehicle will turn up soon. Better go do some scouting around."

"Sure. It will make a change from shovelling up dead fish."

*   *   *

The chief didn't hold out much hope of recovering Tripp's machine.

"I doubt that a fancy, new vehicle like that will ever turn up on the retrieved property list."

Pete had got into the habit of checking the list daily for the Jardine chain saw. Curious, he moved the cursor to ATV thefts.

"Listen to this -- last week, there were twenty ATV thefts in Eastern Ontario alone."

Halstead snorted, "A popular item. How many found?"

"One abandoned roll-over in a ditch. Front wheel wrenched."

"Ouch, that would smart. Any accident reports?"

"Looks as if the thief preferred to stay anonymous."

"Ah well, wouldn't be Barry's vehicle yet."

"Right model, wrong colour anyway."

He continued on down the list. "There's a couple of chain saws here. I'll jot down the info for Bert Jardine but of course he's got no way to prove the equipment is his, even if he does recognize it."

"Any leads there?" Halstead asked.

"Just a spite call, reporting on a neighbour's son. When I went to check, the kid hadn't even been at home that night. He's gone to Saskatchewan to work."

"Think this ATV incident is connected with the others – the Jardine theft and the break-in at the hydro station?"

"Could be. We'll see what Jory finds out."

He studied the computer screen for a few minutes.

"Hey, listen to this. Chain saws and ATV thefts are just small potatoes these days. Thieves are moving into heavy equipment theft for the big bucks. It's a multi-million dollar, international problem. Construction equipment, like back hoes. But even that stuff is beat out by farm equipment. It's so specialized nowadays that a machine like a combine harvester can cost half a million bucks."

He read from the list. "Even a plow can cost $60,000, a hay baler $100,000, a combine $200,000. Makes sense of that joke about the farmer who won the lottery. Said he was going to pay off his debts to the bank, then buy a lunch pail and get a job somewhere. Now he's got to worry about his equipment being stolen before he's made the first payment on the machine."

Halstead shook his head, marvelling. "What do they do with the stuff – how do the thieves get the machines to the buyers?"

"Apparently they stow the stolen tractors and other equipment in those big shipping containers and ship it out to countries like Africa and Dubai. There's a huge market, this article says. With some of the stuff like the tractors, they strip the motors and batteries to sell on the black market here."

"And get this, only nine percent of stolen agricultural machinery is ever recovered."

"Shouldn't affect us much," Halstead chuckled. "Never mind Dubai, how would they get the stuff fifty miles away? We live on an island. How would anyone spirit away a combine harvester – on a boat?"

"Trucks go back and forth on the causeway all the time," Pete pointed out.

"O.K. maybe you could move out an ATV but that's about it." Halstead shook his head. "Good luck to Barry then if that's what happened. And goodbye to his ATV. It's probably on the way to Quebec by now."

"But we've got enough headaches right now. I'm not about to start worrying about some international equipment thieving ring."

"*Why is a baseball umpire like an angry chicken?*
They both have fowl mouths."

Pete waved from the cruiser at a quartet of women in sports gear, running along the side of the road. Hoped there was no fish offal awaiting them on the trail. So far there hadn't been another incident.

He'd been listening to the CKAS morning news, which always included a short humourous commentary. The guy was no Robin Williams but he was pretty good. Corny but good.

> "*How about those Jays? Did you get that pitch last night – Ouch !*
> *Come on trade-offs !*
> *What do baseball players put their food on?*
> *Home plates*
> *And in local news, what about that construction on Johnson Street? I'm not criticizing our roads department but really ..... three weeks to fill a couple of pot holes?*"

Unfortunately this was followed by Don Rusher's call-in-show, *Your Turn*. Rusher's Turn, more like. It seemed that no matter what a caller said, Rusher disagreed. Usually mockingly. Often caustically. But the callers must like the abuse because they kept calling in. And people kept listening.

These days Rusher shamelessly used his show to plug his team's participation in the Marathon and announce how much they had raised in pledges so far. He'd even erected a big red and white fundraising thermometer on the street outside the station. Because of course the publicity wasn't hurting the station either.

Now he boasted. "Hey folks, have you checked our thermometer lately? Rusher's Runners have already raised $10,000 in pledges. Our closest competitor have only raised $7000."

"But hey, all the money is going to the hospital, so we're all winners here. Just sayin .... Some of us are better at bringing in the moola. And we haven't even got to the actual run yet. So come out this evening and watch our practice at Bonville waterfront park. Or better yet, join us ! Let's double those pledge numbers."

Pete wondered what Andy Kovak thought of all this razzing and how he could combat it with his own publicity. If it was winter, he could easily present an exhibition hockey game, local team vs old-timers event. But that wasn't an option in June.

As he drove, Pete automatically scanned the properties, fences, and yards along the way. He stopped briefly to check with Bill Baird at the hydro station. Various crew members were getting ready to head out on the road. The burly boss was in the trailer going over schedule sheets. He looked up and greeted Pete.

"Head office approved the alarm system," he said. "The alarm company guys are coming this morning."

"Good," Pete said. "Noise is really the most effective deterrent. At least if there's anybody around to hear it."

Baird nodded. "There's been a couple of break-ins in the northern stations too. The systems will soon be mandatory for all the field offices." He looked out at the yard.

"We patched the fence. Any follow-up yet on who tried to get in?"

"Not yet. Like you said, it doesn't look as if any of your guys were involved."

"I heard about some kids pulling tricks on the Marathon Trail – think they might have been at our fence?"

Pete laughed. "Not unless they planned to leave you a bunch of dead fish ! And it would take some strength to use those wire cutters."

He stopped for gas at Byer's station and Vern's son Tom came out to the pumps to say hello. Father of twin toddlers himself, young Byers was as cheerful as his his parent was gloomy. Still, he was concerned about the ATV theft at Barry Tripps.

"I lock up every night of course," he said. "But I'm thinking of getting one of those new computer type systems. The ones you can check even if you're on vacation. Of course Dad thinks that's nuts. He says that nobody ever stole gas from him, that folks used to be honest."

Pete swiped his credit card. "Guess your dad is conveniently forgetting the hundred years of smuggling on the lake here."

Tom laughed. "I guess he is."

"Yep, crime never goes away, criminals just update their methods."

At the station, the front desk was empty, Jane had gone to the post office for the mail. He found the chief and Jory in the lunch room, with coffee and a bag of double chocolate chip cookies between them on the table. They had the door open to listen for any visitors at the front. Jane was likely to be awhile, the village post office was better than the newspaper for 'gathering news' as she called it.

Pete poured his own coffee and joined them. Jory was in the midst of reporting that he hadn't heard or found any information on the ATV theft.

"Sorry, not a thing. No boasting about the theft. No stories or hints."

He took another handful of cookies. "And it hasn't turned up in the ditch anywhere either."

Halstead looked askance at the fast-emptying bag.

"When you've done stuffing your face, Stutke, I've got something else for you to look into. Turns out the thieves weren't the only busy folks out and about last night.

Jane got calls this morning regarding three more vandalism incidents on the Marathon trail route. A direction arrow moved, landing a runner in the swamp. Another smelly fish treat, and a pile of dog doo at one spot."

Jory rebelled. "You're not sending me out to clean that one up, Chief! Someone on the Marathon committee can handle it. Beside how do you know it isn't just some lazy dog walker who isn't picking up?"

"Because she'd have to be walking an elephant," Halstead said drily. He scowled. "These tricks are getting to be a real pain in the butt."

"Where are the incidents happening?" Pete asked. "Near any particular spot or all over the place?"

Halstead looked at Jane's notes. "The fish incident was at marker K3. Looks as if the other two are near markers K5 and K6."

Pete took up the map of the marathon route and smoothed it out on the desk.

"The road doesn't intersect at all of those markers. How are they getting there?"

"I've seen bicycle tracks." Jory said.

"Kids, like we thought." Halstead shook another cookie out of the bag. ""Where do you think they're getting the fish guts? That's pretty smelly stuff to cart around."

Jory nodded. "I thought about that. I think it's the remains of dead carp. There's always a few who get stranded and die at the lake edge at spawning time."

"Ugh," Pete said. "Corinne said she had to throw those sweat pants out. The Wash and Go folks wouldn't allow them in her machine."

Jory laughed. "You have to hand it to those kids though, they're determined. They must have bagged the stuff up somehow and dragged it to the trail. I don't know how they do it without throwing up."

"It's not funny," Halstead glowered. "We get one marathoner with a sprained or broken ankle and we're looking at a harmful mischief charge, maybe more."

"So, no ideas at all re the perps?" Pete asked Jory again.

Though Pete had learned a lot about the local residents in four years, Jory was a born and bred Islander. Raised on a dairy farm, grew up with manure on his boots. Had attended the Island school and knew all the families.

Jory shrugged. "There's a new crop of kids every year. Can't be high school kids though, they have to catch the bus to Bonville too early to get the pranks out. Besides, the stunts seem pretty dumb. I'd expect the older kids should have more imagination."

He chuckled, remembering. "Like the time that Zak Sorda and some buddies dragged an old privy out to the school front yard and left a scarecrow sitting in it. The scarecrow looked like a teacher we all hated."

"Lucky it's not them, then"

"On the other hand," Jory continued, obviously enjoying the novelty of his superiors asking for his opinion. "really young kids couldn't get out that far on the track. Not without their parents noticing. So I say we're looking at the 12 to 14 year old group."

"Ali's kids," Pete said. "The grade sevens and eights. I'll talk to her, ask if she's heard anything, To keep her ear to the ground."

Halstead scowled, "There better not be any more nasty surprises coming up. Seems these days it's busier at night on the Island than in the day. We'll soon have to change our shifts."

He handed Jory the report sheet which Stutke reluctantly took.

Pete collected the cups. "I suppose we could look on the bright side, maybe the kids will spot the thieves or vice versa."

Middle Island Elementary schoolyard rang with the excited shouts of eighty-nine children, this year's entire student body. The one-story yellow brick building was build in a utilitarian el-shape with a flagpole out front. What it lacked in charm or grace, was made up for by extensive grounds that many an inner-city school staff would have envied. The building housed classes from kindergarten to Grade Eight, older Island students then took the school bus across the causeway to Bonville.

Today was outdoor field day. In the senior playgrounds, Ali Jakes and school principal Eileen Patrick were overseeing the grade eight students relay race. Both women held stopwatches and shouted out encouragement as each runner completed his or her lap on the quarter mile oval track that circled the field.

There were nine boys in the class this year and seven girls, divided up into two mixed teams to race each other on the split track. Now the second last relayers were finishing up their stint and the last two relayers waited to grab up their batons.

So far, with the occasional lag, offset by a burst of speed, the two teams had pretty well kept in tandem. But Team A had an advantage in reserve. Tiffany Stenhouse, a pony-tailed, long-legged soccer player and the best athlete in the school. Ali clapped as Tiffany scooped up her baton and running flat out, easily left Trevor Corman in her dust. Seconds later, she skidded into a long slide at the orange chalked finish line.

"How did we do Mrs. Jakes?" she gasped, looking up at Ali.

"You cut off two minutes," Ali said. "Great run everybody," she added as the rest of the relay runners straggled in.

"Have a break and get yourselves a drink." She nodded at the cooler under the tree.

Eileen grinned happily. "This marathon excitement is a wonderful boost for our physical fitness program, I must say. No more complaints about practice."

The relay runners had spent some time choosing team names. Some Ali had to reject out of hand. The boys all wanted some superhero reference of course *New Ninjas, Spidey's Speeders* and the like. They rejected with disgust names like *Run for Fun,* though *Run Like a Girl* got some votes. The girls liked *Fast Women* and *Wonder Women.* Eventually the groups settled not too reluctantly on the *Island Contenders* led by Tiffany vs the *Victory Laps,* led by Trevor.

Of course the marathon wasn't supposed to be a competitive race but tell that to the kids, Ali thought. And there was no harm in the teams practising with a goal to achieving their personal best.

The marathon event had prompted lots of research and interesting discussion in class. Trevor had come up with the technical definition of a marathon -- a long-distance running race with an official distance of 26.219 miles or 42.195 km.

"Does anyone know how this distance was decided on?" Ali asked.

Tiffany had obliged with the information that the distance was roughly the distance in Greece from Marathon to Athens. The original marathon had been instituted in commemoration of the fabled run of the Greek soldier Philippides, who had run from the Battle of Marathon to Athens, to report a victory.

"He died after giving the message," Tiffany finished.

There were groans. "Gee thanks, Mrs. Jakes," said Trevor. "That's kind of a downer."

"You're not running the whole twenty-six miles," she pointed out dryly.

Tiffany continued, "The Marathon was revived at the beginning of the modern Olympic games in 1896."

Jason, the class math whiz, had the timing statistics.

"Nobody knows how long it took that guy Philippides to run the twenty-six miles. But in 1896 the winning time was 2 hours 58 min and 50 seconds or nearly three hours. Only men ran then. In 2008, the winner ran it in 2 hours, 6 min and 32 secs. So in a bit more than a hundred years, the men's time has been cut by almost an hour."

"Women have been running marathons too", Tiffany bristled, switching her pony tail. "Even though they weren't allowed to compete officially. It was felt the exercise was too taxing," she added indignantly.

"But in 1967 a woman named Katherine Switzer made history when she became the first woman to officially run in the Boston Marathon. No one noticed she was a woman until two miles into the race. Then a race official ran after her and tried to pull off her bib number ! But she kept on going. Someone took a picture of the incident and that got other women involved in changing the game for women athletes."

She paused to look at her classmates, particularly the girls. "There was still a long struggle ahead though. Women were finally allowed to run in the Boston Marathon in 1972. In 1984 the women's marathon was introduced at the Summer Olympics and won by an American woman with a time of 2 hours, 24 minutes and 52 seconds."

"And "– Tiffany finished with a flourish – "in 2017, fifty years after her first run, Katherine Switzer at seventy ran the race again with the same number that she wore in the famous picture."

"Thank you Tiffany," Ali clapped. "Excellent research."

The girl grinned impishly. "I forgot to add one thing. In 1977, women runners designed the sports bra and shorts."

Hoots and catcalls from the boys.

"Why aren't you running in the Marathon, Mrs. Jakes?" A girl asked.

"I'm supervising your relay race, remember? But I did run 10 ks on Sunday with my husband," Ali said. "I believe my time was a respectable hour and ten minutes."

"Not bad, Mrs. Jakes," Tiffany approved.

"Thank you. But I will now rest on my laurels. I prefer cycling."

* * *

"So, what do you think?" Ali asked Eileen later, in the office. "I hate to believe that any of our kids messed up the trail like that."

Eileen shook her head. "These pranks are going way beyond fun now."

Ali agreed. "This will give you a laugh, though. Pete asked whether any of the kids have been acting strangely."

Eileen rolled her eyes. "They're thirteen years old, did you tell him they all act strangely, all the time !"

On her desk was a printed list of the school's senior students. Sixteen grade eights and fourteen grade sevens. The women didn't need to look at the list, they knew all the children well.

Eileen sighed, said practically. "Someone's doing these pranks. And Pete's right, the perpetrator is probably one of our little darlings here."

Reluctantly they agreed on some possibile suspects, all boys.

"I suppose we're being sexist," Ali said.

"No," said Eileen, "just realists. It obviously wasn't Tiffany or anyone on her team. They're too wrapped up in the run."

"Trevor then? Or someone on his team?"

"I can't see Trevor doing it," Eileen said. "Maybe someone else on his team though."

"But why? It's not as if they're achieving anything with the tricks. Tiffany isn't going to be scared off. It doesn't make any sense."

Eileen laughed, "Of course not! Teenagers don't make sense."

Ali joined in. "Still," she said finally, "we'd better have a talk with the class. You can do it, Madam Principal and I'll case the room for tell-tale smirks or giggles."

The classroom was the usual noisy melee when Ali opened the door. They quieted though, at the sight of the Principal. Eileen was popular with the children, had known most of them through all the grades in the Island school. She spoke in a friendly tone.

"I'm sure you've heard of the recent incidents on the Marathon Route."

A chuckle from some of the kids. "Something fishy, you mean," somebody said.

Eileen smiled. "Yes I can see that could seem sort of funny at first. But the woman who fell into the mess had to get all her clothes cleaned. And she could have seriously hurt herself. The same with yesterday's incident of moving the signpost. We don't want any of these visiting Marathoners from the city to get lost, do we? Some of you will be going to high school next year. You don't have to stop having fun but you do have to start thinking like an adult and taking responsibility for your actions."

"Why do you think it's one of us?" asked Jason. "Isn't that kind of unfair? Aren't kids innocent until proven guilty too?"

"You certainly are," Eileen agreed. ""We're not asking anyone to be a tattle-tale. The community has put a lot of effort into organizing this Marathon and we want it to be a fun occasion for all. Think how badly you'd feel if anyone got hurt."

*   *   *

Kedi took up most of Nevra's pillow. He liked story-time too.

"Why do I have to go to bed now, Daddy?" Nevra asked. "It's not dark yet."

"It's eight o'clock though, honey," Pete said. "Look at your clock. School will be over soon and you'll be able to stay up later."

"How late – till morning?"

"You wouldn't want to do that. But here, listen to this poem. It was written by a Mister Stevenson a hundred years ago. It's about a little boy who felt just like you."

In winter I get up at night
And dress by yellow candlelight
In summer, quite the other way
I have to go to bed by day.

And does it not seem hard to you
When all the sky is clear and blue
And I should like so much to play
To have to got to bed by day?

Nevra was thoughtful, running her fingers through the cat's thick fur.

"How could he be a boy if he's a hundred years old?"

Pete closed the book. "Good night, you two."

He found Ali in the red chair, bare feet curled up, finishing her wine. She'd already reported about her session with the students that afternoon and that she had no suspects.

"It's not possible that any of your little darlings could ever get up to some tricks?" Pete was skeptical. "We'll see."

Now, cheerfully ignoring the sheaf of English papers waiting for marking, she flipped idly through *Runners World* magazine.

"Wow, seems the Marathon craze is sweeping the world. And it's a bonanza for business. Steph says there's been a run on stopwatches at the Bonville Walmart. Some of them are pretty fancy. And expensive ! The gadgets measure everything from your heart rate to something called your cadence."

"What the heck is that?" Pete asked.

"Apparently the number of strides the runner takes per minute." She showed him the picture. "Your old stopwatch is obviously hopelessly out of date."

"It'll do," he said, though mentally making a note. Stutke would be measuring his cadence, no doubt.

"It's the same with the clothing," Ali marvelled. "We won't even talk about the shoes ! But jackets can run from $200 and up. Depending on lightness and portability,"

"And on brand names of course," he said dryly.

"Maybe I'll order one of these," she pointed to a canary yellow jacket. "We could get matching ones," she teased.

He rolled his eyes, "No, we couldn't."

"Ah come on, it could spice us up a bit."

"Do we need spicing up?" he asked absently, reaching for a couch cushion.

"Maybe," she tossed the magazine aside and joined him on the couch.

"Guess what comes up next month?" she poked him with her elbow. "Our seventh anniversary !"

"You didn't give me a chance to answer," he protested. He dropped his arm around her shoulders. "Seven years," he mused, "I'll never forget the first time I saw you at the school. All the kids were staring at you too. You were so pretty, like a flower in that wasteland."

She turned to look at him. "And now "?

"Just as gorgeous," he assured her, stroking her long dark hair.

"Maybe, but I'm not twenty-four anymore."

"Neither am I," he said reasonably.

She sighed, "Sometimes I wonder how we're going to keep our love fresh and alive."

He nuzzled her neck. "I hope you're just kidding. The romance is still very alive and kicking as far as I'm concerned.'

She turned and snuggled into his embrace. "Oh you know what I mean. That's *now* at anniversary number seven. But what about anniversary number ten, or fifteen?" Look at the statistics."

"We'll beat the odds sweetheart."

11

Bonville and District Courthouse
Courtroom Three
Hon. Margaret Pinder presiding

M onday morning session at the Bonville Courthouse. Pete
noted the usual suspects, loosely scattered over the first
three rows of benches. Some with their own lawyers, others with
appointed legal aid juniors. The judge hadn't yet arrived, the dais
was empty.

He made a quick survey of the benches. Three speeders he
guessed and likely more than a first offense, at least one impaired
charge, a couple of scared shoplifters and maybe a minor assault.
He sometimes thought that those facing charges missed the
sheltering corners and darkened alcoves of the old courthouse. The
new building with its large, high windows and bright fluorescent
lighting was not kind to unfortunates who were wincing from
hangovers, or suffering from withdrawal of various substances.
Most were subdued by their experience and dully accepted their
due from the judge of the day.

However there were always a few who wanted to dispute the charges, especially speeders. Then there was the case of Island resident, Ernie Perkins, who had not been jailed but was being charged for non-payment of the $300 fine for illegally parking in the handicapped spot before the Island Public Library. This was his second offense.

A judge couldn't allowably roll her her eyes, but Pete was pretty sure he heard Madam Pinder sigh. Perkins was defending himself. His right of course, but a tedious process.

Pete was called to describe the reason for the charge, which he did succinctly, finishing with, "The handicapped spot in question is well and properly marked both on the pavement and with signage warning of the fine imposed for such an offense."

The bailiff asked the defendant to stand. Perkins, a heavy man in his sixties, hauled himself off the bench with much heaving and puffing. He stood with his cane.

Madam Pinder gave the standard warning re the risk of defending oneself.

"This is your second appearance before this court, sir. I ask you, has anything changed in this situation? Have you done as I ordered and applied for the handicap sticker for your vehicle?"

"I shouldn't have to," Perkins said trucelently. "I have a right to go to the library, same as anybody else. This isn't a police state, not yet anyway. It's a *public* library, says so right on the sign."

Madame Pinder knocked her gavel.

"I have warned you that I will not tolerate such frivolous waste of the court's time and expense. $300 fine and the next time you come, there will be a sentencing."

Pete had spotted a fellow officer in the room. Randy Miller from the Bonville OPP detachment.

"Coffee?" he signalled.

After the session, they took the stairs to the cafeteria on the second floor. The room was airier and lighter than the former facility in the basement of the old courthouse. But the machine-generated coffee was as vapid and from experience, Pete knew better than to pay for a sandwich from the other machines. He settled for a bag of corn chips and a coke. Miller braved the coffee.

He'd been in the courtroom regarding a contested speeding ticket. When the accused was confronted with the actual camera evidence that he had been travelling at 140 km/hr. in a 100 km zone, he claimed that the camera had messed up.

"They'll try anything," Miller said philosophically. He was about Pete's age, but had been on the provincial force since police college and spoke from experience.

"And now the texters are even worse. I stopped a woman last week – I'd been watching her at the stoplight. She was holding the darn gadget in her hand and she tried to deny it."

Pete shook his head. "Texting, like the police needed another headache. So dangerous too, as if impaired driving wasn't bad enough. What's the scoop on that backhoe theft up near the highway? I heard about it on the radio, coming over here."

The operation had been brazen. Apparently the thieves had arrived at the Case Equipment sales lot, just before closing. The manager was in his office going over the day's sales, there was no window at the rear of the building. The thieves just backed their own trailer into the lot, loaded up the brand new backhoe and drove away down the highway.

Miller nodded ruefully. "Quite the haul. The machine was worth $200,000."

Pete whistled. "Wow. And nobody saw them?"

"If they did, they didn't question it. Would you? It's not like some guy running away with a snatched purse. It would have just been a truck pulling a trailer, a sight we see everyday around here."

Miller grimaced at the last swallow of coffee. "They've got balls, I'll give them that. Either they're real smart or just dumb lucky. You should have seen the look on the Case manager's face. The guy just couldn't believe the machine was gone."

"That sounds like more than dumb luck," Pete said. "They must have had some inside information."

"We'll be looking into it, that's for sure. We had a briefing the other day even before the incident. The higher-ups are starting to think there could be a gang operating in the area."

"I've read about those overseas markets. Pretty lucrative. Looks like a lot of planning and a lot of work."

Miller smiled wryly. "Yeah, but who couldn't use an extra million bucks? And it's not always outside thieves doing the stealing. I saw a report where a farmer in Western Ontario stole a bunch of equipment from his neighbours. Tractors, hay balers, Dodge trucks, he took it all. And nobody suspected him."

"Now doesn't that just warm your heart."

Miller shrugged. "Keeps us working anyway."

"Probably won't affect Middle Island folks much," Pete said.

Miller differed. "Seems like a prime target area. All those farms, lots of pricey, tempting equipment. And you said that ATV hasn't turned up anywhere yet."

"An ATV weighs maybe five or six hundred pounds," Pete said. "Even a mini backhoe weighs a ton, let alone one of the big diggers. You'd need a big, visible trailer. Who's going to risk getting that off the Island? And I doubt these gangs are much interested in chain saws or ATVs."

"Somebody's buying them."

"True," Pete acknowledged. "Hopefully folks have learned a lesson and will keep better track of the serial numbers on their equipment."

"We can hope," Miller said. "On another note, how are the Marathon plans going?"

Pete groaned. "Like all plans made by a committee. Too much discussion. But they're not a bad bunch, they're pulling it all together."

"I guess you've been hitting the trail regularly?"

"Now and then."

"Go on," Miller scoffed. "I bet you're out there every chance you get. How's your time?"

Pete knew that Miller and another officer were running to represent the OPP.

"1:45:2 last time I ran."

Miller was impressed. "What about that kid Stutke? I hear he's pretty good."

"Hey it's about personal best," Pete protested. "Not a race."

"Sure, Pete, all us old guys tell ourselves that."

They took their garbage over to the waste bin. "See you on the trail,' Miller said.

There were more dejected looking people waiting outside another courtroom for the afternoon session. It was a relief to open the big plate glass door and step out into the warm afternoon. Pete stood on the steps, glad to leave the building and all those convoluted lives behind.

* * *

Jane was watering the geraniums at the front of the station. She carried a bright yellow metal watering can, which she filled from a hose at the side of the building. She waved cheerily to Pete.

"Everybody's out but me. The coffee's on. I'll join you in a minute."

When she came in, he filled two cups and brought them out to the front desk, where he hung about indecisively.

"What's up?" Jane asked, noticing at last.

"You're a woman," Pete said.

"Last time I checked," she said drily. "I might be a tad over the hill or at least looking down the other side. But still a dame."

He looked abashed. "Sorry. I just need some female advice."

She sat down, pushed aside a pile of reports and said happily. "Fire away."

"Ali mentioned our anniversary last night," he said. "Our seventh."

Jane clapped her hands. "Congratulations! That's so nice."

Seeing his face. "It isn't?"

"It's great. It's just that I think Ali would like me to come up with something special this year. And I haven't got a clue what that would be."

"What did you do last year?"

He shrugged. "We went out for dinner at a nice restaurant."

Jane nodded, "Traditional, but always a winner in my book. Tom and I are coming up to our thirty-second. What did we do for our last anniversary? – Oh yes, now I remember – we were in the maternity ward at the hospital, waiting for our granddaughter to be born. So can't top that for excitement."

Pete smiled.

Jane continued in happy reminisence. "But let me think back to the early days. We never had much money and of course Tom was on the road so much – in fact we could almost count on it that any special occasion, kids birthdays, whatever, he would be called in to drive."

She paused, "But our thirtieth was special, our daughters held a party for us and invited all our neighbours -- maybe you could hold a surprise party."

Pete looked dubious.

She chuckled and patted his shoulder. "Don't sweat it handsome. You and Ali are in no danger of losing your spark. You come home with a fistful of flowers, a dinner invitation, and your smiling face, that's all any woman wants."

"If you say so. Thanks anyway."

"I say so. How was court, the usual suspects, I suppose. Nothing new, or interesting?"

"Not on the docket. Theft of a backhoe though, at Case Equipment up by the highway."

He described the incident.

"That's a little different," she said. "And here the chief is always complaining that criminals have no imagination these days. Wait till he hears about this."

"Miller thought it was more dumb luck than any imagination."

She shrugged. "Oh well, better boring though, than all that shooting and violence in the States. Me, I'm sticking to my battered Agatha Christies for my bedtime reading. Did you know she's never gone out of print?"

"You have to wonder what she would have thought of cyber-crime though."

Jane tutted. "I'm sure that she wouldn't have been surprised at anything criminal that humans got up to."

She waved him away. "Now, be off with you. I've got reports to get at."

He headed for his desk, regretting that he hadn't checked out the jewellry store when he was in Bonville. Although he hardly knew what to get. Ali already had a nice turquoise necklace and earrings, that had once belonged to her grandmother.

"Turquoise is the French word for Turkish," she'd informed him. "Because the mineral was first brought to Europe through Turkey, from mines in Persia. So it's not surprising that I adore the colour."

He could picture the necklace on her now, it certainly complemented her honey-coloured skin. Sigh.

Maybe he should get her a nice combine harvester or a backhoe for a gift. Sounded as if the machines were more expensive than most diamonds.

What do other men do to celebrate anniversaries, he wondered. He might ask the chief, he must have some ideas. Whereas Jory probably couldn't even imagine an event so far in the future. He was probably years away from settling down yet.

12

Jory turned into the by-way at Simpson's side road and parked the cruiser. This was the closest access to the Km 9 post. Jane's note said a couple of runners had noticed some damage to the post, thankfully no fish or dog crap today.

He had the Marathon map in the car but hardly needed it. He knew pretty well every inch of the route, had worked with the volunteer crew himself to mark it out last week. The km posts were of course set a km apart but had been placed as near as possible to local lanes, crossroads, farms and corners for quick identification.

Some of the posts had been quite a job to put in, luckily they'd had a post-hole digger. But the trail shoulder was a bit looser here and he guessed the work hadn't held. He only had to walk a short distance before coming upon it, like all the others a three foot pole of raw lumber, with a yellow stripe and black number painted on the top.

But Km 9 was leaning over drunkenly. As if somebody or more likely somebodies had tried to snap the post off completely but hadn't succeeded.

Well isn't that the limit.

He grasped the post, trying to push it back in the ground. But it had splintered near the bottom, the thing was a goner and would have to be replaced. He yanked it fully out from the hole and tossed it on the grass. Brushed his hands off on his uniform pants, then looked thoughtfully up the track.

It was a pretty spot, and on a June day, looking its very best. The leaves on the bending maples were at their fullest, shading the track from both sides. A mourning dove cooed. Simpson's tractor, a mile beyond the farmhouse, buzzed softly as a far-off bee.

Jory shook his head. Dammit, you kids, now you're starting to tee me off. You think I haven't got anything better to do than go around cleaning up your messes?

Joke's over, enough's enough. A lot of folks are looking forward to this Marathon run and you're not going to ruin it.

On the way back into the village, he veered suddenly into the Canadian Tire parking lot. Not because he had a dire need of motor oil or a flashlight battery, but because he saw Livy Bind stepping out of a car at the chip truck. It was just about lunchtime. He often stopped at Benny Sorda's truck on the store lot for a burger. The sight of Livy there was just a nice bonus.

Livy was at the counter, waiting for her order of fries. She smiled at Benny. "Still my favourite place to eat on the Island."

Benny smiled back. "And that will get you extra ketchup my dear."

"Seems to me I heard a rumour you were retiring."

Benny made a face. "Maria says I'm underfoot at home, so I come in here a few hours a day. For better or worse, but not for lunch she says."

"Mom tells my Dad that too," Jory said. "Could mean more business for you though, Benny. All the retired guys can meet here for lunch – you could start a club."

"Did you get the bike fixed?" he asked Livy.

Today she was wearing jeans, a plaid shirt and a baseball hat that read Kyoto Japan. He of course was in uniform, basic black short-sleeved shirt, with a yellow stripe down his pant legs.

"Yes thanks," she said. "But I'm driving today. Mom sent me into town to pick up some plants."

She indicated the back seat of the vehicle, crammed with pots of begonias.

"She's got an entire garden at the Retreat but she decided to put hanging baskets on the guest cottage porches as well. Bud says he's going to bunk in his man-shack for the duration."

Jory laughed, then nodded at her cardboard plate of fries. "Take out, or eating here?

She eyed him. "Here I guess. You too?"

"Yep, my lunch-time burger."

"I'll get us a table."

There were a half dozen wooden picnic tables placed on the pavement apron before the chip truck. Some were occupied, though many of the customers carried their burgers and cold drinks back to their own vehicles and drove off to their respective work sites.

"You didn't get a fish burger," Livy teased, when Jory joined her.

He grimaced. "No way, I probably won't eat fish for awhile. That was disgusting."

"Any sign of the perps yet? I heard they've been at it again."

"Several times," he said ruefully. He itemized pranks one, two and three. "Number four you don't want to know."

"And no clues at all?"

"I found some bicycle tracks."

She laughed. "Not mine, I hope?"

Through a bite of burger, he shook his head. "Not yours. I've got a few ideas but the mafia's got nothing on those kids. They're not going to crack and rat on their buddies."

She grinned. "Can't really argue with that. And they're pretty smart too."

Like Jory, she probably knew every inch of the trail. Island-born, they and their playmates had wandered the Island back-ways and by-ways on foot or on bicycles, throughout their childhoods. The spots that the kids had picked to lay their messy booby-traps were the locations that they would have chosen as well.

"Still, I hope they lay off now," she said more seriously.

"Before Marathon Day anyway. We don't want anything screwing that up."

"I certainly hope not. A lot of people are involved, and a lot of money for the hospital too. Mom says that you're already getting two hundred dollars a kilometer in pledges."

He raised his paper cup, saluting his sponsors. "My practise time is pretty good. I should be able to get it close to an hour and half. That's the goal anyway."

"So you're pretty sure of yourself," she scoffed.

"Have to be. I've been razzing my partner Pete Jakes about him being an old man and how I'm going to beat him."

"Officer Jakes?" Livy said. "He looks in pretty good shape to me."

"How about you?" he challenged. "Thinking of entering?"

"Mom wants me to help at one of the water stations. I'll probably do that."

She finished her fries and wiped her fingers on the napkin. Looked around.

"Will you be going travelling again?" Jory asked diffidently.

Livy shrugged. "It's a big, interesting world. I'm going as far as Ottawa next week for a job interview with a foreign aid agency. What about you? Still happy on the Island?"

"Sure, I guess so." Thought he'd been. Up to now.

A little silence. She balled up her napkin.

"I'd better get those begonias out to the Retreat. Mom will be waiting."

She turned as a rusted blue pick-up came spinning into the lot, almost causing another patron to drop her drink.

All the people at the picnic tables looked up.

"Who's that jerk?" Livy asked.

"Just a jerk," Jory said sourly. But he knew the guy, a thin, dark-haired wiry fellow in jeans and a feed cap who now came slouching out of the truck. "His name's Rick Farron. He went through high school a few years before us. He doesn't like cops since the chief put his brother away in the nick."

"What had his brother done?"

"Beat up another guy in a bar. Pulled a knife on him."

"Ouch."

"Rick's not that bad. He lives with his mother actually, and even has a respectable job, driving for Samson's the Mover. I'm still glad that it was Pete not me, who had to book him for speeding last winter. Farron has enough against me just for being a cop."

"It must be hard sometimes being a policeman in the area where you grew up," she said sympathetically.

"Sometimes," he agreed.

As Farron passed the table, he tipped his hat and said with a smirk.

"'Lo Stutke."

"'Lo Farron. How's it going - I see you got your license back."

"Ought never to have been took in the first place. I had to thumb a ride into work every day for a coupla months."

"Just doing our job. The police don't make the rules, we just enforce them."

Farron snorted derisively. And he kept on going.

Livy looked to be going too. Jory couldn't think of a good reason to keep her there.

She did smile though and say it was nice to run into him.

"I'm off on Saturday," he called after her. "How about a bicycle ride down the Point?"

"Sure," she said. "As long as we don't ride into any dead fish."

He watched her leave. As he backed out the cruiser, he saw in the mirror that Farron was giving him the finger.

That was definitely one of the down sides of being an officer of the law – he couldn't return the gesture.

13

The new ATV glowed like a shiny black and gold bee even in the dim recesses of the old barn. A beam of sunlight cut down through the dust of the empty loft, to caress the metal curves of the vehicle parked in a bed of straw.

Bobby Jardine sat on the black leather seat, leaning like a race car driver over the handlebars.

"Vroom, vroom," he cooed, startling the swallows who were nesting high up in the hewn wood rafters.

Tufts of his fair hair stuck out from under his baseball cap and with his round pale blue eyes, he seemed more like a big kid than than a thirty year old, two hundred and twenty pound man.

"Cut that out," Rick Farron said. "You'd better get off the damn thing. You'll scratch it."

Bobby looked pained, on his strangely flat face all his expressions appeared exaggerated, like those of a silent movie actor.

"I won't scratch it. Look I got my special soft sneakers on."

Rick sighed, "OK but be good and quiet – I need to put this new padlock on the door."

While Rick worked with hammer and screwdriver, Bobby vroomed quietly and watched the swallows swoop in the sun-dusted upper reaches of the barn.

Then he chuckled. "Hey Rick, did you hear about the lady runners sliding into the dead fish on the trail – that was funny. And yesterday somebody changed the signs so the runners went in the wrong direction."

"Yeah I heard about the fish, must have been somebody as dumb as you who carried them out there."

"I wish I did do it, I thought it was pretty smart. But they say it was likely just some kids."

Rick wiped his hands on his jeans and tested his work a couple of times. He'd debated about using the padlock at all. Even though the barn was disused and way up Turners Lane that nobody had driven along for years, the sight of a new padlock could look suspicious. On the other hand, he didn't need some nosy kids discovering the hiding place.

"I wish I could ride it for real," Bobby said plaintively. "You don't need to have a driver's license to drive an ATV, so I'm allowed."

"Well you can't ride this one. Come and help me put some straw around this stuff."

Bobby grabbed a pitchfork, then easily hefted a bale.

"That's a pretty nice chain saw. Dad paid a lot for it. Serves him right though, he'd never let me touch it. He doesn't think I can do anything right."

Farron grunted as he dragged over another bale. The barn was on an abandoned property and the only window was twenty feet up in the loft. But he wasn't taking any chances.

"I guess I was lucky. My old man took off when I was a kid."

"Was he nice to you?" Bobby asked. "Did he say you were smart and stuff like that?"

"No. Like I said, we were lucky he left."

"Yeah well I wish I was lucky like that."

He stacked another couple of bales. "What time is it? I gotta go real soon."

Rick looked at the wall of straw they were making. "Where do you have to go?"

"I just gotta go. I got an appointment."

"With a doctor or what?"

"I just gotta go."

"OK whatever. Just help me finish with this friggin' straw first, though. Hurry up!"

Rick bumped the pick-up carefully back down the half-mile of laneway. The dirt ruts were stone-hard and deep. Where the lane met the road, both men got out and dragged brush across the entrance. Farron dropped Bobby off in the village and watched him lumber away.

What a clueless oaf. Strong as an elephant though, really strong. Comes in handy And that ATV is gonna make me some money. Those guys over in Bonville said they'd give me twenty percent.

* * *

Middle Island Library
Open Mon. Wed. and Fri, noon till four.
Saturday, ten till two.

Miranda Paris turned the sign on the front door to *Closed*, and withdrew to the back room where she kept her coat and purse and various office supplies. One wall of shelves was neatly stacked with bins of materials for the children's Saturday morning craft activities. In an alcove, there was a small fridge from which she now took out a pitcher of lemonade and a plate of her own home-made gingersnaps.

Emily her border-collie mix lay down on the floor to guard the cookies.

"Patience, my dear," Miranda said. "You know Bobby will give you a bite."

She sighed. Emily was probably Bobby Jardine's biggest fan, and heaven knows, the young man could use a friend or two.

He hadn't done too badly in public school on the Island where everyone was familiar with his slower speech and slightly lumbering gait, but once he took the bus over to the high school in Bonville, he'd been teased pretty unmercifully and on a regular basis. Like baiting a bear, Miranda thought.

And poor Bobby's response seemed to be OK if they think I'm dumb, I must be dumb. There was support from the teaching staff at the high school but with no back-up from home, they could only help so much. It was a foregone conclusion, Bobby had left high school as soon as his dad got sick of trying to force him back there.

He'd spent the last few years working on his parent's farm, though by all accounts, without much thanks for his efforts. And little pay.

Things changed though a year ago, when Miranda had hired Bobby for a few days to help with spring cleaning at the library. Part of the job involved moving out boxes of used books that were going to benefit the humane society sale in Bonville.

At one point she found Bobby turning pages in a children's story book that featured photos of a cocky little Jack Russell pup. He was chuckling at a photo of the pup being chased by a big white duck.

She laughed herself, "I like that story too."

"We had a duck like that at the farm," Bobby said. "We were all scared of her."

"Would you like to keep the book?" Miranda asked.

Bobby shook his head. "Nah, that's OK. I've got other books. I just liked the pictures in this one." He replaced it carefully in the box. "I can read grown up books you know."

Miranda spread her arms, encompassing the stacked shelves of the room. "You haven't had a library card since grade school when you came with your class. Why don't I make you out a new card now."

At the end of the day, she handed him the card. "A travelling pass to other worlds," she said.

The next day Bobby approached her hesitantly. "I heard you can get that high school diploma thing without going to school," he said.

She nodded. "Would you like to do that?" she asked.

"Yes ma'am. Then I could get a driver's license and have my own car."

"It's not easy. It doesn't happen overnight."

"As long as I don't have to go to school. Have them all laughing at me."

"There are places where people won't laugh at you. Where there are other students who learn differently."

"I'm not going to any kind of school, no ma'am."

Miranda considered. "You could come to the library when it's closed and I could help you with what they call qualifying courses. When you've done well in them, we'll see."

"It would have to be a secret ma'am. In case I don't pass. Then nobody will know."

"You'll pass." Miranda said.

In fact after months of hard work, Bobby only had one more qualifying course to go. He'd still have months if not years of hard work after that, but as Miranda told him,

"Knowledge shouldn't be rushed. You can take all the time you need."

As Bobby was emphatic that the lessons be kept secret, she wondered how he would get to the sessions. But Bobby said his mother drove into the village most days and could drop him off at the Island Grill. Other times he just hitchiked in. Everybody knew Bobby Jardine and didn't mind giving him a lift.

He was certainly one of the most eager students she had ever taught. He would tap softly on the front door, the tap out of all proportion to his size and greet her with a big smile. Then tiptoe elaborately in, after taking an exaggerated view of the street. He seemed to love the clandestine nature of their project.

Then he would make a big fuss over Emily and slip her a cookie.

The lesson took about an hour. Some hours were harder than others. Discussing R.L. Stevenson's poem about the summer sun, for instance.

Though closer still the blinds we pull
To keep the shady parlour cool,
Yet he will find a chink or two
To slip his golden fingers through.

It was that 'golden fingers' metaphor part, that was the difficulty.

In her years of teaching, Miranda had always found it horribly ironic that the most difficult course for many students was English grammar and literature. The student's own language. Bobby had a particularly difficult time of course, but they struggled on.

Privately she wondered what poetry had to do with getting a drivers' license. But her short-range goal was to hopefully help him pass a qualifying test on English proficiency. And in the long run, who knew? In the meantime, a little learning could do the man no harm.

At the end of the session, Miranda would pour more lemonade and they would sit and chat for a moment. Emily leaning in bliss, as Bobby knew the special place to scratch behind her ears.

"Are you practising for the Marathon, Bobby?" Miranda asked today.

He shook his head. "Dad says the marathon is for morons." He laughed. "He calls me a moron though, so maybe I'd be good at it. That'd be a good joke on him."

Miranda clucked with frustration. "Your father's wrong, the marathon is for heroes, it's named after a hero." She told him the story of Philippides, the Greek solder who made the original run.

"That's a good story,' Bobby said. "Too bad the guy dies at the end. But like you say he was a hero."

Miranda smiled. "So perhaps you might run in the Marathon after all."

"No ma'am, maybe sometime. But I'm too busy right now. Real busy."

"That's good Bobby, I'm certain you are a big help to Mr. Samson with the moving."

"I've got other business too, important business. But I can't say nothing about it right now."

"That's all right. Just keep making time for your lessons. That's important too.

"And remember your grammar. "It's 'I can't say anything.'

*   *   *

That evening at home in her celery coloured house across the road from the Jakes' home, Miranda sipped her wine. She was watching a television documentary that Charlene had mentioned. The story of a big city Marathon.

"What is this compulsion to run?" she asked Emily. "Oh, I know your reasons for running, you just think it's fun. And you come from a long line of doggy forebearers who had to run to chase down dinner."

She looked back at the screen. "But these people are just moving from one flag to another, nothing is being accomplished. And they seem to take it so seriously. Look at their faces, the strain. What's wrong about a pleasant walking pace, when you can hear the birds, smell the flowers, talk to a neighbour?"

There was the obvious observation she supposed, that running was literally an escape from troublesome events or thoughts, even if only temporary.

For some it seemed a kind of meditation.

"It just feels marvellous," the girl with the glowing face was saying on the television.

"It's something direct and positive to do," said a young man. "A clear goal to shoot for. An achievable goal, not like most of life's challenges."

"A statement for health in an unhealthy world," said another.

"Peace and solitude," said a young matron fervently. "Just me and my I-pod".

Hmm. Miranda took another sip and shook her head.

"No sirree," she said to Emily. "That wouldn't be my idea of solitude. Not in a packed run with hundreds or even thousands of other people. If I'm seeking solitude I'd rather walk or sit on a log, or a rock by the lake."

An ad came on and she pressed the mute button.

"But it's a shame that Bobby thinks he shouldn't run," she said. "I could just shake that Bert Jardine for the way he treats that lad. It's no credit to Bert that Bobby has turned out to be such a nice fellow. It's a wonder he hasn't gone bad."

14

The big snapper turtle swims through the thick, green water. Her camouflage is almost perfect, there are even patches of slick green vegetation growing on her carapace. She's lived in the swamp now for twenty years, content among the reeds and cattails. Her life little varied and uneventful, but pleasant.

But this year is different, something more is required of her. She's beset by an unaccustomed restlessness. A need to leave the confines of the water, but to go …. Where?

She's got huge, clawed feet for digging. She wouldn't look out of place in prehistoric times. And now they will be needed for a new kind of digging.

She feels the strange, new compulsion strongly this morning.

But just as she's about to pull herself up on the road, there are more of the pounding feet.

Then a high-pitched wailing sound.

It's not a hawk, or a crow or any other bird.

It's like nothing she has heard before.

15

Sun streamed into the Retreat kitchen, bathing the owner in its warm glow. Steph, wearing an elegant Japanese robe - a gift from Livy - sat in her favorite window seat, going over a list of the day's tasks.

She heard Livy on the stairs. Her daughter was staying in her old room and this morning in cotton pyjamas, with her hair touseled and rubbing her eyes, didn't look much older than her former eight-year old self. Of course that little girl hadn't craved caffeine.

"Coffee's hot," Steph said, looking up from her notes.

Livy poured herself a cup, left it it black and ambled over to the window. "I'd forgotten how pretty it is here in the morning, by the lake with your peonies bobbing in the sun. You've made a lovely place here, Mom."

Steph smiled. "Thank you sweetie. There were definitely a couple of scary decisions to make along the way, but they seem to have worked out. I haven't gone bankrupt yet, anyway."

"Oh mom!" Livy bent down to hug her. "You never will. Opening a haven for tired businesswomen to recharge their batteries was a great idea."

And so it had proved to be, almost instantly popular. Guests were welcome to cook meals in their individual cottages but Steph provided kitchen facilities for some larger gatherings in the lodge in the evenings. Groups of women would book the Retreat for various pursuits. The lawn could be dotted one week with easels, and ladies in sunhats painting scenes of the lake. Another time with prone bodies on yoga mats.

Steph had a helper for cleaning and housekeeping tasks, and she hired a cook/caterer for the larger events.

Livy noticed the calendar in her mother's lap. "More bookings?" she asked.

Steph nodded. "Yes, for September. Another sketching group, they want to catch the fall colours."

"And we haven't even had our first swim of the year yet!" Livy protested.

Steph flipped a page. "I could show you a booking for Thanksgiving."

Livy emptied her cup, and looked a bit wistfully out at the lake. "I wonder where I'll be in September."

"Wherever you like, dear," Steph said with wary gaiety.

Just not as far away as Japan, please. Not nearly as far.

"You're happy to perch here for awhile dear, aren't you? At least for the summer. There are other attractions than just the lake – there's that handsome Stutke boy."

"He's cute," Livy agreed. "But hardly enough to keep me here on the Island, Mom, if that's your game. Honestly – you're so transparent!"

"Can't blame a Mom for trying," Steph laughed. "Here comes Bud."

"I'm on the run," the chief said. "Late for an appointment with Vern."

"What, no breakfast?" Steph teased. "We've got croissants."

She popped a couple in the bag for the ride.

At the station, though, he found Jane and Pete hunched together over the dispatch phone, faces looking serious. He didn't need Pete's upraised hand to know enough not to interrupt. Jane seemed to be doing the talking, obviously trying to calm the caller down.

"Please ma'am, just try to describe what you're seeing, where you are, any landmarks. Then we can get an ambulance out to help your husband."

She turned to Pete, mouthing the woman's words "..... Pine trees, a farm-house not too far back. You parked the car, then you were running for about ten minutes ... can you see a kilometre post?"

She looked up at Pete. "They just passed K4, near the beginning of the swamp."

There were numerous crossroads and lay-bys where people could park and enter the trail and run as far as they liked. On a warm day, the shade of the old swamp maples that lined both sides of the trail, was a popular section.

Luckily the spot was close to a junction with the main road, Island Road 2.

"You stay on the phone with her Jane," he gestured. "I'll call the ambulance."

"A couple of marathoners out for an early morning practice," Pete said to Halstead as he punched in the ambulance number. "The man apparently collapsed. Luckily she had her cell phone with her."

"Is your husband breathing?" they could hear Jane ask.

She nodded to the others.

"Keep him warm," Jane said into the phone. "We're calling the ambulance and the officers will be there soon."

They ran for the cruiser. The ambulance had to come across the causeway from Bonville and would take longer.

"I'll drive," Halstead said. "We'll stop at the fire station and you can run in and pick up the defibrillator. Sounds as if we might be looking at a heart attack."

The fire chief himself, Jeff Waverly was there. He looked up as Pete ran in and breathlessly explained the situation.

"I'll come with you," he said, grabbing up the equipment.

The three men were silent during the fifteen minute trip. It was another fine morning, the dew rising as a fine mist off the passing fields. Nothing in the pastoral view hinted at the awaiting drama on the trail.

They had arrived at the junction lane. It was a quick run up to the trail at this point, Pete leading the way and Waverly carrying the defibrillator. Pete spotted the scene right away, only a few feet away from the yellow painted kilometer post. A woman leaning over a prone shape on the track.

She was about fifty, short silver hair, stylishly cut. She wore a blue sweatsuit and expensive looking sneakers and looked totally distraught, in a state of panic. Pete didn't know her, and the chief made no sign of recognition either. They must be visiting runners.

She didn't rise, could barely speak, "Thank God you're here. …. Please … please … can you help him?"

Quickly they introduced themselves as police, while Waverly knelt on the track. The man there lay on his side, curled in the foetal position.

"Your husband, ma'am?" Halstead asked.

She nodded, wide-eyed. "His name is Greg…. Leduc" she quavered. "I'm his wife, Adele."

Greg Leduc was also wearing running sweats, his were grey. Pete could only see his face in profile. What he could see was contorted in pain, like the rest of the man's body.

Waverly gently pulled him over to lie on his back. He felt for a pulse.

He nodded. "Looks like a heart attack."

"How old is your husband ma'am?" Halstead asked.

The woman was wringing her hands, staring helplessly down at her husband's unresponsive face.

"Fifty-eight, but he's always been in great shape. He works out twice a week at the gym. Oh god, I'm the one who suggested we come here and run in the marathon….. we were only going to run the 10 k. If only we'd never come !"

Pete turned at the sound of the approaching siren. "Here's the ambulance."

He went to greet them and show the way. The paramedic, a young woman, was already running along the path. Two others were unloading a stretcher from the van.

Waverly gladly ceded his position to the paramedic.

She moved briskly, talking as she worked. "How long would you say your husband has been unconscious, ma'am?"

Adele Leduc looked dazedly at a big round watch on her wrist.

Halstead intervened, "She called us about twenty minutes ago at the station."

The paramedic nodded. "So, say a half hour then, ma'am?"

"Yes. I saw him fall, I called his name and saw he couldn't talk to me.... thank God I had the phone with me."

But she sounded frightened. "That's too long though, isn't it? That's not good."

The paramedic didn't answer, she was beckoning to her co-workers who had now appeared at the entrance to the trail with the stretcher.

Halstead helped Adele to her feet. She clapped her hands to her face, overcome as the crew carefully transferred her unresponsive husband to the stretcher.

"It was all so lovely, running along the quiet road, just the two of us in the mist," she said tearfully. "Until that awful banging started."

"What banging?" Pete asked abruptly.

"I don't know," she gulped, taken aback. "It was loud, from somewhere in the bushes by the roadside. And then something jumped and ran across the road in front of us. It startled us – that's when Greg fell."

"Something ran across the road?" Halstead asked. "What the h....." he caught himself and began again more quietly.

"What do you think it was, ma'am?"

"I didn't really see much more than a blur," she said helplessly, her attention distracted by the activity at the stretcher. "Greg was a couple of feet ahead of me."

The attendants were headed for the ambulance now, manoeuvering carefully over the uneven terrain. Adele started to follow. Halstead moved alongside, trying to control his impatience.

"Was it an animal do you think? A rabbit, a squirrel, something like that?"

The attendants were lifting the stretcher up into the ambulance.

"I'm sorry I just don't know, I think it was bigger than that though. I forgot all about it till now, things were so confusing. You don't think that caused Greg's attack ! It's impossible, he's a perfectly healthy man. Oh, if only we'd never come."

Halstead had to let her go with the ambulance. He'd promised to make arrangements to pick up the Leduc's car and get it to the hospital.

"I guess you don't need me either," Waverly said. "I'd better get back to the station."

Halstead nodded, "Thanks, Jeff. Great to have you available."

"Happy to help, Bud. We'll be on hand on Marathon Day as well."

Halstead returned to the roadside, his expression sour.

"What do you think – someone shooting rabbits, or another prank?"

"I sure hope not," Pete said. "But guess we'd better check it out."

They each took one side of the roadway. In a few minutes Pete called out.

"What is it?" Halstead asked.

"Broken branches, somebody or somebodies were waiting here. And their bicycles. Probably had a tin pail or something to bang on and make the noise. Maybe a corn popper."

"And they chased something across the road."

"Or scooted across themselves. Mr. Leduc might be able to tell us more – if he wakes up."

"God damn it," Halstead said. "There's nothing funny about this joke. We've got to find those kids before they do any more damage."

"They wouldn't have known the prank would give the man a heart attack."

"They'll know now. We'll get this out on the radio and the TV."

"Kids don't watch the news," Pete said. "Best make an announcement at the school."

"I'll phone in to the station and get Jane on it." Halstead said, checking his watch. "School's just starting now. "They wouldn't even have needed to play hookey."

He phoned from the cruiser while Pete checked the other side of the road.

"So still think these kids are no older than twelve?" he asked when Pete was back in the car.

Pete shook his head. "I hope anybody older would have more sense. This is pretty serious stuff. Let's hope it doesn't get any worse."

It got worse. When they arrived at the emergency department of Bonville Hospital they were told that Greg Leduc had succombed on the way over.

"Yes it was actually a heart attack," the doctor reported. "Not because of age, but a weak aortic valve. Could have happened at any time, but yes could have been brought on by a sudden scare."

"Damn," Halstead said. "This sure opens up a can of worms."

He asked where to find the victim's wife and was directed to a waiting room.

Adele Leduc didn't look up at their entrance, but the man sitting with her did. At the sight of the two officers, his eyes widened. He rose and strode across the room in a few broad steps.

The Chief was a tall man, and this fellow was nearly as tall, broader built and younger. Angry too.

"Are you the police officer responsible for this investigation?" he demanded. "My sister has lost her husband, dammit. On your Island, in your jurisdiction. I want to know what you're going to do about it."

Halstead held up a restraining hand. "And you sir, are?"

"Patrick Cowes," the man said impatiently.

"Then if you don't mind, I'm here to check whether Mrs. Leduc is O.K. and to offer my condolences."

"She doesn't need them," Cowes spat out. "She needs answers. And we're going to get them. Be warned that I'm calling my lawyer as soon as we get back to the city."

Adele Leduc looked up then and said wanly. "Oh please Patrick, not now. The officers were very helpful. We can talk about that all later. Please."

Cowes still bristled, but he lowered his voice.

"You'll be hearing from me."

Of that, Halstead had no doubt.

16

"*Three, Two, One .... And you're ON AIR.*"

The radio technician made the thumbs up sign for Halstead to begin talking. He'd been on the radio before from time to time in his work, but still found it strange to be in the booth and sending his words out over the airways to an invisible audience.

He briefly described the incident on the Marathon trail that morning and expressed condolences for the Leducs.

He emphasized that so far, the police had no suspicion of criminal intent.

"But we are asking that parents and friends who might have any knowledge of the circumstances leading up to this unfortunate occurrence, come forward and contact us. You're not being a friend to let this tragic and unnecessary event pass without dealing properly with it. The perpetrators, no matter their youth, must realize there are consequences to their actions.

"Above all, I'm stressing that these reckless incidents must stop immediately."

Halstead followed the announcement with the telephone numbers of the Middle Island police station, as well as Crime

Stoppers. He waited for the off air signal from Don Rusher, who had been listening from the sidelines, before saying anything else.

"Thanks, Don, for recording the spot so quickly."

"You bet," said Rusher. "Hell of a thing to happen so close to the run."

The station manager frowned, his sharp features creasing. "I sure hope there's no talk of cancelling the Marathon though. I mean I feel sorry for this Leduc guy but it just seems like some crazy freak of a thing. So a rabbit or something ran out on the track in front of him. Nobody else would have croaked – he just had a bad heart and sounds as if he was out of shape."

Hardly a sympathetic view of the circumstances, Halstead thought.

Rusher indicated the sponsorship chart on the station wall. "My team's raised $20,000 in pledges. We can't cancel the run, the hospital foundation needs that money."

"And then there's that bet you go on about every day on your show," Halstead added drily.

"You've got that right. No way I'm going to end up waxing one of Andy Kovak's old Chevies on national television."

Everyone knew that Kovak collected vintage cars and liked to drive them to local events. Rusher's tone was vehement though, out of all proportion to the community spirit of fun in which the challenge had been made. He was an intense fellow at any time but the mention of Andy Kovak seemed to rattle him even more.

"Hardly national television," Halstead said mildly.

"You wait, any mention of a hockey has-been gets a story. That's why it's going to feel so great to win the challenge." Rusher grinned, but it wasn't pleasant. Halstead was thoughtful as he left the radio station. He wondered if indeed, there was anything to the old rumours. Maybe some old feuds did die hard.

Just another sour note in this Marathon event that was rapidly souring altogether.

* * *

Middle Island Town Hall.
Vern Byers, Mayor's Office Main Floor.

The building was blameless, a tidy two storey red brick with white trim, whose basement or second floor was busy most nights of the week with boys and girls club meetings, or pilates classes. But Halstead always climbed the steps reluctantly. He imagined most folks did. This was the place where you paid your taxes or parking fines and purchased licenses for everything from your dog to a fire burning permit. Usually a costly visit.

For Halstead, there was more. Every March, he had to get the police budget approved by council and every month he, or more likely Jane, had to submit a report on how he'd spent the money. Today was different, but almost as bad.

Vern was at his desk, drumming his fingers in agitation on the wood. He jumped up at sight of the chief and began sputtering at once, disjointed phrases tumbling out.

".... total disaster ..... public relations nightmare .... . you'd better fix this….."

Bryan and I …."

It seemed for once, Vern and the Bonville mayor were in league together.

Halstead sat down himself, though not invited. He explained about the radio broadcast. About the ongoing investigation of the incidents on the marathon route. How Jory and Pete had been all over the site, looking for evidence of the perps.

Vern kept sputtering. "But there could be booby traps anywhere along the route. How can we guarantee safety for the runners? What about liability, that could run into the millions. The family haven't contacted us but they will."

"What can they ask for?" Halstead asked. "A man goes out for a run, he has a heart attack. Sad no doubt, but them's the breaks."

He reflected that now he was sounding as callous as Don Rusher.

Vern sank back into the chair, folding his heron-like skinny limbs.

"There's the event insurance of course," he said, as if comforting himself. "Charlene arranged for that months ago. Costs a bundle, $800 for a $1 million policy for the day, but necessary to cover any property damage inflicted by the runners along the route."

"And the policy includes liability coverage for personal injury and associated costs such as medical expenses, though that's not as important here as in the U.S. But you don't usually expect anything more serious than a sprained ankle. Not an incident like this !"

Halstead frowned, "Just back up a minute, Vern. You said the Committee has contracted for event insurance. Correct me if I'm wrong, but there wasn't any event this morning. In fact the event isn't happening till June twenty-second. So what liability are you talking about?"

Vern didn't look cheered. "What if something like this happens on event day?"

Halstead rolled his eyes. "What if the sky falls in? What exactly do you want us to do Vern? There's more than twenty kilometers of track to cover, most of it unpopulated, most of the time. Or maybe you want to ask your new friend Mayor Bryan to lend us some city staff to help patrol the route. We could call in the OPP too. Those fellows might enjoy the break from real crime busting."

"I don't know Bud, just *do* something. Maybe your boys could at least run the track in the mornings, see if it's clear."

"Sure thing, Vern. They can give up two hours of police time every morning on a wild goose chase, no sweat."

Vern groaned. "We can't cancel."

"Up to you two mayors to make the call," Halstead said. "I'm just the policeman."

"But what do you think Bud? Really."

Halstead sighed. "I think it will be alright. You'll have a great run."

He only hoped that was true.

* * *

Stephanie sighed. She could see that her husband was still a troubled man, even after downing his suppertime beer and a plate of his favourite garlic ribs.

"It will be O.K. Bud," she soothed. "The Marathon will come off fine."

"How can you say that? I bet your Committee members have been burning up the telephone circuits all afternoon."

She couldn't deny that. The news of Greg Leduc's death had circulated quickly via the local grapevine and only a little less speedily to the radio and television news networks. She had fielded a call from Charlene (furiously demanding) and Carol (utter panic – *It's an omen, an awful omen!*)

Apparently the Marathon website and e-mail had been flooded with registrants seeking assurance that the run was still on and that the run was still safe.

"This will all settle down," she assured, as confidently as she could. "Charlene and Barry are meeting tonight to check the insurance policy. She's pretty sure that the insurance is limited to accidents that occur during the event or activity schedule."

Steph could see that her words brought little comfort. Though Bud was normally of a fairly even temperament, he was unhappy when his Island wasn't happy. And it was certainly in turmoil tonight.

He fetched another beer from the fridge but didn't open it, just held the cool can against his forehead.

"What possessed Leduc? Haven't the doctors given us men enough warnings about heart attacks? The man was fifty-eight. He could have worked out a couple of nights a week on a stationary bicycle, instead of trying to run the four minute mile for our Marathon."

"You should have seen the books in the Leduc's car," he marvelled. *The High of Running, The Science of Running, Running at any Age.* That one was about a hundred year old man who finished the marathon in just over eight hours. A hundred year old man!"

Steph shrugged. "For some people, running is a kind of quest, I've heard. A spiritual thing."

"Humph. I might have known. Nothing is simple anymore, everything's got to be fancied up. Look at the ads in these magazines - $300 shoes, just to pare a mille-second off your timing. It's not like they invented running. Our high school football training was a lot tougher than this marathon stuff. You had to run *and* ram."

Steph wrapped her arms round his shoulders. "You don't have to prove yourself to me by running a marathon, my love. You certainly don't have to get into some rutting testosterone-filled rivalry, as Don Rusher seems to view it. That man is taking this run way too personally."

They looked up as Livy passed through the room, on her way to the sunporch. She wore her bathing suit and was carrying a sandwich, a glass of lemonade and a paperback book.

She had obviously heard the last part of the conversation and smiled as if at a pair of doddering seniors.

"You shouldn't overthink this running thing folks. For a lot of people, marathons are just plain old *fun*."

Halstead watched her leave, then shook his head. "For Greg Leduc, running meant a fatal heart attack. Nothing fun about that. Dead fish, fake detours, heart-attack-inducing noises. Not to mention a new batch of Island thieves sprouting up. Makes you wonder what's going to happen next?"

He opened the can with a wrenching pop.

"Plus it doesn't help that the local police force look like a bunch of incompetent fools. "Hell we can't even collar a couple of bratty kids, let alone attend to these thefts."

"Nobody thinks you're a fool, Bud."

"I feel like one. I feel worse than that – the poor fellow *died*. I don't know, maybe it's time that I retired."

Steph laughed affectionately, "Seems to me we have this conversation every year about this time. And you're still on the job."

She went to fetch the strawberry shortcake. It might help a bit.

Privately though, she couldn't help but wonder if the incident might indeed overshadow and spoil the run.

17

VISITING MARATHON ENTRANT
SUFFERS HEART ATTACK
VICTIM OF MYSTERIOUS PRANK?

"That isn't confirmed yet." Halstead reminded Bob Denyes, friend, fellow member of the Bonville curling team, and editor of the Bonville Record.

Denyes scanned the Dockside Restaurant menu, though he always ordered the chowder, followed by cod and chips. "I spoke with the victim's brother-in-law, he seems to think it's confirmed. He's talking about suing somebody."

Halstead ordered the chowder too, the best in Bonville. The day was pleasant so the two men had taken an outside table on the deck overlooking the Bay.

"I can see how he feels of course, but we're talking about some kids here. How's he going to sue some kids?"

"Who knows? Maybe he'll sue the Marathon Committee. Or even you."

"Me?" Halstead shook his head. "I feel sorry for the family of course and I'll keep them informed of any charges or arrests arising out of the incident. But that's the extent of my duty."

Denyes raised an eyebrow. "You're the police, you're responsible for safety on the route."

"On the day of the actual run," Halstead objected. "We can't supervise every keener who's out checking the route a week ahead of time. And even on Marathon Day, standard practise is that all participants will be signing a waiver. We hardly have the manpower to hold every runner's hand through the run." He shook his head, "We've become safety nuts in this country."

Denyes started in on his soup, he'd heard the chief before on this subject.

"So, any leads on those kids yet?"

"Hopefully we've scared the bejesus out of them so there won't be any more tricks. But I doubt they'll turn themselves in, would you? Remember when you were a kid and in trouble."

Denyes nodded. "I'd just lie low and hope it would all go away. No TV sitcom stuff where the kid confesses and everybody smothers him in forgiveness."

Halstead crumbled crackers into his bowl. "You heard me on the radio this morning, we're doing what we can. So we'll just have to hope that's the end of it. Pete's going to the school today to have a chat with the class."

"Hell of a thing, though." Denyes said. "But enough of the kindergarten crimes. I heard there's been some thefts over on the Island."

"A few," Halstead admitted reluctantly. "Some equipment and an ATV."

"I heard it was a pretty nice ATV."

"Yes, it's worth a few bucks. At first we thought somebody took it for the usual joyride and that the bike would turn up in a ditch somewhere. But so far, there's no sign of it."

"There is some talk about a gang operating along the 401," Denyes said. "There was that backhoe theft near the highway the other night."

"We don't even know yet that our Island robberies are connected," Halstead scoffed. "Let alone that they're part of a gang operation over here."

Their main course arrived and they ate industriously for a bit, in the easy silence of old friends. Denyes eventually pushed his plate aside, virtuously leaving the last few chips untouched and plied his napkin. Halstead, lucky devil, never had to worry about extra calories but had stayed rangy and lean even into middle age.

As the waitress re-filled their coffee cups, Denyes hailed a fellow coming onto the deck.

"Andy – over here."

Halstead moved to make room, as the hockey legend pulled another chair up to the table. He wore a t-shirt and summer slacks, and sported the marathon cap on his prematurely silver hair.

There was a round of "How's it going?"

Denyes grinned at Kovak, "Have you thought about joining the curling club next winter?"

Kovak made a face. "I'm not that far over the hill yet. Not like you two old codgers."

Denyes was unfazed. "It's only a matter of time. There's a jersey with your name on it."

"How's the marathon training going Andy?" Halstead asked. "Is your team going to whup Rusher? I'm thinking of proposing a little betting action here with Bob."

Kovak spread his arms. "No contest. I've been working out every morning on the waterfront trail. Only problem is which one of you gets to bet on me?"

The waitress had brought him ice water and he took a long draught.

"Say Bud, I hope the Committee hasn't got any crazy idea about cancelling the run. Debra says most of the members feel there's no reason to. I mean we all feel sorry about that Leduc guy and his wife, but the hospital could sure use that money."

"You probably know more than me," Halstead said. "I'm meeting with the Committee this afternoon. But I very much doubt they'll cancel the run. There are too many people already involved. All those months of organizing, and advertising. And of course there's been all that publicity – you and Don Rusher all over the TV and radio."

Kovak scowled, "You mean Rusher's on the radio. He manages the station, so no wonder. I can't turn the darn car radio on without hearing how he's going to clobber my team."

Denyes laughed. "I doubt the coffee-swilling office staff from the station are going to beat your team of high school athletes. I saw you putting them through their paces at the park last night."

Kovak brightened. "They did look good." He reached into his pocket, "Say have you seen the brochure for the hockey camp? Hot from the printer."

He spread the brochure out on the table.

Hockey camp ! A challenging opportunity for your boy or girl.

Combines developing skills in hockey with a summer camping experience.

10 intensive hours of ice time per week, scrimmage games, plus a special goalie program.

$1000 a week.

Halstead whistled at the price, remembering his own summers cycling and fishing on the Island, free gratis.

"Cost of ice time," Kovak explained. "It doesn't come cheap to keep an arena open in the summer. Bonville can't afford it, that's why I'm working with a partner in Oshawa."

"Looks good," Denyes said. "Here's to your new venture. Just remember to save some nights for curling this winter."

"Don't hold your breath." And with a wide wave, Kovak left to join his lunch companions.

"Cheerful guy," Halstead observed.

"Salt of the earth," Denyes agreed. "Always has time to visit kids in the hospital, sign autographs, the lot."

"How much is there to the old story?" Halstead asked.

"You mean the jilted lover?"

Halstead described the incident at the radio station that morning. "Rusher's been married to somebody else for years, isn't he over it yet?"

"There's always been a tension, that's for sure. And this city is as bad as the Island for gossip, makes it difficult when the couples bump into each other. Then there was the blow-up this winter at the rink. That fired up the gossip mill all over again."

Halstead looked the question. "I must have missed that."

The waitress arrived with their bills and Denyes paused before continuing.

"There was an NHL scout at the rink that night. Rusher claimed that Kovak had deliberately kept his sixteen-year old stepson on the bench most of the time and wouldn't let him play."

"That would make a dad mad alright. Was it true?"

Denyes shrugged. "It was an important game to win the championship in the local series. Kovak said he had put the players out who could do the best for the team. There was a real dust-up in the arena lobby, almost came to blows."

Halstead sighed. "No wonder Rusher is determined to win in the Marathon. You should have seen his face when he swore he'd never be waxing Andy's car. Looked more as if he'd rather blow it up."

He picked up his complimentary peppermint and popped it in his mouth. He wasn't looking forward to his next stop.

*   *   *

It was a tense group gathered in the committee room of Bonville City Hall. Some of the members were close to panic.

Charlene had no qualms however.

"Of course Mr. Leduc's death is sad, but not out of the ordinary for a middle-aged man. We'll be going ahead with the Marathon. The insurance policy is quite clear. The liability is limited to accidents that occur during the event schedule. It protects our volunteers and covers damage to property.

We do have the requisite warning in our brochure that entrants should be in good health before running and must be careful to choose a distance category that they're comfortable with. That is the entrant's responsibility and each runner signs a waiver accepting that."

"What about these awful tricks though? What will happen next?" Carol said fearfully. "The high school has had calls from concerned parents."

"Thirteen year olds are hardly likely to suffer a heart attack," Barry reminded her.

Carol wasn't to be soothed, she fussed again about bad omens.

Charlene was firm. "We're not going to let a few malicious tricks frighten us. We've got nearly two hundred runners and many volunteers who have been practising and looking forward to this event. We're not going to just turn tail and run."

"However, we do need to reassure our participants that they will have a safe and well-conducted experience. Debra and I have been drafting a release for the media."

Debra handed copies round the table. "First thing of course, we sent our condolences to the Leduc family. I believe Vern Byers and Mayor Sheehey are also issuing a joint statement."

There were approving nods around the table.

"Chief Halstead is here today to answer questions." Charlene said, looking expectantly towards him. "Bud?"

He knew almost everyone there and wouldn't have tried to fool them anyway. He confirmed what Charlene had said, then added.

"I hope the severity of this incident has scared the pranksters off. But in any case, we'll be scouting out the entire route early on race day. There will also be patrollers through the race."

They sat silently, considering his words.

At length, Charlene clapped her hands and said briskly. "So we're done here, troops. Onward and upward."

On the way out, Miranda nudged Ali and murmured. "I thought it wasn't appropriate to remind the Committee members that Philippides, the original marathoner, collapsed and died from his exertion !"

18

A fine morning, in an unbroken chain of fine mornings. Mourning doves cooed in the soft green maple tops, and dewdrops still glittered on the weeds by the roadside. Pete's t-shirt was sweaty but he felt good. The tranquility of the morning was his favourite time of day, and this bit by the swamp, the best part of the run.

He wasn't being a slave to a stopwatch either, though couldn't help but be pleased that he'd cut another minute off his time. Plus he'd seen a fine box turtle by the swamp and spotted a snapper in the water too. If a female, she'd be emerging soon to cross the road and lay her eggs.

So far then, a perfect June. Ali said that ironically some of the Marathon organizers who had fussed about the weather for weeks, were now almost wishing for rain to get it over with. Some folks were never satisfied !

He trotted the last few yards up his own driveway. Paused to sluice his face and neck generously from the garden hose and grabbed a towel from the clothesline. In the kitchen, he leaned over Nevra and shook water out of his hair.

"Daddy!" she protested. "Stop it! You're silly."

She wore her kitten patterned pyjamas, her taffy-coloured hair still uncombed. Spooned cereal out of her kitten-patterned bowl, while the big orange cat sat patiently at her feet waiting for the bit of milk she always left for him.

Nevra was four now, with a four-year old's deep questions. Yesterday she had asked Pete where the sky stopped. The day before that, why water at the beach got deep. The questions reminded him of the astronomer Carl Sagan's comment re childhood observations – that he had never got over this stage himself.

Now she asked, "Where are you running to, Daddy?"

"Nowhere special sweetie, just running."

"Why are you running then?"

"Just for fun" - he looked up as Ali entered the kitchen, dressed but yawning. "And to stay the buff army man your mommy married."

"What's a buff, Daddy?" came the inevitable question.

Pete laughed, signalled to Ali. *Over to you.*

She kissed her daughter's cheek. "A buff is a silly man, my darling."

Nevra asked to play with Pete's stopwatch. "I'm going to time how fast Kedi can run," she said, half-carrying and half dragging the big amiable fellow towards the door.

"Good luck," Pete said.

He poured coffee into two cups and kissed his wife's hand. "You look especially lovely this morning."

She tossed her hair seductively, "It's that seven-year glow."

She'd marked the anniversary on the calendar for July. He'd peeked and looked ahead. Three exclamation marks. !!!

He'd better come up with something good.

* * *

Jane looked warily down the hall. The chief's door was rarely shut but this morning, firmly closed. He was probably tossing paper clips into the wastebasket or staring moodily out at Baker's field. The chief much preferred to run a happy ship and lately the ship was definitely foundering.

He'd stamped past her on the way in, barely acknowledging her own cheery greeting.

"What's good about it?" he grumbled. ""The Leducs are threatening to sue, thieves are running rings around us and my officers can't even manage to catch a couple of prankster kids. I'm not here."

Patrick Cowes had followed up on his threat. The letter from the Leducs' lawyer had arrived yesterday. Halstead had been expecting it and in fact had consulted directly after the trail incident with Ken Connors, the lawyer who from time to time advised the Island municipality on legal matters. Connors had sent notification that the police were currently conducting an investigation of the incident and would keep Mrs. Leduc advised.

Seeing as the so-called investigation was getting exactly nowhere, none of this served to improve Halstead's mood much.

So Jane tapped quietly on Pete's cubicle wall when the call came in. Jakes was at the computer as he was every morning these days, going over the stolen property lists. So far none of the recently stolen items had turned up.

She screwed up her face in an apologetic wince. "Line 2, Pete. You're not going to like this. Another ATV theft."

Pete groaned. "Not from Barry Tripp's again? I thought he'd be more careful now."

"Not directly from Barry. But the victim – Jim Szabo at the garden centre, bought it from him a week ago. He'd barely got the price tag off it."

"Jeez."

"Apparently one of his employees left it outside the greenhouse last night."

He took the call, and grabbed up his jacket.

"Have fun telling the Chief, Jane."

"Gee thanks."

He drafted Jory who was just on his way in.

Jory made a face. "Not more crap on the trail? Or did they knock down another post?"

Pete explained, as they got in the cruiser.

Jory shook his head. "Makes you wonder what the heck is going on around here these days. It's like there's some kind of jinx operating."

"You're not hearing anything at all?

Jory shook his head. "If anybody is running Barry Tripp's ATV on the island, it must be alone and in secret and what fun is that? The fellows I know, would want to show off that machine, not hide it."

Pete stopped the car to wait for a turtle to cross the road. A Blandings turtle with a bright yellow throat.

Jory hung his head out the window, "Come on Rocket, get those eggs laid and get back home to the crik."

"Rocket?" Pete asked.

Jory nodded. "She crosses here every year, for years now."

"How do you know it's the same one?"

"I just call them all Rocket. Have called them that since I was a kid."

He laughed, "Imagine a turtle marathon, I wonder how long that would take?"

Pete started moving again. "So back to these ATV thefts, where are the things ending up? And did the same perps take this one? Is there some secret ATV club roaring around a field under the stars?"

"Snowmobilers go out at night," Jory said. "But not ATVers. Too dangerous."

They passed the spot where Jory had fixed the post.

"Do you think there's any connection with the trail pranks?" he asked. "That maybe it's not young kids doing them after all?"

"I wondered that too," Pete said. "But to what purpose? It's not like they're diverting us from the thefts."

Jory shrugged. "Unless they're just thumbing their noses at us, getting our goat."

"They're certainly starting to make us look bad. It's getting to the chief."

"So maybe he was wrong and that equipment gang is working down here now."

Pete was skeptical. "These are just a couple of ATVs. That gang is interested in bigger stuff. To move anything like that, they'd need a really big truck."

*　　*　　*

Samson the Mover. Local and Cross-Province Service.

The blue truck was parked in typical stance, on the front lawn of a house. A sturdy ramp reached to the front porch and Rick Farron and Bobby Jardine were struggling to carry a full-size dining room hutch along its length.

Bobby was doing the hardest part, moving backwards down the ramp and through the front door into the house. Farron steered and called out instructions. "Just keep going straight. Be careful ! Don't scratch the wood against the door."

Jeez, the guy was dumb as a doornail. But strong, that's for sure.

It was a short distance job, just delivering a couch and a dining room set from Sears in Bonville. Barely a quarter-load. They wrapped up the job in another twenty minutes and Rick drove back to the boss's place, out on Route 4. The Samsons had a neat white frame house, set back from the road and surrounded by clumps of lilac bushes. Gerry's office was to the side of the house, really just a room that he had drywalled in the garage.

Rick left Bobby in the truck. Samson was at his cluttered desk. A brusque, sturdy sixty, with oversized biceps from his own years of hauling heavy loads, he never seemed at ease with paper work.

"Got her all done? No damage?"

"Yeah, yeah," Rick said. "All done."

And no frigging damage – just because we screwed up and dented some dame's microwave once...

Samson nodded, "Good. You remember Rick that you've got that long-haul on the twentieth." The client had got a new job in Hamilton and was moving his family. The wife and kiddies were already there.

"Yeah, yeah," Rick said. "I got it on the calendar."

Gerry paid them as usual, in cash. Bobby never got over this exciting novelty and kept counting it over again when they were in Rick's pick-up.

Rick smiled thinly. "It's different for you Jardine. You don't have any bills. Me, I sweat like a pig all day and collect a few lousy bucks that barely keeps gas in my own truck. I can't wait till I get some real money, instead of peanuts from Gerry Samson."

Like the money for that ATV last week. A cool thousand for that one. And now I've got another one. Those guys want lots of other stuff too. Like that big job where they got the backhoe last week, man somebody must have made a bundle on that.

That's the business that I want to get into, not just stashing a bunch of small stuff in the barn up Turner's Lane. I need a big job, to make a stake and get away from this jerk Island forever.

Good thing that I've got this dumbo to help me, as long as he can keep his mouth shut. It's pretty easy to keep him happy though. Like now when he's counting up his money. He even says he feels lucky that I got him the job with Samson. Meanwhile Samson can't believe the guy comes so cheap when he can practically move a piano by himself.

Bobby was looking happily out the window. "When are we going to do another job, Rick? Getting that ATV at the garden place was cool."

"Not now," Rick said impatiently. "I told you we have to lie low for awhile between jobs. We don't want to put folks too much on their guard."

"O.K. Rick, you're the boss." Bobby frowned then, remembering. "I just wish I coulda kept that ATV you sold."

"Well now you've got another one."

"The first one was nicer. And what fun is a ATV if you won't let me ride it?

"Just stop talking about friggin ATVs," Rick snapped. "And let me concentrate. If we pull off a big enough job, you can buy your own ride. But my contact says I gotta find something a lot bigger to heist, if I want to get in on the real money. These guys don't want frigging chain saws. Even the ATVs aren't really big enough. Now a backhoe or something like that, would get me five thousand bucks or more."

"Is that a lot of money?" Bobby asked.

"You bet it is, man. And no kindergarten cop like Jory Stutke is going to keep me from getting it. I'm not going to get put away like my jerk brother."

It was pretty handy too, last week when that old guy died on the trail. Talk about lucky. Those kids pulling the tricks are keeping the cops busy.

"I'm gonna drop you off, Jardine," he said as they were nearing the village. "I've got some folks to talk to over Bonville way."

"The folks who buy our stuff?"

"Maybe."

"Why can't I come?" Bobby asked. "I could help with the plans."

"Ha. You'd probably blab it all to somebody."

"No I wouldn't."

"I'll tell you all you need to know when the time comes."

He's probably said too much already. Trouble is he doesn't have anyone else to talk to about the jobs. At least dopey Jardine is some kind of an audience.

"I don't want to come anyway," Bobby said proudly. "I can't. I got an appointment."

"What's with all these appointments? I hope you're not gonna get sick on me."

"I'm not sick. I never get sick."

"I bet you've got nothing to do," Rick sneered. "You've never got anything to do."

"A lot you know."

19

Late afternoon sunbeams slanted across the library floor. Miranda looked up from her desk, shifting Emily off her feet. The Wednesday afternoon seniors' book club had just wrapped up a session. The club members made up a list of choices in September and Miranda endeavoured to get multiple copies, often through a shared arrangement with inter-library loans. There was usually a theme to link the monthly choices – this year's had been *Mysteries Set in Exotic Places*. Readers had been thrilled, horrified or merely cozied in venues as far-flung as Hong Kong and Reykjavik. This month's choice had taken them to Venice with Commissario Brunetti.

Now the six women came out from the other room, still talking animatedly. Not about crimes in sunny Venice it seemed, but rather events much closer to home.

"I can hardly watch the television these days for all the trouble in the world," nattered Alma Pitt. "Lately it's getting where you don't even feel safe on the Island any more with all these robberies goings on."

"And then that fellow dying on the trail," said Louisa Scott. "Because of some prank ! Gives me shivers, thinking about all sorts of weird folks creeping around at night."

"Oh come on, Louisa," Miranda chided. "Kids have always been getting up to tricks. Remember what Hallowe'en was like when we were growing up. Privies tipped over, rotten eggs, the lot."

Louisa was indignant. "Yes, but we never *killed* anybody."

"Nor was any killing done here," Miranda said crisply. "It was unfortunate that the man had a bad heart."

Louisa obviously preferred her version of an Island stalked by murderous miscreants. The ladies left, still a-twitter. No doubt their next stop would be tea at one of their homes where they could chatter the way they liked.

Quarter to four, almost closing time. She turned the door sign to *Closed* and walked over to the long reading table by the windows.

"Boo !" she said to Ali Jakes. "I almost forgot you were here, you've been so quiet."

"I'm sorry Miranda, I didn't notice the time."

"No matter. If you're taking those books out, I'll put them through the scanner."

"It's O.K. thanks. I was just browsing."

Miranda noticed the titles. *The wonders of Butan. Hiking in Wales. Amazing Australia.*

"Are you planning a trip?"

"Not really. I don't think so. Maybe."

Miranda raised a quizzical eyebrow. Her friend was not usually prone to vagueness.

Or blushing, which she was doing now.

"It's just a silly thing," Ali explained. "Our wedding anniversary – our seventh - is coming up at the end of the month. I'm trying to think of some special way to celebrate."

She hastily gathered up the books. There were also a couple of magazines, the type whose covers showed handsome couples in sailing or skiing gear against brilliant blue skies.

"A trip to New York might be nice," Miranda suggested. "All those beautiful art galleries and museums, such as the Smithsonian."

"Maybe. But it can get pretty hot this time of year. Sometimes I think we should just go for silly. To Dollywood, for instance. Or even Graceland."

She picked up her purse and shopping bag. "Truth is, I don't really know what I'd like to do. I just want to keep making our anniversaries a celebration."

Miranda chuckled. "I'm a happily single spinster my dear. My idea of a celebration is an extra piece of pie for dessert. I'm sure you'll think of something nice. Just let me know if I can help with Nevra sitting."

"You're a dear," Ali said affectionately. "But I should go. Won't Bobby Jardine be here soon?"

She'd stopped by the library one Wednesday to drop an overdue book in the mail slot and had inadvertently seen Bobby leaving. Miranda had explained and Ali swore not to tell.

"It's wonderful what you two are doing," she said now. "What a surprise it will be for his parents! I know you've booked him for the qualifying test at the end of the month."

"I'm actually a bit concerned," Miranda said. "I've noticed his attention has been wandering the last couple of visits. He seems to be losing his concentration and is always eyeing the clock."

She sighed and crossed her arms. "I hope I haven't been pushing the fellow. But he's the one who so badly wants a certificate to show his parents."

"He's probably just excited about his job. Gus was telling me that Bobby loves working for the mover."

Miranda frowned. "Well he'd better get excited about this test again. I had to make special arrangements at the college for him to take the test orally."

"He's probably just running a bit late," Ali soothed.

And indeed, here he came charging up to the door, childish face pink with excitement. He stooped to greet Emily, then looked a bit flustered at seeing Ali.

He held up a video. "I got here just in time. Don't want to make this overdue and pay a fine."

Ali winked at Miranda. "That's a good movie," she said to Bobby. "I liked it too."

*   *   *

"And he hits it! Bottom of the 8th, the Yankees have two men on base."

"Ugh," Pete turned down the television sound and wandered into the kitchen to get a beer.

Ali looked up from marking papers. "Jays suck?" she asked.

He nodded. "Tonight anyway." He stared restlessly out at the back yard, which un-cooperatively didn't need mowing. It hadn't rained for nearly two weeks.

She pushed aside the papers, recognizing his mood. In the winter months, he spent many evenings coaching hockey. He needed action, especially when he was trying to figure out a case.

"Suppose I could get the weed whacker out," he said. "Weeds grow, no matter what."

"I suppose you could go out there in the dusk and make a meal for the mosquitoes," she scoffed. "Or you could get your wife a glass of wine and we could put our feet up in here."

He smiled sheepishly and fetched her a glass with ice cubes.

She pushed her hair up and held a cube to her neck.

"Still thinking about the ATV thefts?" she asked. He'd been talking about that over supper, how there'd been no progress. "At least the trail pranks seem to have stopped. That's good, isn't it?"

Pete nodded. "Hopefully."

"I've noticed that since the chief's radio broadcast, the kids at school aren't joking anymore about the pranks."

"That's something anyway."

"Do you think you'll ever find out who did the tricks?"

"Oh, someday I imagine." He made his hands into exaggerated vampire claws and hissed *"Secrets Will Out."*

She tinkled the cubes in her glass. "It probably isn't a good thing though, if the perpetrators do get away with it. Not good for them anyway."

"You mean maybe they'll proceed with a lifetime of crime? ... *if only my boy had been taught the right way, back then*...... sort of thing?"

"I'm serious Pete. If we never know who did it, there might always be suspicion on completely innocent kids. Even *I* find myself doubting my own judgement when I look at the class now. It makes you think about what particular factors do create criminals."

He nodded. "Poor economic situations can obviously have a lot to do with certain crimes."

Ali shook her head. "At least those crimes are logical, *I need this, so I'll take that*. I'm thinking more of trying to figure out a kid's psychology and upbringing. Parental influence is huge, for instance. Lousy parenting can really mess up children."

"True. Yet for all those harmful instances, which unfortunately happen every day to thousands of kids, most of them don't turn out to be lawbreakers. And yet some kids who have none of those factors working against them, take up crime just to get kicks."

"Is that what you think of the trail pranksters?"

Pete sighed. "I think they're just kids having fun who made a mistake. And I bet right now they're feeling pretty scared and not interested in a life of crime at all."

Ali looked at the pile of marked papers, the work of her students. *I liked this story because....*

"You're probably right. I'm reassured. But what about the ATV thieves? They're older obviously – what's their psychological profile?"

Pete shrugged. "I know one thing, somebody wants to make some money."

Ali looked out at the gathering dusk. The robins were quiet now, asleep with their young. "I wonder who the thieves are. I wonder *where* they are. Do you think they're dangerous?"

"Not so far. But thieves can be put under pressure, like any of the rest of us."

"Do you think most criminals are smart?"

"These thieves are smarter than us at the moment." He smiled. "Nevra's smart, are you worried we're raising a criminal mastermind?"

Ali laughed. "No, I think that's more Kedi's line. But I'm smart, and I bet I can beat you at Scrabble."

And she did. 320 points to his 280.

When they finished she gathered up a handful of letters and spelled out.

WHAT DO ON ANNIVERSARY.

"Very clever," Pete said.

"I made do. There are no question mark tiles."

She reached for her tablet. "I've found some interesting suggestions of what we could do. And don't wince, some of them are cute."

Grinning, she read out.

Ten Romantic Ideas. One. Recreate your first date.

He laughed outright. "Didn't we go out to the little bar in Kandahar? I think we literally got bombed, or nearly anyway."

In fact, it was two days later that the flimsy structure was demolished. The fate of many a structure in Afghanistan settlements.

"O.K." she ceded. "Here are some more."

Do something new. Skydiving, ballooning.

Go to a spa, boutique hotel, dude ranch, or an exotic atoll.

"We aready live on an Island," Pete pointed out. He leaned over her shoulder. "What about this one?

Just be together.

She leaned back against his chest. "Sounds dreamy – but we're going to be together somewhere else !"

R eport of texting violation, Island Road 3.
    Presiding officer, Jory Stutke.
    Suspect vehicle was travelling extremely slowly, as approached Benson Crossroads. Female driver, was obviously typing a message on a cell-phone. When pulled over, she said that she was on her way to Collier Cove but had lost the address and had to text her friend for directions.

Paperwork, the bane of any operation. Jane kept a daily log for each officer, where he travelled and what task he was working on. Halstead was going through the week's reports and now tossed this one disgustedly on his desk. A new type of traffic offense, as if the police needed one. And not just among teenagers. Jory said this woman looked to be in her sixties. You'd think she'd have more sense.

"Why did she have to text her friend?" he demanded of Jane. "I bet she already had an entire satellite positioning gizmo on the dashboard. Could have found her way around in Tuktayatuk."

The next item wasn't likely to improve his mood either. Jake's report on the ATV theft at the garden centre. Another Yamaha machine, not quite as fancy as the first, but still with a list price of over $6000.

Jakes had interviewed the owner, Jim Szabo. Also Andrew Terry, eighteen, employee and the last person to use the bike. The person who said he'd forgotten to bring it into the garage at the end of the working day. Szabo himself vouched for Terry, said he was a good honest kid who had worked summers at the garden centre since he was sixteen.

Investigation on-going. In other words, no leads.

When Jane called him from the front desk, he welcomed the diversion.

"Hey chief, better get out here."

At first glance, there seemed to be a small crowd. This sorted out to two adults, a man and a woman, and two boys, who looked to be about twelve or thirteen years old.

'Hello there," Halstead nodded to Lloyd Storms who managed a hardware store in Bonville. A tall, active man, he also helped often in the store yard, loading lengths of pipe and board.

Jane made the other introductions. One of the boys was Lloyd's son Owen. The woman was Helen Copps, she was with her son Jason. The Copps ran a small resort on the south shore. He'd passed the place often but never had occasion to drop in.

The two adults looked uncomfortable and extremely serious. And when Halstead looked behind them to the two lads slinking by the station doorway, he could guess the cause of their discomfort.

"Why don't you all come into the office," he invited.

He fetched a couple more chairs from the lunch room, making a tight squeeze in the small space. Opened the window wider to let in some air. The business of getting seated done, there was a silence in the room.

Neither boy met Halstead's gaze. They wore the standard teenage boy outfit of cargo shorts and t-shirts, sneakers and ball caps, which their parents hastily snatched off. Halstead waited, looking an inquiry. He imagined that round faced Helen Copps was generally a cheerful woman but today she just looked anxious.

Finally Lloyd Storms cleared his throat.

"The boy's got something to say to you about the tricks on that running track." He glared at his son, "Go on boy, say it."

The boy was a scaled down version of his father. Already lanky, with long, serious features under his dark hair. He looked down at his sneakers.

"It was us did those tricks," he said, almost inaudibly. "Me and Jason."

"Are you Jason?" Halstead asked, turning to the other boy.

"Yes he is," said the mother. "And he's very sorry, aren't you?"

"Yes," he said and nodded, but not very sincerely, Halstead thought.

This boy had the blond hair and almost cherubic face of his mother. But he had a sly, unrepentant look about him. No contrition or regret there, not like Owen Storms. Not a whit. Halstead knew the look, though he usually saw the expression on someone a little older. The only lesson this kid had learned from the experience was not to get caught.

Have a good gander around a police station, kid. You'll likely be seeing more of the place in future.

He turned back to the Storms lad. "You seem like a smart boy – why did you do such a dumb thing as that?"

The boy shrugged helplessly. "For fun, I guess."

Halstead took in both kids with a severe gaze. "I sure hope you're too smart to ever do something like that again."

"Yessir."

"They never meant any harm," Lloyd said. "It was just kid stuff, fooling around."

"It was a little more than that, Lloyd. They were warned at the school."

"Well what are you going to do with them? Lloyd asked. "They're too young for jail."

Owen blanched.

Helen Copps uttered a little muffled squeak.

Jason just looked cockier.

Halstead stood. "You boys go sit out front and wait with Mrs. Carrell. I want to talk with your parents."

He ushered the boys out and shut the door.

"They're thirteen years old," Helen Copps protested. "Still in public school." She looked an appeal at Storms.

"I can punish my own kid, Chief," Storms said. "You can be sure of that."

"We will too," Helen said eagerly. "Grounding, no allowance, anything you say."

Halstead sat back down. "It's not that simple."

Storms would discipline his son properly for sure, and it was obvious that the kid was already suffering guilt. Learning too, that actions had consequences. But he doubted that an old-fashioned licking, let alone any of these soft punishments would affect young Copps much.

"There could be legal consequences, if not for the boys, for you parents," Halstead said. "The dead man's brother-in-law is already threatening a suit."

Another squeak of dismay from Helen Copps.

"You're going to have to jump through some hoops, likely starting with some family counselling. I'm going to order that they perform some community service too. Probably not anything to do with the marathon," he added drily. "Folks wouldn't be too happy to see the boys anywhere near the route. But maybe they could help with the clean-up afterwards."

The two parents rose silently from their chairs, thinking all this over. In the front office, Halstead spoke a final word to the boys.

"I'd better not hear of any more nasty tricks from you lads ever again. Or you'll find the young offenders quarters at Bonville Detention Centre are really nasty."

The group marched soberly out to the parking lot.

Halstead turned wearily to Jane. "Well that's one headache solved. What a thing, though."

*　*　*

"I can hardly believe it !" Ali cried. "Owen Storms and Jason Copps ! I don't want to believe such a thing."

"Sorry, but it's true," Pete said. "The chief told us all about it."

She dropped her briefcase on the table. "Their parents must have been shocked. I bet they feel terrible. I know how I feel and I'm only their teacher. Although it's awful to say, but I'm not quite as surprised to hear that Jason is involved. Owen's a nice kid though, but more of a follower."

She sank into a kitchen chair, and took a big gulp of the glass of lemonade Pete had poured out for her.

"You'd better tell me what they said. Everything."

He gave her a succinct account.

She kept sadly shaking her head but made no more comments, save for an agonized groan every now and then.

"So what's going to happen?" she asked dejectedly when he was done.

"I'm sure their parents will figure out some punishment on the home front. We're still waiting to hear how far the Leducs will take things. The boys are minors and there was no real malicious intent. And since they're minors, their names won't be published or announced anywhere. But of course the news will get out fast enough."

He explained some of the options. She agreed that it wouldn't be a good idea to let them participate in any way on Marathon Day.

"Eileen and I will have to deal with the boys too." Ali said. "We'll talk to them privately of course, though as you said, it will hardly be any big secret." She sighed, "At least the pranks will stop now and nobody else will get hurt."

Pete nodded. "That's the Marathon trail problem cleared up. One mystery out of the way. Now we've only got to catch some thieves. Should be a piece of cake in comparison."

21

The Bonville and District Detention centre, a low-slung block of featureless concrete, was not a sight to lift anyone's spirits. Nor was there any cheer to be gained at the view of the paved exercise yard, surrounded by a barb-wire topped fence.

These days there were all these TV programs trying to make it cool to be wearing an orange convict jump suit. There was even a comedy set in a prison. But Rick Farron wasn't fooled. No way was he going to end up in a dead-end joint like this. Tony had been too full of himself, too much of a show-off, always mouthing off. No surprise that someone had finally hauled off and hit him at that bar. And then Tony acts really stupid. He pulls a knife.

Luckily, the bouncer had kicked it out of his hand before Tony cut anyone. But that's the end of that career. For two years, anyway.

No use standing around out here though, better go on into the dump and get the visit over with. He was used to the routine by now, once a month like clockwork. Ma insisted. He'd brought her over once in the beginning but she'd started to bawl and Tony got all mad and said things are crummy enough in here, who needs that. Don't ever bring her here again.

So it was Rick who brought the bag of treats from Ma, as if he was visiting a monkey at the zoo. He stood resignedly for the patting down by the guard and waited in the visiting room. Not much of a crowd today. Just a dragged out older woman like Ma, and a skinny girl with a tattoo that reached from the back of her halter top up to her neck.

Tony came in, it was always a bit of a shock to see him in that baggy orange suit. All the time growing up, he'd been the older brother. The cool guy, who always looked better in clothes, who drove faster than anybody else. Always the leader of any group.

Now Tony just looked like the other prisoners. He even walked like them, with a sort of weird shuffle, not cocky at all. His face, once lean as Rick's, was getting puffy and doughy looking. He sounded the same though, that hadn't changed. Real bossy and always telling Rick what to do. Tony didn't seem to get the point that it was him who was trapped in this hole of a detention centre and little bro Rick who could leave any time he wanted.

But he had to admit, it was Tony who had put him on to the guys who would buy the stolen ATVs. Some connection he had made here.

"So, how's it going?" he asked Rick now. He always liked to hear details, probably because his life inside was so boring. He had been in the detention centre for almost a year now and was hoping to knock six months off his sentence for good behaviour.

Another reason why he was so interested in the thefts, he wanted money for when he got out, to buy some clothes and a car. He figured he deserved a cut on the jobs for getting Rick started. Rick didn't mind that part, but he didn't like to tell Tony too much about the jobs. And he for sure wasn't going to tell him about future plans. He didn't trust Tony not to blab to some other guys at the jail.

So he just said that he was lying low till the Marathon was over.

He felt bad, walking down the hallway, leaving Tony there. But hey, it wasn't his fault that his brother was dumb. And he was sick of feeling bad. About Tony, about Ma. He needed to feel good about something.

If you don't like your life, change it. Like some of those TV talkers said. And that's what he was going to do. He whistled, going down the steps.

Before leaving the city, he drove past the Case heavy equipment yard, his favorite place these days. All those rows of gleaming tractors and back-hoes, lined up on the lot. And each one worth thousands and thousands of dollars.

Some pretty sight.

* * *

Halstead left the 401 highway and took the turnoff for Cobourg. Traffic had been light on this weekday, the sky was a clear, pastel blue and the low, green hills had rolled by easily and soothing to thought. Ten minutes later he drove into the parking lot of the Ontario Provincial Police station, his expression a mixture of pleasure and resignation. Pleasure because he'd be meeting up with Chief Clark Barnard, an old friend, and resignation because Barnard wasn't above chaffing an old friend re the 'mickey mouse' detachment of Middle Island.

And so it might seem, compared to this impressive three story structure of glass and concrete, the nerve centre of an operation comprising some fifty officers, fifteen cruisers and a full office staff.

The sergeant at the front desk directed him to a meeting room where waited a dozen representatives from various detachments. All were here to co-ordinate efforts in the investigation of the heavy equipment thefts along the highway corridor.

Barnard waved from a knot of people mingling by the doorway.

"Hi Bud, I'll see you after the talk. Help yourself to coffee and take a seat," he motioned to the row of chairs.

Barnard moved to the front of the room where a power point screen was set up. He introduced Officer Kathy Pearson, who had prepared the day's presentation.

"As you are all aware" she began, "there's been a string of equipment thefts in towns along the highway. Many of these towns have been hit already – we've marked these with a red circle."

"These thefts are part of an international criminal operation. An annual billion dollar business, all built on a series of local connections, in many countries."

Some pictures came up on the screen.

"Here are some of the items of choice. Anything from John Deere, or Case or any of the other big name manufacturers. Including backhoes, forkifts, tractors, Gator side by sides, mowers and tillers. All of these have been stolen in the area in the past six months. And when we look back, we can see they might even have started a couple of years ago. But the trend is noticeable now."

Halstead raised a hand. "It still seems impossible that they can move the stuff so easily without being caught."

"Not so easily now," Kathy said. "Since we've been putting out more surveillance, they find it's harder to ship the equipment out right away or all at once. Their practise now is to stash the stuff in out of the way, empty spaces like old sheds or barns. Then move it in trucks, but inconspicuously as possible at night when there are lots of other truck out on the highways.

"We can't stop and search every truck or tractor-trailer on the highway. But we did find one of the barns, just outside Colborne. It was jammed with the stuff stolen from the Case dealership a couple of weeks ago. We figure that there has to be a network of local contacts, working for the ring. Someone who can inform the gang when there's an opportune time to make the grab."

She clicked off the power point and turned to address the audience.

"We have to make things tougher for these thieves. More observance in your jurisdictions. A tighter watch on known perps. Monitoring large structures such as warehouses and empty buildings. Highway patrols will double up on checking out large transports and trailers. They'll be pulling over anyone who looks suspicious. The weigh stations operations offer a good opportunity for this."

"These gangs are really getting under our skin. It's time to stop these thefts. Good hunting!"

At the end of the presentation, Halstead joined Clark Barnard in his office.

"Good show," he said. "You have to hand it to the bad guys, they're always coming up with something new."

"They keep us on our toes, that's for sure."

Halstead looked sceptical. "I doubt they're operating down our way though."

"I thought you mentioned some thefts."

"Just home-grown thieves. They crop up every few years."

"Could be," Bernard said. "We've found this gang or gangs usually hit one area for no more than a day or two, then move on before folks and businesses get more cautious and security conscious."

Halstead nodded. "We haven't had any thieving activity this week. Hopefully whoever they are, the perps are lying low because the Island is so busy with folks involved in the Marathon. I can barely get around myself."

"You're probably right. But keep an eye out. Think who a local contact could be in your patch."

"I still think our thefts are home-grown. Nobody's sending Bert Jardine's chain saw over to Dubai."

Barnard grinned. "I thought they got an ATV too."

"OK I guess that might get all the way to Montreal."

Shop talk done, they chatted briefly. Asked about each other's families. Bernard's eldest daughter was expecting. He seemed a bit bemused that he would be a grandparent.

"I'm a grand daddy twice over," Halstead said, pulling out a picture. "I highly recommend it. You have all the fun but get to hand the kids over when they get cranky."

Bernard made suitable admiring comments re the picture.

"And I suppose life on the Island is as serene as ever. With a bit of dog-catching or an occasional smash and grab at at the convenience store to liven things up?"

Halstead was loathe to mention the trail vandalism, which would just give his friend more ammunition for jokes. Also easy to imagine what Clark would make of Jakes' spring-time rescue of three fox cubs from the church basement. Or the various by-law infractions that came up, such as Mrs.Bigg's permanent yard sale.

"Oh we get the occasional murder or two," he said. "In among the traffic offenses."

He drove away, saying it was good to catch up. And it was. He had known Clark a long time and was glad to see his friend successful in his element. He supposed Clark really did wonder how he could spend his life in the quiet backwater of Middle Island. Not so surprising for himself of course, he was nearing sixty.

But what about young Jakes, he wondered. If the Middle Island force was to be swallowed up some day by the provincial or Bonville force, would he want to stay?

Maybe he should discuss it with Jakes some time, over a beer.

Any doubts he had for himself were allayed as soon as he reached the causeway and started across the sparkling Bay. He hadn't had his boat, the *Lazy Loon* out on the water much. Maybe when this Marathon Mania was over. He supposed he shouldn't be such a curmudgeon. The Marathon was good business for Steph and the other accommodation people. Plus inexplicably, most people seemed to be having fun.

There was more to life than battling crime. And nothing wrong with living in a peaceful backwater, untouched by far-fetched notions of international crime syndicates.

22

Jory tapped on the cruiser dashboard, beating out a cheerful tattoo to the music. He felt pretty good. He'd shaved another two minutes off his running time and there'd be no be no more shovelling duty on the trail. The pranks were over, the tricksters caught and turned in by their own parents. Poor kids, they'd only been pulling the type of stunts he and his buddies would have got up to at that age. It was just terrible bad luck that runner had a heart condition. Terrible most of all for Greg Leduc of course.

Still, cleaning up after the pranks had been turning into a real headache.

So he didn't even mind that Don Rusher had boasted on his show this morning, how his funding thermometer total had passed $15,000 bucks. Big deal, Rusher had a whole team, where Jory had raised pledges of $2000 on his own.

Stopped at an intersection, he saw Gerry Samson's big blue moving truck. Rick Farron and Bobby Jardine were in the midst of a job. Bobby was carrying a heavy box up the ramp but he still stopped to wave and give a big grin to Jory. The Jardine's farm was down the road from the Stutke place and Jory had always felt bad for Bobby, the way his Dad treated him. Bobby was a nice guy, happy to throw a ball or kick a soccer ball around with Jory and the other little kids.

Farron hollered at Bobby now. "Watcha looking at - get a move on !"

Geez, what a miserable jerk. Still, Bobby enjoyed having a job and making some money of his own. And he didn't have many options, so maybe it was worth it.

Jory was grateful for his own parents. Of course he had his wrangles with them, especially during his teens but overall they were pretty cool. Maybe it was because he had a couple of older sisters who kind of broke them in. Now Jen was married and living up in Stirling, with her husband and the twins. But it was Patty who had saved family feeling in a big way. Like many farmer's kids, especially sons, Jory had been aware as he grew up that his parents would like him to continue running the dairy farm. And he hadn't minded the planting and the haying, even the milking was an automated efficient procedure. But he didn't love it. He wasn't sure exactly what he wanted, but he knew he wanted more than sameness every day.

There wasn't a big split in the family. Dad and Mom were disappointed but not furious or bitter like Bert Jardine because Bobby's brothers weren't interested in farming. It was more a gradual thing, everybody just eventually getting used to the idea. And then Patty who had been doing all the same work as Jory through the years, came home from university with her new degree in animal husbandry.

Plus a pretty new ring proclaiming her engagement to Bryce McKenny a neighbour, who with his father, ran the farm next door. Jory's Dad and Mom would be farming for a few years yet but the news opened up all sorts of possiblities, still being discussed.

And Jory was free to pursue his own way.

All sorts of possibilities there too, still being thought of. Such as Livy Bind, sigh. No chance of seeing her today, though. She had gone to the city for the day, to a job interview. At least not the ESL job, for teaching abroad. Not yet, anyway.

He swerved, as a runner abruptly changed direction and darted across the road. They were everywhere now, new ones popping up as fast as the orange daylilies in the ditches. This guy was wearing earpods and listening to music. Classical, country, whatever, it was a dangerous practise and not allowed during the actual Marathon. Unfortunately there was no authority to control what the practising runners wore.

He checked the clock on the dashboard. There was time to stop at the Grill before going on to the station. Have a quick check of the blackboard, see how his pledges were mounting up. Gus was a good guy, had started Jory's sheet off with a $200 pledge and now it had grown to ten times as much.

He deftly nosed the cruiser into a tight spot on the street, marvelling at the number of cars. In the winter, you had your choice of spots. He noticed too, the No Vacancy sign on the driveway going to the four units out back.

Gus was behind the counter, polishing a glass. "Congratulations," he said. "I just updated the scores this morning. You're up to $2500."

"The Old Codgers aren't doing badly either." Jory said charitably, mentioning the local Elks team.

A man paying his cheque at the register, said "Those two Bonville guys are really pulling in the dough too. Over $10,000 each I heard."

"Yeah well there's a lot more people over there," Gus defended Jory. "A lot more money too."

The man shrugged. "I hear there's betting going on too. You should put up another board Gus, we could get some action going here."

Gus nodded judiciously. "Sure, not a bad idea. As long as we give half the winnings to the hospital fund."

He turned as a burst of laughter went up from the back room. Jory moved to the door and looked in where the regular were watching the noontime news.

Gary Plug was doubled over and laughing so hard he could hardly sputter out his words.

"Big news, it was just on the television. What a joke ! Somebody stole Rusher's goddamn fundraising thermometer."

"No kidding !" Jory snickered. "That's a good one!"

Probably not admirable behaviour for a policeman, but who could resist?

"Rusher didn't say anything about it on the show this morning though." Gus said.

"The parking lot is at the back," Plug sputtered on. "I guess nobody checked the front of the station till now, and then noticed that the thermometer was gone. They figure it happened last night when only the midnight guy was on. Probably just pulled up on the street out front with a pick-up and tossed the stupid thing in the back."

"No prize for guessing who," said another regular.

Gus nodded. "Somebody from the Kovak team for sure. Though Andy might not have known about it."

"I bet Rusher's blowing his top," Plug cackled, "He's been boasting about that thing on every show. What can he do though? Post a reward? The police aren't going to give a hoot, eh Jory?"

Jory grinned but said virtuously. "A theft's a theft, if it's reported. Depends what Rusher wants to do."

"Yeah well depends how embarrassed the guy wants to look I guess. I'd sure like to have seen the look on his face when he found out."

Gus went back behind the bar to switch on the radio. "The staff at the radio station wouldn't have wasted any time in telling him. And the way he's been going on about Kovak already – he'll probably be threatening bloody murder now."

Jory left reluctantly, hoping that Jane would know more. Her nephew was taking the journalism course at the College and hosted a program of local music one night a week at the CKAS station. And yep, she had her little desk radio turned on low.

He looked around, but Pete and the chief seemed to be out.

"It's delicious!" Jane crowed. "Don Rusher just made a special announcement on the news. He called the theft a puerile prank."

She pushed a chair over to Jory, and turned up the volume. "Here, listen."

Rusher's talk show tone was always caustic, today he was positively vitriolic.

"So here's my message to the perpetrators. You know who you are and I know who you are but I'll allow anonymity, though you don't deserve it. Nor will the station press charges for destroying property, though you don't deserve that exemption either.

"You've had your fun, now it's time to grow up. This kind of scurrilous behaviour from a fellow team is hardly helping our cause. The Marathon committee, not to mention the hospital foundation, would like the funding thermometer returned, no questions asked. Since you prefer to sneak around in the dark, you can do the same again tonight. No one will be watching. I have better things to do."

Jane switched off the set, grinning widely. "I bet the switchboard will be jammed with calls from folks who wanted to razz him."

"Must have been someone from the Kovak camp," Jory said. "It's pretty obvious."

"I don't know," Jane chuckled. "It could just as easily been some of Rusher's co-workers. My nephew Kevin says there's been lots of jokes about the thermometer at the station. Some of them were pretty rude about measurements, you can imagine."

Jory laughed. "I'm kind of sorry Rusher isn't pressing charges. Could have been fun getting the victim's statement. *And what exactly would be the dollar value of the stolen goods, sir?*

Jane shook her head. "Even he must realize that would make him look an even bigger ass than he already is."

23

Bert Jardine pulled the tractor into a tight turn in the driveway. The flock of gulls that were following him across the field, rose in screeching complaint. He drew up before the little group of watchers at the edge of the field. Marg, his wife, still trim in jeans and denim shirt, her gray hair twisted up with a bright pin into a tidy knot. Tyler his younger son, dark-haired, tall and rangy. And Bobby the lout, uselessly massive, with his mother's blue eyes.

The metal tractor flanks gleamed in the morning sunshine. Fire engine red, like a dazzling toddler's toy.

Burt beamed proudly. "Looks pretty good, eh?"

He stepped down to the ground and started to walk around the machine, extolling its wonders like a salesman. And well he might, he had just invested over $70,000 in the tractor. It was one of the newer compact models, a tough, versatile machine that with added attachments could excavate, front load, bale hay, cut brush and forklift. Just like its bigger counterparts.

"Quiet operation," he said. "Remote controls and all the bells and whistles, a beauty."

"C'mon Tyler," he invited, "Have a spin, try her out."

Tyler looked bored.

"C'mon," Bert urged. "After lunch we can start clearing those rocks up the lane. Put this baby through her paces."

"Take Bobby," Tyler said. "He wants to go."

Bert rolled his eyes, "I haven't got time for that right now. This is an expensive piece of equipment. We've got to go through the manual and work out the kinks first."

Tyler turned to Bobby and shrugged apologetically. *I tried. Maybe next time, buddy.* He stepped up into the tractor.

"Oh Bert," Marg said crossly. "Can't Bobby come too?"

But her words were drowned out as the others roared off in the machine.

She patted Bobby's shoulder, her eyes brimming with sympathy. The entire family were aware of the unhappy situation that had been going on for years. They just lived with it and Bobby stayed out of Bert's way as much as possible.

"How about some ice cream?" Marg asked. "I've got a new tub of tiger tail, your favourite."

Bobby just kept on looking after the dust of the tractor's wake.

"Or we could go to a movie in Bonville. Your pick. I have to go to the mall anyway."

Bobby turned around. "Thanks Mom," he said. "But ice cream doesn't help much anymore. Not like when I was a kid."

Marg's smile was watery. She gave him a hug. "You're a good boy, Bobby."

She dropped him off in the village, giving him another hug before driving away. He stood irresolutely in the park, squinting in the sunshine. He had a neat pair of sunglasses but he must have left them in the car.

Ice cream for a good boy!

He knew his mother loved him but she still treated him like a little kid, not a full-grown man. Even now, when he had a full-time job. But he did have a job and it was great to drive with Rick up Main Street and across the causeway in the big blue moving truck.

He had a plan now too. Soon he'd have enough money to get a place of his own in the village. Away from the farm, away from the old man. For awhile there had been a For Rent sign above the convenience store. Someone else got that place but he thought that after the summer, he might see if he could stay in one of Gus' places in back of the Grill.

He pictured it now. He'd bring the bed and dresser from his bedroom and his TV. He could put all his clothes in some big plastic bags and hang them up in the closet at the new place. Put his posters of race cars up on the walls. Rick could bring the truck and help him move. He wouldn't need help from anyone at the farm, he had his own buddy.

He saw the room all fixed up, himself lying on the bed watching Monday night wrestling. If he wanted a beer or a bag of chips or anything, he could just walk over to the Grill. Watch the baseball game with Gus or whoever else was there in the restaurant. Maybe he could even get a microwave and one of those little fridges. Then he could keep some beer himself, for guests.

Like, say if Rick wanted to drop in some night. Or maybe Tyler. He'd need a couple of chairs too. He should make a list. Miranda would help him. *The Pathway to Independence.* That was the name of the program they were working on.

He would be independent.

Free from the old man. Never have to listen to him calling me stupid again.

It was hard work studying with Miranda. That poem stuff about the sun's golden fingers and everything. But it was worth it.

He was on the pathway to independence.

He liked that word.

* * *

The Farron house, on Island Road 4 was not exactly an eyesore on the otherwise neatly kept road, but getting there. A storey and a half building, it was clad in white siding that had never been installed properly around the windows. A sparsely branched spruce tree drooped by the front door. The lawn was mowed but there were no flower beds, just the usual day lilies which would grow anywhere and a patch of scraggy untended daisies.

Inside the house in the kitchen, Brenda Farron looked anxiously at the clock and tugged at a strand of her fading red hair. A thin, wiry woman of fifty, she had once had a pert charm but both the confidence and the looks had become blurred over the years.

A restless woman who had survived a difficult life, her salvation had always been hard work in various local nursing homes. But since she'd strained her back in lifting an elderly patient in January, she'd been on sick leave. Now she was sinking into bitterness at the inactivity, and the prospect of her future on an inadequate government cheque.

Her first husband had left years ago, though she supposed she was still married to Rick's dad. Not that there was any money coming from that bum, though he owed her years of unpaid child support. Last she'd heard the guy was down in Mexico or somewhere, living in a hut and smoking dope on the beach. Some people just had it lucky.

She looked at the clock again and absently stroked a grey and white cat who lay on the table. Even more than her paycheque, she missed the company of her workmates and getting out for a beer now and then. She knew she was always bugging Rick to do things for her and sometimes she even felt bad about it. But damn it, kids owed you something. And with Tony her oldest son, sent away for the next two years – that kid got his old man's messed up brains, that's for sure -- there was nobody else to help.

Oh sure, there were a couple of fellows who were fun to drink with but they'd dropped off too since her injury. So these nights it was just her and the meds and whatever junk was on the television. Which was even worse after you'd watched it all day.

At least there was beer, as long as she could keep affording it.

Here was the boy driving in now, lord bless him, he hadn't forgotten.

Not that he was much company these nights, always with his nose in some farm equipment catalogues. Not much to talk about there. He said he was studying, if you could believe it.

Rick entered the kitchen, pushed the cat off the table and deposited the box of beer. "Geez ma, you could keep it off our plates at least."

But tonight his complaint was half-hearted. He had other things on his mind these days than his mother's sloppy housekeeping. He'd even picked up her Tuesday night chicken wings special.

Brenda perked up, that he'd remembered. She limped over to the fridge and reached for fresh plates. Luckily, there were a couple.

"Are you going to eat?" she asked.

"Yeah I guess, then I've got some more studying to do."

She looked disappointed, but put the plates on the table. Then added a couple of wings on her plate and four on Rick's, plus the little containers of cole slaw and sauce. She cracked open a couple of beers and sat, wincing a bit.

"Get my pillow will you Rick."

She pulled over one of the catalogues and flipped a page.

"I don't know why you're looking at this stuff all the time. It's not as if we need anything like that for this place, even if you could afford one of the things. My goodness, even the lawn mowers cost $5000."

"I told you it's for work. I have to know all sorts of details, like how much things weigh when I'm using the trucks. How much they can carry."

"Doesn't your boss look after that sort of thing?"

He snatched the magazine away. "Maybe I don't want to have a boss all my life."

"I could help," she said. "Give me the magazine and I'll test you."

"Maybe sometime Ma. Not just now."

She cast about for another topic, spotted the calendar, which still featured the February picture, a white Persian kitten sitting on a heart-shaped chocolate box. She liked cats.

"You're making a long haul sometime soon, aren't you? All the way to Owen Sound, isn't it?"

He grunted, chewing on a wing and already immersed in the catalogue.

John Deere 4520 series – cab and loader. Used $40,000. LD 4760 $86,000. duals, power shift, hydraulic pump.

They finished the meal in silence. At least there was Canadian Idol on tonight, she thought. She was going to vote for the eleven year old dancer.

24

Only ten days to go till Marathon Day ! Get your souvenir hats and t-shirts here!

The village Main Street was already getting busier as Marathon Fever gripped the Island inhabitants. It seemed that every second person Halstead met was wearing the Marathon cap and t-shirt. Many others seemed to be visitors, drawn to check out the Island by the recent spate of publicity. Local business owners were ecstatic. Pott's Grocery had no more bread and the convenience store was out of ice.

"If it's like this now," Halstead complained. "Imagine what it's going to be like next week for the actual run. With all this great weather too, there will likely be people coming out just for the drive."

There was a line-up at lunchtime at the Grill. He battled his way to the counter where Gus didn't even have time to chat. Both dining rooms were packed and loud with conversation. The blackboard had been hoisted up into prominence above the bar. If there was any actual betting going, Halstead was technically unaware. However, folks could buy tickets to predict who would raise the most funds. The ticket money would go to the fund as well.

Gus waved from the happily beeping cash register.

"A twenty minute wait for a table," Tammy apologized.

"The chip truck?" Pete suggested.

"And if there's a line-up at Benny's," the chief said. "I'm heading to my daughter's in Kitchener. She's got two kids, but it's got to be quieter than here."

They ordered burgers and found two empty spots at the end of a picnic table, The rest of the table was occupied by three fellows from the hydro road crew, a reminder that the generator hadn't turned up anywhere yet. Work had been completed on the poles by the causeway though, so no detour was needed for the Marathon run at least. The crew were just finishing up their lunch and soon departed with their trash for the bin.

Jakes had spent the morning going over security arrangements with the volunteers. Halstead would have preferred to discuss anything but the Marathon, but he gracelessly submitted to a working lunch.

Jakes now unfolded a map on the empty end of the picnic table and gave an overview of the plan. Halstead supressed a smile, thinking that the former army lad had actually enjoyed the tactical part of the job, mapping out in detail the positioning of the various volunteers along the Marathon route and informing them of their responsibilities.

"The ambulance will be parked here," Pete pointed to a dot by the causeway.

Halstead winced. "Hopefully we won't need it !"

But he nodded approval. "Looks good. It's a big job, a big responsibility, funneling all those people safely along the trail. I'll be glad when it's over."

Pete folded up the map. "All the volunteers will have cell phones in case of any emergency. Which there won't be," he said sternly. 'I'll check out the entire course myself the evening before," he said. "And Jory will be running on the day."

"So, no head to head race for you two?"

"It's not a race."

Halstead laughed. "Sure, I believe you."

"O.K." Pete grudged a nod. "It might be a bit of a contest. But we'll just have to trust our timers and compare stats later."

Halstead moved to the next table for a moment to talk to an acquaintance.

"Anything else?" he asked on returning. Jakes hadn't moved.

"Ali wants to do something special for our seventh anniversary," Pete said reluctantly. "Any ideas?"

"Me?" Halstead laughed. "I just throw myself on the mercy of Angie at the flower shop. She makes me a nice bouquet.'

Pete shook his head. "I don't think that will do for me this year."

"I thought the women had the ideas and we just waited for instructions. Haven't you got your instructions yet?"

"I wish it was that easy." Pete picked up the tray to return to Benny at the truck window.

"Tell him I might be here for supper too," Halstead said gloomily. "Steph's all wrapped up in Marathon preparations and I'm just in the way. At this rate, I might not make it to *our* next anniversary."

*   *   *

"These two boxes have the maps," Steph said, opening the top of one carton with an exacto-knife. "And the boxes over there have the schedules."

She handed Ali a stack of maps, wrapped with an elastic band. They had set up a work space in the big lodge room at the Retreat. Ali began to lay out the items in piles on the long dining table. Each registrant would get one of the specially made cotton tote bags sporting the Marathon logo. A kit would contain a souvenir schedule of the weekend events, a map of the Island and the actual course, the logo stamped refillable water bottle, and a numbered runner's bib in the blue and cream Marathon colours. There were also vests for the volunteers.

Steph held a bib up against her chest. "These are cute."

They quickly set up a system. Each would pick up a tote bag and work her way up the table. After stuffing a kit, would stack them against the walls. Livy and Halstead would help load them in the Retreat van the night before the run. In the morning – a very early start – Steph would drive the kits over to the park.

"Did you hear Don Rusher's program this morning?" Steph asked.

"Yes I did," Ali said with a shudder. "You mean what he said about the "scuzzbags" who stole his funding thermometer?"

Steph smirked, "I heard they found the thing in the town dump, covered with garbage. He was furious that it hadn't been returned to the station."

"What a baby, you'd think he'd realize it was all just a joke." Ali said crossly. "He's way over the top. What's the matter with him? This Marathon is supposed to be a fun-filled community event. It's bad enough that we've already lost one runner in tragic circumstances. We really don't need any more unpleasantness."

Steph carried a stack of filled tote bags over to the wall. "Men! They have to take everything so seriously."

"What must it be like for his wife," Ali said. "So embarrassing, how can she take this?"

Steph nodded. "I've met Arlene. She's nice, works in Bonville social services. Probably can't wait for all this nonsense to be over. Her first husband died young, but they had a son who's now sixteen. She and Don have a daughter a few years younger."

"Are the stories true then, that Don and Debra Toller nearly married? And then she fell for Andy Kovak?"

Steph shrugged. "Sure, but that was a long time ago.".

"And do the Kovaks have any children?"

"No, they seem to be happy in their respective careers. I imagine Debra and Andy are fed up with this public rivalry though. They probably regret ever getting involved."

Ali agreed. "Debra looked pretty icy at the Marathon Committee meeting yesterday."

"Steph sighed. "It's so ridiculous. They're all in their forties, passions long cooled."

'Don't say that!" Ali protested.

Steph looked startled, "I didn't mean that feeling was over, just that jealousy is over, everybody has moved on."

"Sorry," Ali said, "I didn't mean to jump on you like that. Pete and I are coming up on our seventh anniversary and I've been thinking about love and passion a lot."

Steph frowned, "No trouble, I hope in Jakes-land? Anyway you're nowhere near forty, you're just a couple of kids."

"No," Ali said hastily. "Nothing like that. Just me, being silly."

Steph sat down and patted the chair beside her. "Give. I'm all ears."

Ali hesitated but began,

"Our wedding wasn't a well-attended event, neither Pete's Dad or my mother Nuran came. I think it would be nice to do something with Nuran and Walter. But that would be a big deal, and way too complicated to arrange for this year. I haven't even mentioned the idea to Pete. Anyway, he would rather just do something together. What we usually do."

Steph nodded. "That can be nice too."

"It's the word *usually* that bothers me. Are we already at *usually*?"

Steph was back to frowning. "Are you worried about Pete's feelings for you?

"No, never. He's as sweet and loving as ever."

"Then what are you worried about, your own feelings?"

Ali shook her head. "I guess I just don't want to lose our fire, our passion. I don't think I could ever bear to have Pete look at me and wonder where that all *went*."

Steph smiled. "There are many different phases to love, my friend."

Ali nodded, "Of course you're right. As I said, I'm just being silly."

Steph was thinking. "I didn't mean you couldn't shake things up a bit from time to time. What would you like to do?"

Ali blushed. "I find myself reading headlines on the women's magazines at the supermarket. You know the type of thing, *How to spice up your marriage.* Or looking up honeymoon trip packages on the Net. Even the really silly ones."

"You mean the hot tubs in the Pokonos?" Steph teased. "Plastic rose petals on the bedsheets?"

Ali laughed. "Can you picture Pete Jakes in that setting?"

"Where might Pete like to go then – some magical tropic isle?"

"If it was February maybe. But it's hard to top the beauty of the Island in June. And he travelled so much in the army, he's been a lot of places. Definitely seen enough of the Middle East anyway."

"What about the Far East? Livy could fill you in about Japan."

Ali patted her friend's shoulder. "Thanks for listening, but we'd better get back at stuffing these kits. Maybe I'll just get some new lingerie, that at least has a proven track record."

"You know it, girl !"

25

"How much weight can a big truck like this carry?" Rick Farron asked. "Like in a full moving load."

Gerry Samson could be forgiven for looking surprised. His employee rarely spoke beyond a sullen compliance with the instructions of the day. Had never offered an opinion on the weather, let alone shown any interest in the technical details of his job. This was a first.

The two men stood in the Samson driveway, looking at the vehicle.

Samson answered enthusiastically. "This 26 foot truck has a capacity of 1600 cubic feet, about right to haul furniture for a four bedroom house, as you know."

"But what weight is that?" Rick asked again.

Samson considered. "About 10,000 pounds. That's easily enough to handle most furniture loads, even with appliances."

Damn, a backhoe and bucket weigh 14,000 lbs.
A tractor weighs 20,000 lbs
The truck's OK for carrying the 500 lb ATV or a lawn tractor
But how am I gonna transport any thing like a backhoe for the big bucks?

Warmed at the presence of an audience, Samson expanded. "Those you-haul type businesses have really made a name for themselves but there's lots of older folks out there too. They don't want to haul furniture and heavy boxes around. One bad move could cause a back injury that lasts for months, if not permanently." Samson even used a cartoon showing this in his print advertising. Two older guys bent double carrying a couch. Over their heads, a speech balloon saying a big OUCH!

"That's where you boys come in."

That's what the job was today, as a matter of fact. A senior couple in Bonville moving from their home of fifty years to an apartment. Downsizing, they called it. A hectic time for movers was coming up, as they approached the end of the month. Lots of back and forth movement in the Bonville apartment buildings. The boys would be busy.

Rick didn't thank him for the information, merely nodded abstractedly before climbing up into the cab. But that was O.K. Samson looked musingly after the small dust storm he left in the driveway. It was good that Rick was interested at all.

He gave himself a mental pat on the back. He had been right to take Rick on, despite the warnings.

The Farrons are low-life, trouble.

Look at his jail-bird brother.

But the fellow was working out fine. Shows what a bit of trust and encouragement could do. Sometimes you had to give people a chance.

* * *

Farron drove away, his mind buzzing.

Damn, this was gonna take some figuring. Unless he just wanted to keep on taking small stuff and ATVs.

But there were some lighter tractors in the catalogues. Japanese compact machines, about half the size.

Maybe he could scout out one of those.

He picked up Jardine at the Grill and headed across the causeway, his thoughts on equipment weights and dimensions. Luckily he was a good driver, as he was hardly aware of his surroundings. When they arrived at the job, he got out of the truck and went around to the back to drop the loading ramp.

Jardine grabbed the other side. Belatedly, Rick noticed that the dummy wasn't his usual self. He hadn't been telling any of his goofy stories that Rick never listened to. Hadn't said a word, come to think of it, since he got in the truck.

Now he nearly dropped the loading ramp on Rick's hands.

Rick just managed to pull away in time. "Watch it dummy ! You could have smashed my fingers !"

Bobby's big bland face went through an amazing transformation. Rick even backed away, the guy looked so angry.

"Don't call me dummy," he said savagely. "Not you or nobody else. I'm sick of it."

"OK, buddy," Rick said. "Settle down." He waved his hands. "See, I'm O.K. No problemo."

He grabbed up a length of cotton tarp and headed for the house.

The old people were there, hovering on the porch. He wished they'd gone away for the day but people always did that, like they needed to direct the move.

"Maybe you want to take that hutch last," the old guy said. "It's going to our daughter's house, you can drop it off on the way."

Rick looked at the big mother of a thing, six feet tall and heavy. *Fine with me to leave it for now. With Jardine in this nutty mood, I'd be glad to wait a bit. I don't need a hutch dropped on my foot.*

"What's up, Jardine?" he asked when they got into the living room. "Get out on the wrong side of the bed this morning? You look like you want to pound somebody."

"I do want to pound somebody," Bobby said in that same raw tone. "My dad is such a jerk ! He's had the new tractor for a week now but only him and Tyler are allowed to drive it. I only wanted to sit in the driver's seat and see what it feels like, but he won't even let me touch it. He says I'm too dumb to learn the instructions."

Your old man's likely right.

Rick Farron had no tact but he knew better than to say this aloud.

"What kind of tractor is it?" Rick asked idly. He knew the Jardine place was a big operation, using major equipment.

"It's real nice," Bobby said truculently. "Not big like the field one but it can do everything around the yard. It's even got a backhoe you can hook up to it."

"What make?" Rick asked, not so idly now.

Bobby shrugged, "They said it was forring or something like that."

Could he mean foreign?

"I'll show him, though," Bobby said. "I'll go out there some night and drive that tractor so far into the woods my Dad will never get it out."

A light dawned in Rick's eyes.

Was it possible? If it was like the tractors he'd seen in the catalogue, it could be worth as much as $80,000.

What would a tractor like that weigh? He'd have to check that. Still, it was one heck of an idea.

And I've got that long distance run this week. Could move everything out from the barn at once. The generator, the other ATV and a tractor! What a haul that would be.

He looked almost benevolently at Jardine

The dummy would be some use to him yet. He could probably get hold of the keys to the vehicle. Hell, the dog wouldn't even bark at him. This could work.

He clapped Bobby on the back. "We get this stuff moved quick today, buddy and we can go for a beer."

Surprised, but gratified, Bobby grinned and picked up a big heavy armchair. By himself.

Invitation
Ms. Ali Jakes and guest
To the annual Gala-Fund-Raising Dinner
of the Bonville and District Hospital
In the Banquet Room at the Commodore Hotel

The invitation had arrived two weeks ago.

"We're all invited," Steph said. "The entire executive of the Marathon Organizing Committee. And their spouses. We're being included as special guests this year because of our – and I quote – amazing fund-raising efforts toward purchasing new hospital equipment."

"A posh card," Ali said, fingering the deckle edged cream-coloured invitation.

"It's going to be pretty posh altogether," Steph said. "The Hospital Board of Directors will be attending of course, some staff doctors and head of departments. Also our Member of Parliament, the two mayors and their wives, and various Bonville luminaries and business people who have collectively and generously donated millions to the hospital over the years."

"Goodness !" Ali said. "Sounds impressive."

Steph frowned. "I may have to go to T.O. and buy something new to wear. Of course I'm sure that Debra will outdo us all with some fabulous designer creation."

She paused and looked warmly at her friend. "Though she could never outdo you, my dear, even if you wore a flour sack. What will you wear, by the way. Do you want to come shopping with me? We could make a day of it."

Ali smiled. "Thanks but Nuran sent me a lovely dress for my birthday in the winter. Red silk, with a gold thread running through it. I haven't had an occasion to wear it yet."

"Sounds exotic ! "Steph said. "That will jazz up the group picture, for sure" She pirouetted. "I believe we're being presented with a plaque."

At supper, Pete had found the card propped against his water glass.

He read it, and looked up to see his wife's eyes bright with mischief.

"Closest thing to a ball we've ever been asked to," she grinned. "Aren't you excited?"

"I'm surprised that you're excited," he said warily. "Don't forget I've heard your opinions and Miranda's about some of these folks over the last few months."

She shrugged, said airily, "Let bygones, be bygones, I say. I guess I just feel like doing things differently this year. Special things, like dressing up, dancing even."

Pete winced. *Oh, oh there's that dreaming look in her eye again.*

She bussed his cheek. "We'll have to get your suit cleaned."

"I'm the Marathon security adviser, remember," he protested. "I should probably be in uniform."

"No way," Ali laughed. "I'm sure some OPP fellows can handle that. You'll be at the Committee table with the rest of us."

And now the big night was nearly here.

"You're going? Halstead asked gleefully that morning. "You actually got roped into going? I knew I did the right thing giving you the job."

"How are you getting out of it?" Pete asked enviously.

"I'm not on the Committee," the chief smirked.

"Steph didn't want you to come?"

"It was a bit tricky," Halstead acknowledged. "I insisted that someone has to be on call here on the Island." He lay luxuriously back in his chair. "Of course I'm sorry to be missing all the glamour of a gathering of the Bonville luminaries and hospital donors. Oh and the riveting speeches of course, particularly from the mayors. That's probably the best part."

He picked up the Marathon cap and spun it playfully on his finger. "But I'll be all ears to hear details, Prince Charming. The menu, the band. What the ladies were wearing."

Pete swiped the hat out of his hand and sent it flying to the floor. "You owe me." Which for Jakes was a pretty stern comment.

* * *

Ali swirled around the the living room in her new dress, to her daughter's excited approval. It was a dress made for swirling. The shimmering silk gold top, sleeveless and scoop necked, and the red full skirt swinging out below.

Nevra clapped her hands, "You look just like the princess in my books, Mommy." She called up the stairs. "Daddy, come and look."

"Yes come on, Pete," Ali added. "It's almost time to go. We've still got to drop Nevra off at Holly's house." The little girl was staying at a friend's house overnight, which made an exciting evening for her too.

"Oh don't you look great," she said as he came down the stairs. "Look at Daddy, Nevra. There's something about a man in a well-cut jacket. And the smell of after-shave – yummy!"

She took a couple of dancing steps towards him and gave him a kiss, which he returned heartily.

Only Ali heard the husky murmur in her ear. "Lucky we've got an audience, honey. Or that dress wouldn't stay on you long."

"Later, my sweet," she murmured back.

Nevra took a picture on the phone, small face earnest in her task. Her parents at first made funny faces but were strictly reprimanded.

Across the road, Emily dog looked forlornly out the kitchen window as Miranda stepped into the car.

"I told her I'd bring back some tasty treat," Miranda said. She was wearing a sand coloured blazer and trousers, with a rose coloured scarf for colour.

"Aren't we all fine," Ali enthused. "No hicks us, we Island folk. Fit to rub elbows with the elite across the causeway."

Miranda tssked. "It's easy to outshine those Bonville upstarts. My family took up residence on the Island when it was an Island, a hundred years before Mayor Sheehey's people had even boarded the boat back in Ireland."

Ali pretended shock. "And I thought you didn't put much stock in ancestry. That it was probably peopled with thieves and pirates."

"Only when it's called for, my dear. There are times when the blood rises."

* * *

Unlike most of Bonville's chain hotels, situated at the north end of the city near the highway, the Commodore fronted on a large treed park beside the lake. Designed in the lavish sixties, when the city downtown hadn't yet lost out to the malls, it had a sweeping drive and an entrance fit for the arrival of movie stars. In fact, that very entrance had once been the setting for a television commercial for a famous shampoo with an equally famous actress. There was a framed picture in the lobby.

Talk was that the hotel was suffering from a loss of custom to the chain operations and that the air conditioning in the rooms was often faulty. But in the mellowing sunlight of a June evening, the Bay waters sparkling in the distance, the place had a nostalgic charm. Ali thought the chrome and concrete chain hotels couldn't hold a candle to it.

Pete drove up the curving drive and stopped to let the ladies out. "I'll catch up in a minute."

"Look, there are the kids with their camera equipment," Miranda said.

Students from the community college media course were making a video of the event as a term work assignment. They had taken up positions on both sides of the steps.

Ali opened the door of the car with a flourish, her eyes sparkling with excitement. "Come, my friend. Our moment of stardom awaits!".

Pete grinned, driving away.

Maybe there is something to say for getting fancied up, once in awhile.

Ali took Miranda's arm and they swept up the few steps to the grand entrance, waving graciously to the cameras. The actual annual meeting consisting of auditor's report, board elections etc. had taken place already, during the afternoon. Now the lobby was decorated with tall vases of purple and gold irises.

Steph, wearing a slinky tropical green top over cream coloured slacks, came forward to greet them. "We're in here, ladies."

The door was open to the high-ceilinged, spacious banquet room, which could easily accommodate the tables set with flowers and candles for a hundred guests. Wine glasses and cutlery sparkled in the light from the chandeliers.

Before Steph could usher the others into the room though, she paused, aware of some sort of disturbance in the lobby, near the entrance.

Curious, Ali looked back. "I wonder what's going on."

People seemed to be crowded around the doorways, looking out at something happening on the steps. She could hear raised voices.

Leaving Miranda behind, Ali and Steph pushed their way through.

"Oh no !" Steph clapped her hand to her mouth. "That's some bad timing."

It seemed that by some awful coincidence both the Kovak and the Rusher couples had arrived practically on top of each other. Andy and Debra Kovak looked to have arrived first and were in the midst of posing and being interviewed by the media students.

Debra in a silver sheath, struck a pose that managed to look both natural and stunning. Andy, his broad shoulders impressive in formal wear, flashed a proud smile. The couple joked and talked easily with the students.

The Rushers were stuck at the bottom of the steps. Looking fed up, the radio station manager roughly grabbed his wife's arm and started up. One of the students noticed, and smiling, reached out, saying something like. "You're next."

Arlene Rusher, startled, stumbled slightly and bumped into Debra Kovak.

Both women swayed precariously on the steps and reached out for their menfolk.

Rusher was almost knocked off his own feet. Either he hadn't noticed the sequence of events, or was too blindly angry to care.

He shouted at Andy. "Watch where you're going, you big stupid buffalo. You almost pushed Arlene down the stairs."

Kovak steadying his own wife, turned in surprise, his anger flaring up quickly in return.

"Who are you telling to watch it, jerk? Shut up or I'll be happy to give *you* a shove."

Debra and Arlene now stood together safely at the top of the steps, staring with embarrassment and horror at the scene.

Rusher, now really incensed, scrambled closer to Andy. The students moved nervously back from the two men. Just as Rusher seemed about to launch himself at Andy, Pete appeared at the bottom of the steps. Assessing the situation immediately, he ran up and grabbed Rusher's arm.

"Hey men, let's settle down. Take it down a notch. There are people here waiting to go into dinner."

Andy Kovak glared but stepped back. "Just keep this lunatic away from me." He moved to join his wife.

Rusher was still rigid with anger. He looked blankly around at the shocked students, the waiting people, the two women standing at the top of the stairs.

He took a deep shuddering breath, his hands slowly unclenching.

Pete waited till the Kovaks had disappeared into the lobby. Then let go of Rusher's arm. "OK now?"

Rusher nodded tightly, then moved quickly up the steps to where Arlene waited, her face furious.

"I suppose there's no possibility of a joint photo?" Steph asked brightly.

*   *   *

"At least they're sitting at different tables," Ali muttered to Pete.

The Kovaks, in recognition of their many city fund-raising efforts, were seated at the head table. Through the opening speeches, Debra wore an expression as cold as the ice cubes in the water glasses. Meanwhile the Rushers sat at a table for local business sponsors. Arlene Rusher looked as if she wished herself a thousand miles away.

Miranda unfolded her napkin and said drily, "I wonder how much the kids will edit the film. If there's anyone there with real journalistic instincts, they'll keep all the juicy parts."

"Miranda !" Charlene admonished. "We don't have to fan the flames."

Charlene was obviously prepared to enjoy the evening. She wore a purple pantsuit and looked like a happy plum. Barry and Joyce were attending with their spouses and even Carol, in a summery print dress, seemed to have put aside her pessimism for the occasion.

The chicken cordon bleu was good, wine flowed. There was a cheerful buzz of conversation around the room. After dessert, people were mellow enough to sit through more inevitable speeches and thank-yous. One of which was to the Marathon Committee and their fund-raising efforts.

Charlene rose to her public moment, speaking for all of the members of the team. She ended with a rousing invitation to the audience.

"I hope we see some of you out in your sneakers next Saturday. We'll give you a commemorative hat !"

She received enthusiastic applause.

Ali noticed that the Rushers had left quietly and unremarked, at some point. The band began to play then and Andy Kovak escorted his wife out onto the dance floor that had been cleared at the end of the room.

Steph offered to drive Miranda home, if the Jakes wanted to stay.

"We accept !" Ali said, taking up Pete's hand.

Steph smiled. "Just doing my bit for romance." She leaned in to whisper, "But judging by the look in your husband's eye tonight, I'd say you two are good for another sixty years."

27

Halstead found Jakes at his computer post, scanning the provincial daily list of thefts and property recoveries. He sat in the other chair, said cheerily,

"I guess I missed some excitement last night at the Gala. Steph told me you had to break up a potential punch-up."

Pete grimaced. "Yes that was fun. I had to stop Don Rusher from attacking Andy Kovak. Maybe I did Rusher a favour, I doubt that he would have won."

He pushed away from the computer. "What is wrong with that guy? He seems to have a good life. A nice wife and kids, a good job."

Halstead shook his head. "He's a real sorehead on that show of his every morning. Maybe he can't shake the personality when he's out of the studio either."

"Yeah well, he could sure use some counselling and he'd better get it soon before he causes any more trouble."

"Andy didn't want to press charges?"

"No, he's a good guy. I think he and Debra found the incident embarassing enough. They just wanted it to end and not ruin the Gala evening for everybody else."

"Lucky for Rusher."

"I told him that. I also warned him that police can lay charges of our own if we think it necessary."

"Let's hope that's enough." Halstead looked at the computer screen.

"Turning to other matters, my guess is our stolen ATVs aren't turning up on the 'found items' lists."

"Nada, as usual," Pete agreed. "And no local leads either. But those machines are tasty, hot items. Brand new, with intact registration numbers. The gang would likely ship them away somewhere fast - out of province at least."

"So you're assuming now that the gang has spread its tentacles here?"

"It's a strong possibility, anyway. As Jory says, if those machines were taken by local joyriders, they'd be showing up. The perps would be wanting to show them off. I'd say if another pricey item goes, we'll know for certain."

"So we'd be looking for a local contact, who scouts out the jobs."

"Could be one of ours, or maybe even someone from Bonville."

"Either way, they must have to stash the stuff here for a bit. And that's just great. With all the back lanes and disused farm buildings we've got here, it would be like looking for a needle in a haystack."

*   *   *

Jory couldn't control an involuntary jump as the two barking dogs roared up to him. The one was a shepherd mix, easily a hundred pounds. In his experience though, the other, a smaller terrier type, was probably more likely to bite.

"Call them off, Howard," he yelled up to the house. "It's me, Jory."

There was a whistle and the dogs wheeled in mid-yelp, as their owner, old Howard Peelie came limping down the driveway. He carried a cane, which he wielded in a threatening manner. The dogs weren't fooled at all, but happily circled the old man's ankles, almost knocking him over.

"Sorry Jory," Howard wheezed. "They're supposed to stay up by the house."

"Keep them tied up on Marathon Day," Jory said. "Not everybody knows they're friendly. You don't want some visitor lodging a formal complaint."

By now the dogs were wagging their tails at Jory.

"I will for sure, lad," Howard said. "What are you doing out here on a warm day?"

"Just checking out the trail, making sure it's safe for the runners."

He wasn't running this morning, but driving to the various crossroads and nipping up to the trail. It was actually kind of nice for a change just to be walking and checking off his clipboard. Even nicer, Livy was meeting him with a picnic lunch.

Someone was practicing today though, he heard the thudding of sneakers on the trail. Mrs. Hunter, the high school gym teacher. He'd been her student at one time and supposed he could call her Corinne by now, but it still felt strange.

She didn't pause, but waved. "Hi Jory. No fish guts today, I hope."

"No ma'am," he assured her. "All clear."

Though this was hardly a big feather in his policeman's cap. The kids' own parents had brought them in. Life on the Island didn't involve a lot of major crime-solving. Not like the guys in the OPP, investigating those heavy equipment robberies. But he thought the chief was likely right, there was no chance such a gang would ever look to the Island for thieving prospects. Who would be that nuts?

He was a bit envious though, an unusual feeling for him. What would that be like to work for the provincial police force? Say a fellow wanted to get married someday and his wife wanted to live somewhere else. With the OPP you could get a job anywhere in the province. Somewhere bigger than Middle Island. Or maybe he could even apply to a city force, a city like Ottawa for instance.

Funny how you could be dissatisfied and not even know it till someone comes into your life and changes everything you thought you knew, overnight.

And here she came, riding her bike. A blue plastic cooler bag in the basket.

"Hi," she smiled, on coming up. "What a lovely day!"

He smiled back.

The lunch was pretty amazing. Sandwiches would have been fine, but she'd brought a container of chicken salad, buns and chocolate cookies made by Steph's caterer.

"Leftovers from last night," Livy said.

Jory took another forkful. "Must be nice."

She shivered, "It's terrible to think that man died just back there on the trail. Terrible for his wife too. They must have been enjoying the morning, being together. Thinking it was like any other day – like today for instance."

Jory nodded. "Yep, it makes you think."

"I bet those kids feel really bad. That's a heavy load to carry. Do they know what's going to happen to them yet?"

"Most of the old folks around here would just say they need a good whipping."

"And what would you say?"

He grinned. "I'm an officer of the law. I can't condone violence."

"But?"

"I'm thinking those boys might have preferred that to a whole summer of community service, picking up trash in the ditches, which is what they're likely to get."

She passed him the container full of cookies.

"How's your running coming along?" she asked. "Broken that Olympic record yet?"

"Ha, ha," he said. "I did shave off nearly another minute on yesterday's run though. Down to 1:35:03 now."

"I guess that's good."

"Pretty good," he admitted modestly.

She laughed and punched his shoulder. "Pretty darn good, you mean. I bet Pete Jakes is shivering in his sneakers. It should be quite a photo finish."

"It would be, but we won't be running together. The chief can't spare us both at the same time."

"Well that's no fun," Livy said.

"We'll be timed," Jory said. "That will have to do. We are a police station, you know."

"Think you'll keep it up, run in other Marathons?"

"I doubt it. Some of the people who write in the runners magazine seem a little crazy. Like it's how they get their high. I'm just in it for the glory, myself."

"The glory?"

"Sure – knowing that I'm the fastest man on Middle Island. My fame will be legend."

"You wish !"

They had finished eating. The little silence grew into a longer silence. The hour was so still that they could hear the rustling of grasshoppers in the tall weeds by the trail.

Jory stood and offered a hand to Livy. "Want to go for a walk?"

The afternoon was all blue sky and softly undulating yellow fields that smelled sweetly of hot, recently cut hay. In the distance, a baling machine droned like a benign, monstrous insect, chewing away at the crop.

"Not quite the same landscape as Cezanne's south of France," Livy said, "but gorgeous in it's own way."

"Um huh," Jory agreed. Whatever. Personally, he couldn't imagine a more perfect place. And having Livy beside him was the icing on the cake.

She swirled to face him, laughing apologetically. "Boy I bet I sounded like a snob just then. And I haven't even been to the South of France ! I do love Cezanne's pictures though and I hope to get there sometime."

There she was, going on about travelling again. Still the Island was looking it's best today and she had said it was gorgeous. He couldn't have chosen a better day for a meeting, it was as if the whole universe was helping him out.

She had picked up a daisy, was twirling it in her fingers, then handed it to him.

"Mom mentioned that you were going steady with someone. Wouldn't she have liked to go for a walk with you today?"

"Gayle and I broke up last fall."

Livy looked the question.

Jory tossed the daisy into the grass, said lightly. "She got a job in the city – all you women go off to the city." Then added more seriously, "I think she had kind of a hard time with me being a policeman here. She said that people didn't want to hang out with us any more."

Livy frowned. "That's too bad."

Jory shrugged. "She was probably right. You've seen what I run into with Rick Farron. And he's not the only one. I guess if I stay here long enough, they'll just see me as a policeman and forget they ever knew me any other way."

They watched a hawk circling over the field.

"What about you?" he asked. "I heard you were seeing someone in Japan."

She kept looking at the hawk. "It was too far away, that's what it finally came down to." She turned and smiled, "The airfares alone ..... Mom would have had a fit."

They started to walk again. "So you find your job interesting?"

He grinned. "It's not exciting stuff like cleaning up fish guts every day, but yeah, so far there's been lots to learn. You feel like you're helping people too. Last year we caught a really bad dude, I'll tell you about it some time. And right now we're working to solve some robberies."

"I'm glad you've found something you like to do," Livy said. "I think that's one of the hardest things to figure out in life. That and where you want to be."

She paused to look up a lane, lined by a hedgerow of wizened, crooked apple trees. The entranceway was partly jammed with brush.

"Nobody's been up Turner's Lane for awhile," she said. "Didn't there used to be an old barn?"

"Nothing up there but weeds now, I expect." Jory said. "My dad said the land is low there, too wet for haying. I don't know who Turner was, but he's long gone."

"The trees are still greening," she noticed. "I love old apple trees, they never give up."

He took her hand and they swung back along the trail.

Up Turner's Lane, the swallows swooped in and out of the loft in Turner's abandoned barn.

C alamity !
      Three days days before the run, and after twelve days of perfect, unbroken sunshine, the weather channel was now having the nerve to predict that rain was on its way. A big weather system was moving up from the eastern United States.

There was no joy this afternoon at the penultimate meeting of the Marathon Committee.

"Maybe we'll be lucky and it will by-pass us," Joyce said. "You've seen that happen. Areas north of Bonville will get the rain and we won't."

"Don't let the farmers hear you say that," Miranda said. "They'll throw rocks at you."

"Oh you know what I mean, Miranda," Joyce snapped. "Just this once, when everybody has worked so hard to arrange the run."

"It doesn't matter what we wish," Carol said despondently, all memory of the fairy-tale Gala evening now fading rapidly. "It will rain anyway, we can't stop it. I expected something like this to happen."

"Well now you can relax," Miranda said. "It's going to happen."

Charlene rapped the table. "Troops ! This panic won't get us anywhere. I've been following the weather reports and there's a good chance this storm system will blow over before it gets here. Even if we do get some rain tonight, chances are good the route will dry up and be fresh and fresh and green for the run on Saturday."

Ali raised her eyebrows at Miranda. Charlene must be worried, to resort to such soupy sentiments.

Another rap on the table. "Reports." Charlene demanded crisply.

Members complied, glancing occasionally out the window at the darkening sky.

Debra Toller had e-mailed in her report, citing that she had another engagement. Joyce read it aloud.

*   *   *

4:00 p.m.

Ali ran from store to store, doing errands. So far the rain had held off but the sky was darkening and a wind had come up, blowing dust swirls in the gutters. Last errand was to pick Nevra up from the sitter. On her way through the village, she noticed Miranda outside the library, looking up at the sky.

She opened the window and called out. "Are you trying to tell the rain to go away? I don't think it will work."

"I'm worried," Miranda said. "but not about the rain. Bobby Jardine hasn't arrived for his final run-through lesson. I just hope he turns up next Tuesday for the examination. The supervisor of the correspondence course at the college has set time aside specifically for giving him the test."

"Can't you call him?"

Miranda shrugged helplessly. "He's been so insistent on the whole thing being a surprise for his parents. I think I'll just have to trust that he'll show up."

"Oh I'm sure he will," Ali soothed. "Maybe he and Rick are working tomorrow, and he's trying to get a good night's sleep."

Miranda nodded doubtfully. "Well you're right about that. He certainly takes that job very seriously. I hope his father is impressed."

* * *

8:00 p.m.

Pete and Ali stood out on the back porch, where the big spruce tree soughed in the gathering breeze. She leaned back into his arms and took a deep breath.

"Don't you love the smell of rain coming? The air seems fresher already."

He felt the same. Had eaten enough dust in Afghanistan to last a lifetime.

"Another school year almost done," Ali said. The milestone always brought her mixed feelings. Most of her students would be moving on to the highschool next year.

"How are young Storms and Copps doing?" Pete asked.

"They've been pretty subdued since the accident. I know it was an awfully foolish thing to do but I hope they get their spirits back. They're good boys at heart."

"It was a tough lesson," Pete agreed.

"Ah well," Ali moved from her comfy position. "The year's not over yet, there's still marking to do."

Pete pointed to Kedi who came lumbering out of the long grass at the yard's edge.

"There's somebody who plans to get in before he gets wet."

Ali frowned. "Much as we like rain, you have to admit this is terrible timing for the Marathon. I do hope it isn't a real monsoon."

* * *

Midnight.

"Where are you going Rick?" Brenda looked up from the TV. She had often worked the night shift at the nursing home and now with her current daytime inactivity, was a night owl still.

"I just want to check on the moving job, Ma. I think the wind might blow off some of the tarps and the stuff might get wet."

"It's pretty late, Rick."

"It'll be O.K., Ma. You should try and sleep."

She subsided fretfully back down on the couch.

Rick left the house, his nerves excited but taut. Now it was here, the night when he would carry out the plan he'd been working out so carefully. If only the rain would hold off for another couple of hours.

The big Samson truck was ready on the lawn, waiting to play its part. It had all worked out perfectly. He just told Gerry that it would be handier to have the truck at his place overnight so he could get an early start to the job. They had done that before. Of course the poor sucker never suspected that the furniture never would be picked up.

He climbed into the cab and cautiously started up the truck. The motor roared like a beast anyway and he was grateful that the nearest house was a mile away. He drove across the lawn and rumbled out onto the road.

There was no moon tonight, and the way was dark ahead of him, other than the occasional lights of a farmhouse every few miles. The farms were large, prosperous operations on this side of the Island and the houses were well set back from the road. It wasn't a bad night for driving. If he actually had been doing the drive to Owen Sound, he wouldn't have minded the trip. He liked being out on the road when everybody else was asleep. He liked being on the way to something, even if it was just a job. Better than staying still.

After fifteen minutes, he was nearing the Jardine place, so started to look for the back lane entrance where Bobby should be waiting for him.

And there he was, flashing a light just like he was told.

Rick stopped and Bobby climbed into the truck, gabbling like a goose with excitement.

"Shut up," Rick hissed, trying to quench the flow.

It was a bumpy ride going up the rutted lane, like driving through a long, black tunnel. The branches of hawthorn and other bushes scratched like claws at the sides of the truck.

"How much farther?" Rick asked.

"We're here," Bobby said with a big grin.

They had come out of the tunnel into a field but it wasn't a heck of a lot lighter. He could make out only a faint gleam of the tractor metal in the headlamps.

"You see," Bobby said excitedly, "There it is, just like I told you."

Rick swung the truck around in a wide half arc and turned off the ignition. His heart was pounding like a jackhammer.

He put out his hand. "Give me the key." It felt warm from Bobby clutching it the whole way. The air was warm too, clingy and moist on his skin. Rain was coming, for sure, dammit.

"Get a move on!" he snapped at Bobby. "We gotta get the ramp down."

That was easy enough, he'd done it many times before on the moving runs.

He'd brought along a couple of reinforced ramps and it took longer than he calculated to get them set up. Now came the hard part. Still, the field was isolated enough, that's what they were counting on. The tractor started up right away, as sweet as you could ask for. Guess that's one of the things you got for your money when you could buy brand new.

But dammit, wouldn't you know. Here came the rain. And no sprinkle, it was coming on fast. He pushed the tractor into gear.

Bobby was standing at the side of the ramp to direct him in. They had lined up a couple of spotlights on the ground and another in the interior of the truck, but the lighting wasn't great. It was a lot harder than he figured to steer the tractor on to the ramp.

The first try, Bobby waved his arms frantically, *More to the right!*

Then it was more to the left.

This was not working out at all the way he'd planned.

But then he hadn't figured on trying to do the stunt in the pouring rain either. And was that thunder? Jeezus.

R *AIN!*
At the Jakes' house, Nevra woke on hearing the thunder. Dragging her blanket, she crossed the hall to get in bed with her parents.

RAIN!
In her apartment in Bonville, Carol woke and lay in an agony of anxiety. Picturing great rivulets of water, pouring across the track. Runners in rain slickers, slipping in mud. Or worse, not even starting out. Just sitting in their cars in the park, staring out at the drenched grass, the soggy, sagging ribbons decorating the finish line.

RAIN!
Charlene stirred, groaned and turned over to go back to sleep. Tomorrow was another day.

RAIN!
Miranda slept deeply as befitted a seventy-five year old woman. But Emily dog whined on hearing the thunder.

RAIN!

Halstead got up and shut the bedroom window. *Great, I need this like a hole in the head.*

RAIN!

The snapper heard the drops quicken on the water surface. She raised her snout. The rain smelled fresh and sweet. The coming morning could be the time at last to carry out her great adventure.

*   *   *

Rick could barely make out Bobby through the steady curtain of rain. Just a sodden dark shape, against the wavering lights.

At each subsequent try, the ground was getting more muddy. He could feel the goop sticking to the treads of the tractor wheels.

The task seemed to be going on for hours. Rick felt a rising panic in his chest, that threatened his breathing. The whole plan was turning into a disaster. He didn't even realize the rain had stopped till Jardine said so. Because of course there was nothing to see, only dark. But at least there was no more torrent on his head, in his eyes.

In fact the rain had only been a fierce, short cloudburst that lasted less than an hour. Still, it had dumped enough water to turn the field into a slippery morass.

Nothing to do though but to keep at it. That was one good thing about the dummy. He didn't know when to give up.

And glory be, they finally did get the tractor into the truck. They hurried to anchor the wheels, then fell exhausted to the floorboards.

"We did it," Rick gasped. "We did it, we've got the sucker."

The sky was faintly lighter. *Damn, it must be about 4 a.m.*

They picked up all the flashlights and raised and secured the ramp. This end of the field looked as if it had been clawed at by some monstrous creature, a dinosaur maybe.

"Sure made a mess of Dad's field," Bobby said.

Like that's what he's gonna worry about, you dummy.

Still, the guy hadn't done badly, Rick acknowledged in a burst of well-being. No way he could have pulled off the job without him.

"You done good, Jardine," he said. "Now let's get going. We've got some driving to do."

Two minutes later, he was cursing, no trace of well-being left. The truck was stuck in the mud.

At first Rick didn't think they were going to be able to make it out of the field. Each time he rocked the truck, the wheels just went in deeper. And it was so much heavier than usual, with the weight of the tractor. The struggle was taking forever, just when timing was crucial if they wanted to get through the village and over the causeway before too many people start to wake up. Never mind the Jardines and other farmers right here along the road.

But Bobby had the idea of putting the pieces of reinforced ramp under the tires so Rick could get a grip. They were rolling at last but no high fives this time. It was now nearly six in the morning.

Rick drove recklessly back along the lane, his door half open. He had to keep pushing water-logged branches from the windshield. One whipped back into his face.

"Ouch, practically lost my friggin' eye !"

Finally though, he saw the gap ahead, marking his exit point. By now, totally frazzled and fed up, he revved the engine and made a burst of speed. The truck lurched forward and sped the forty feet to the road.

Triumphantly, Rick made the turn and kept going.

He was vaguely aware of Jardine swaying and clutching at the dashboard. Rabbiting in his ear. "Hey maybe you should slow down Rick. That tractor is banging around back there."

"Can you just shut up for a minute ! I know what I'm doing."

"Look out !" Jardine yelled then. "There's something on the road."

Rick saw it too, a blurred white shape.

He pulled hard to the right on the steering wheel, but there was still a sickening thump as the object bounced off the side of the vehicle into the ditch.

He ground to a stop and both men sat stunned for a moment.

Rick swore. "What was that?"

"We hit something," Bobby croaked. "I think maybe it was a person."

"Nah, likely just a big old dog or a cow or something like that." Rick shook his head in a kind of amazed wonderment, "Must've killed the thing too, I don't hear no moaning or anything."

"I'm pretty sure it was a person," Bobby said.

"Well you'd better get out and look."

Bobby opened the cab door hesitantly and peered out into the fog.

"Get goin," Rick said. And gave him a shove that dropped Bobby stumbling to the ground.

All was silent on the road save for the soft scrape of Bobby's reluctant steps on the gravel. In a few moments he came back. He looked sick.

"It's a person. An old guy in shorts, he must be one of the runners out practising. He isn't moving, just lying there with his face in the ditch."

"So he had a heart-attack, like that other old guy," Rick said. "Nothing to do with us."

Bobby just looked at him, face a blank.

"Damn !" Rick hit the dashboard with his fist. "Like we needed this. You're just a magnet for bad luck, Jardine. I should never have hooked up with you in the first place."

"I didn't run over the guy," Bobby said. "You're the one who's driving the truck."

"Yeah well you're an accomplice buddy, so don't get any bright ideas about bailing on me now."

He drove on, the mood in the truck cab now distinctly sober.

Bobby looking nervously out the window, broke the tense silence. "Maybe we shouldn't go to the causeway. The cops will likely be waiting for us."

"Nobody will be waiting for us, you dope. Nobody knows anything yet. I'm just the guy driving the moving truck over the causeway, like I have plenty of other times."

The truck gave a clunk from its nether regions, then lurched to one side.

Rick clutched at the steering wheel. "Shoot," he groaned, "Now what?"

*I*t's a busy morning in the swamp. The water has been topped up nicely with the night's rain. Lots of juicy insects are moving in the morning sun. The big snapper and the other turtles see the dark shape in the ditch. Most humans keep on moving, but this one is different. It isn't moving at all.

The creatures watch and are wary.

Eventually though, they decide the shape is harmless. It's time to go looking for breakfast. The snapper isn't going to set out yet though. This may not be the day after all for the big adventure.

A while later, some other humans come running along the road. They stop abruptly, noticing the shoes sticking out of the grassy verge that borders the road. The man-made rubber and leather footwear make a jarring note against the backdrop of softly nodding pink and purple phlox flowers and the slender stems of delicate buttercups.

31

"Finish your cereal, sweetie," Ali said. "You have to get to school and Mommy has to get to work."

Nevra scooped up a last spoonful of granola and banana. "How come grown-ups work all the time?" she asked. "Don't they want to play?"

Ali popped the breakfast bowls into the dishwasher. ""We play lots, sweetie. Now go get your back-pack. You can leave Kedi to his nap."

"How come cats don't work?" Nevra asked, scratching the big fellow's ear.

"Good question," Ali said, and kissed Nevra on her forehead. "You're a smart girl."

She quickly ran through the mental check-list for the day's start. Lunch, water bottle and sun hat packed for Nevra, plus signed permission slip for the field trip to the Bonville water park. The rain had stopped during the night, thank goodness and though the morning air was still moist and heavy, the sky was clearing rapidly.

Her own briefcase held a packed salad and a stack of marked student papers. Only five more work mornings to go, the school year would be over and she would be as free as that master of leisure, Kedi.

Pete came down the stairs, freshly shaved and whistling. He kissed his women.

"We're off," Ali said, "see you at supper."

Nevra was outside, scampering down the back steps when the phone rang.

"Don't answer if it's for me," Ali said. "It will just be someone from the Committee telling me the rain has stopped. As if I can't look out the window."

But Pete had switched the phone on and was listening intently.

"OK. I'm coming in now."

Oh, oh. From the look on his face something serious.

"Another theft?" she asked.

"Worse. An accident out on Island Road 2."

Her hand flew to her mouth. "Who?"

He grabbed his car keys from the hook by the door. "Don't know yet, dispatch just got the call and phoned the Chief. Some early morning runners came upon the victim and called it in."

"Dead?" she asked hesitantly.

"I don't even know that yet, honey. Gotta run. I'm meeting the chief at the station."

Heading out to the trail on an emergency call felt like déjà vu. No need to use the siren this time of day. Shallow puddles from the night's rain steamed in the heating sun. The dust of the past few weeks had been washed off the Island trees and fields, leaving shades of green from forest dark to bright lime.

The chief had given out only terse details.

"A couple of women found the guy. They noticed the shoes sticking out of the bushes onto the road."

"Dead?"

"Seems to be."

"They didn't touch him? Roll him over?"

"No, they just said the man wasn't moving and he looked dead."

Pete winced. "Lucky they had their cell phones with them."

Halstead snorted. "Doesn't everybody nowadays?"

"You have to admit they come in handy sometimes, chief."

Pete slowed at the Benson crossroad turn near the km 8 post. He drew up beside a red Honda, the only car there. Luckily this was a section of the Marathon route where the runners travelled right on the actual road, making easy access for the ambulance.

A woman was slumped on the roadside, she looked ill. Another woman was tending to her, offering a water bottle. She looked up as the officers arrived.

"Oh thank goodness," she said fervently, standing up. "Is there an ambulance coming? I think my friend here is in shock."

Halstead introduced himself as Pete moved quickly across the road.

The chief assured the woman that an ambulance was coming. "What's your name ma'am," he asked. "And your friend."

"Sandra Penn and Ginny Carr," she said, dabbing at her friend's face with a damp kleenex. "I think I know you, we're staying at your wife's Retreat. We're members of Rosie's team."

Halstead hadn't sorted out the individual guests yet and this was hardly the time for welcome greetings. Ms. Penn looked to be in her early forties, chunkily built, but in good shape as a result of her running activities. Her friend seemed about the same age, though not looking at all healthy at this moment.

"We thought we'd get out nice and early for our practise runs," Sandra added ruefully, "to enjoy the country quiet."

She took a breath. She seemed a sensible woman and not unduly overcome.

"Ginny was running on that side and she noticed the colour of his shirt, she thought it was a clump of bright flowers I guess. Then the shoes. I had run on ahead but I heard her cry out, so I stopped. She was pointing into the ditch and her face was white as a sheet. When I pushed the weeds aside a bit, I could see the blue and white marathon shirt … on a man," she added.

"Did you touch him?" Halstead asked. "Could he speak?"

"I work at the admitting desk of a city hospital," she said. "I'm not a nurse but I know enough to check for vital signs, to see if he was alive."

That explained her relative calm, Halstead thought.

"He was face down and there was blood under his head," she went on. "I told Ginny to call 911 right away. Then I came to wait with her over here. I went to check on the man a couple of times but there was no change and I couldn't find a pulse. I didn't try to turn him over."

"Chief," Pete called. "Can you come here a minute?"

Halstead excused himself. "Wrap a sweater around your friend," he told Sandra. Keep her warm."

Pete was crouched in the roadside weeds, looking down at the victim.

A man, as Sandra Penn had said. Face down in the dirt. He wore running sweats, the Marathon blue t-shirt, and sneakers. The matching marathon cap had flown off and lay in the weeds some distance away.

"Look who it is," Pete said grimly.

Without turning the man over they had only a view of his profile but that was enough, coupled with that mane of prematurely silvered hair.

Andy Kovak.

"Damn," Halstead swore. "I was only talking to him a couple of days ago. I knew this Marathon business was going to be bad news."

He knelt down, could see that there was no doubt. Sandra Penn had been right, Andy Kovak had drawn his last breath.

Pete indicated the awkwardly sprawled legs, the arms thrown out in a desperate attempt to break the fall. Stated the obvious.

"He's been hit."

The pro hockey defenseman had been powerfully built but not powerful enough to withstand the force of a rapidly moving ton of vehicle. It had tossed him almost entirely into the ditch.

Halstead stood and scowled at the mute trees.

"And the driver just left him here. Didn't even bother to report hitting him. That might have made a difference, saved his life."

Pete nodded. "The coroner will have to figure that out."

Halstead looked again at the body. "So I guess the poor guy was out on an early practise run, like the ladies."

"His car isn't here," Pete said. "He must have parked it at one of the other posts."

Halstead scanned the road, quiet now save for the cooing of a mourning dove. "There could be other runners along soon. Better get Jory out here to tape off the road and mark a detour."

Pete made the call, also updating Jane with some more details.

Halstead waved across the road, "You ladies alright? The ambulance should be here soon."

Sandra Penn waved back. "We're OK, thanks."

Pete switched the phone off, waiting respectfully. The chief had known Andy Kovak fairly well. This couldn't be easy.

Halstead sighed deeply and turned back to the ditch. "OK, guess we'd better see if we can find any evidence of the moment of impact. But first, here's Chris and the ambulance."

Chris Pelly from the coroner's office, was a boyish looking fellow, and usually cheerful despite the nature of his job. He sobered though, at mention of the name of the victim.

"Andy Kovak, damn."

Halstead led him over to the body. "Nasty," Pelly said, looking down into the ditch. "A nasty end."

He knelt and gently turned Kovak over. The hockey player's face was as badly bruised as it must have been several times during his years of active playing. The blood was from a wound at the back of his head.

Pelly felt carefully along the chest. "There's stuff broken in here too. I'll know better when we get him back to the shop."

Halstead nodded. "Injuries consistent with a hit from a vehicle, though, Chris?"

Pelly rose and beckoned to the attendants.

"Sure looks like it. I never heard of any moose running around this far south."

"Who would do such a thing, leave him lying there like that?"

Pelly sighed. "It takes all kinds, that's for sure. And some of them are real bad news."

`What about the timing?"

"A couple of hours at most. He wouldn't have been running in the dark and if it had happened last night, there'd be rigor."

"Jeezus. It's a wonder no one saw it happen."

"Maybe they did."

The attendants gently moved Kovak onto the stretcher. As Halstead watched the ambulance pull away, Stutke arrived in the other cruiser.

"Shoot!" he said on hearing the news. "My dad and I watched Andy Kovak play in all the playoff games. I remember the year they won the cup."

Halstead set Jory to work, taping off the site.

By now, Sandra had got her friend standing up. "We don't need the ambulance for us, thanks. I'll just get Ginny back to the Retreat and we'll have a restorative glass of wine."

The red Honda was the next to leave.

Halstead joined Pete who was pacing off the site, looking for some evidence of a skid. Whether the driver of the truck had even attempted to slow or stop.

They each took a side of the road, walking carefully along, checking the gravel shoulder and the ditch.

"It was early," Pete called across, "He probably didn't expect to see anyone on the road. Maybe he didn't see Andy at all."

"He would have felt something," Halstead said tersely. "You hit a two hundred pound man, that's different than hitting a ten pound raccoon."

It was Pete who found some flattened down weeds and a broken sapling about twenty feet from where they'd found Kovak.

"The vehicle swerved here," he said.

Halstead winced. "Tossed him that far away, eh? Damn."

"I wonder where the driver was coming from this time of the morning?" Pete asked. "A delivery truck maybe?"

Halstead sighed. "We'll have to start checking. But first I'd better alert the Bonville OPP. Someone has to break the news to Andy's wife."

The air in the barn felt damp, even the straw bales that Bobby was sitting on. He sneezed. Sure could use a cup of hot coffee right now.

"What are we gonna do?" he asked Rick again. Rick had told him not to ask that anymore, but he couldn't help it.

Rick was in a really bad mood, the worst Bobby had seen yet. When they'd first got to the barn, he'd just sat there swearing and hitting the truck dashboard with his fist. Finally, he'd slid out of the seat and gone around to the side of the truck to look at the damage again. Then he'd sworn some more.

When they'd swerved so sharply on the road, the truck had scraped against a sapling and torn the front left tire off the wheel rim. They'd managed to limp back to Turner's Lane and the barn on the dented rim, but could never have got through the village or across the causeway like that. Someone was bound to notice that the vehicle was listing badly to one side.

Bobby thought it was lucky it hadn't been the oil pan or transmission fluid or the cops would have been able to follow the trail. But when he said that to Rick, he just got more mad.

"Yeah we're real lucky, alright, lucky as all get out. All I gotta do now is figure how the hell we're going to get out of here."

Finally Bobby had just fallen asleep, leaving Rick to his misery.

There's not going to be any help from my contact, that's for sure. We meet you on the highway, that's the deal. The rest of the operation is up to you.

And it sure doesn't help to have Jardine asking what are we gonna do, every five minutes.

"The plan is changed," he said, when Bobby woke up. "We've got to hide this truck for a couple of days."

Bobby was still thinking of that cup of coffee. "You mean we're gonna stay here? What are we gonna eat?"

"Is that all you can talk about?" Rick said savagely. "With everything that's going on? My ma packed me some sandwiches and pop, you can have some later. Now we have to get figuring how we can get this friggin' wrecked tire back on right."

Bobby shook his head like a dog shaking off a horsefly. "I keep thinking about that guy we hit. He looked pretty dead."

"What are you, a doctor all of a sudden? The guy was probably just knocked out cold for awhile. Somebody will find him and call an ambulance. The hospital will take care of him, he's likely just bruised up a bit."

He looked disgustedly at the tire, hanging off the rim. "C'mon, I need a hand here."

He'd found a spare, though who knew whether it would fit now on the dented rim. Some luck.

*   *   *

The Toller/Kovak home was on the outskirts of Bonville, a tudor style mansion occupying a sizeable lot on the lake side of the highway.

A woman opened the door to the officers. Not Debra Toller, but there was a resemblance. She didn't react on seeing their uniforms, just quietly asked them in. So, obviously their visit was not a surprise. Someone on the Bonville force had preceded them with the sad news. A few details had had gone out over the radio by now as well, although with no mention of the victim's name as yet.

Halstead introduced himself and Pete.

"I'm Debra's sister, Sandra." the woman said.

Halstead expressed their condolences and apologized for the intrusion.

She led them into a spacious room with a ten foot ceiling, creamy coloured leather furniture, and an almost wall-sized window affording a stunning view of the lake.

"I'd like to talk to Ms. Toller if possible," Halstead said. "I'm afraid I have a few necessary questions."

Sandra nodded. "I'll just go up and let her know." She indicated the chairs. "Please sit, if you'd like."

Halstead and Jakes took seats but rose at the sound of voices.

Debra Toller came briskly into the room and greeted the two officers composedly. She wore slacks and a cocoa coloured silk blouse and moved with an innate poise, even under these devastating circumstances. The years of maintaining poses for hours under hot lighting was serving her well. Still, beneath the classic planes of her photogenic cheekbones, Pete saw shock and sadness. People handled grief differently and at different times.

"You've met my sister Sandra," Debra said, raising her chin. "She's been visiting us." Her voice quavered a fraction, and Sandra took her hand. The sisters sank together down to the couch.

"Must you do this right now?" Sandra asked, near tears herself.

"It's alright," Debra said. "Please, officers go ahead."

Halstead plowed on. It was part of the job, an unhappy part.

Debra Toller confirmed most of what they'd already put together. Yes, Andy had been out for a practise run. He liked to go early.

Yes that was very early, but lately he'd been up since five every morning, he was so excited about the upcoming Marathon run. She gulped then, but continued.

"Usually he just ran in the waterfront park here, but this week he's been running on the actual course."

"What time were you expecting him back?" Halstead asked.

She shrugged her elegant shoulders, said helplessly. "I'm not sure. I wasn't worried though when I hadn't heard from him yet. Andy knows ...... knew so many people. They were always stopping him to talk .... Some mornings he met friends for breakfast....."

She stoppped, overcome.

Sandra put a comforting arm around her sister and frowned angrily at Halstead.

"An officer came by awhile ago. We've barely had time to absorb the news."

Halstead had one more question for now, always awkward to put. "And you were both here last night?"

Sandra nodded, not noting the significance of the question. "I was scheduled to fly out to Vancouver today, but obviously not now."

As they drove off, Halstead looked back at the house,

"The media will be by soon, looking for their story. Andy was well-known and not just around here."

Pete nodded. "At least the woman has her sister to ward off the callers."

"Let's pick up some lunch," Halstead. "It seems a long time since breakfast."

At the donut shop, Pete joined the drive-through line.

"Hope nobody takes our picture," Halstead teased. He knew that Jakes was sensitive to the cliché about policemen and donut shops.

After collecting their coffee and sandwiches, Jakes drove down to the park by the lake. It was another beautiful June day, ducks and ducklings bobbed by the shore and the Bay was dotted with sailboats. Halstead thought of his meeting with Andy Kovaks only a short time ago, when the man was so excited about the success of the upcoming hockey camp.

"Dammit, Andy was one of the good ones. Now some coward runs him down and doesn't stick around to help. Doesn't even bother to call it in to 911, I checked. Probably afraid we could follow up on the phone number."

He balled up his napkin. "It's not right! The driver could at least have reported from somewhere anonymously – a phone booth, a restaurant. But that would call for some compassion or at least brains."

Pete's glance followed a gull as it dove cleanly into the water and came out with some small, small shining fish. "So who did it? Who left him to die – an Islander?"

Halstead shook his head. "I surely hope not. But there are lots of strangers on the Island these days, coming back and forth. Maybe Chris Pelly will come up with some forensic evidence to give some idea of the kind of vehicle."

They had put out an all points bulletin through the OPP to alert all nearby police forces about the incident. There wasn't much to tell yet, other than the identification of the victim. There was also a call for any witnesses to please come forward.

"Not that there are likely to be too many folks out on the road at that hour of the morning."

"More than there usually would be at any rate," Pete pointed out. "There were the two runners who found him."

Halstead picked up the phone. "I'm going to check with the radio station and see when Rusher can put me on again. Got to spread the net as widely as possible."

Pete bagged up his sandwich scraps and left the car. Nevra always made him save some bits to feed the ducks. The sun was warm on his face, he was thinking that they could go for a bicycle ride after supper.

When he returned to the cruiser, the chief was just switching off the phone, a curious look on his face.

"Well, there's a strange thing."

Pete waited.

"Don Rusher never turned up to do his show at the station this morning, apparently for the first time in the eight years he's been hosting it. He's always there for the six a.m. shift but when he didn't show, the station intern had to take over and fill the slot."

"Where is he now?" Pete asked warily. "Has anybody heard from him?".

"He wasn't answering his home phone but he finally called in about nine a.m. and said he had overslept."

"For the first time in eight years."

"Yup."

"You don't think Rusher ....?"

"Is that desperate to win that forfeit bet?"

Halstead made a 'who knows' gesture. "What about that dust-up at the Gala the other night? The rivalry's been getting pretty tense. And now the competition's gone." He snapped his fingers, "Just like that."

He looked frustratedly out at the water, where a couple of gulls had chased away the ducks and were screeching raucously over the last few bits of bread. Competition was pretty fierce in the natural world too.

Pete started the car. "Debra Toller said that Andy was running that stretch of the trail in the mornings, this week. Maybe Rusher knew that too."

Halstead nodded. "See if you can chase him up at home. You can drop me off at the hospital and I'll talk to Chris."

33

Pete sat for a moment in the cruiser, looking up the walk at Don Rusher's house. This was going to be interesting. That was one word for it, anyway.

The house was 'well-appointed' as the realtor ads would likely describe it. Not nearly as grand as the Toller/Kovak home but a still newish-looking, split-level, situated in one of Bonville's mid-priced suburban crescents. Bicycles and portable basketball nets cluttered many of the driveways, though this one looked as if it hadn't been used for a while. But then by all accounts, Rusher's stepson was more focussed on hockey.

Pete hoped fervently that the kid wasn't at home just right now. Or Rusher's wife. From the information he'd got at the radio station, Rusher was usually at home this time of day, having a nap. He got up early most days to do the six to ten a.m. shift.

But then today had been different, remarkably different, according to the staff at the station.

There was no car in the driveway, maybe nobody was home.

But Rusher himself opened the door to Pete's knock. He wore jeans and a plain t-shirt, not the cream and blue Marathon version.

He was bleary-eyed and barefooted, definitely not looking like his sharp-edged radio persona.

He opened the door a bit wider. "Officer Jakes," he said wryly. "Long time, no see."

"I wasn't sure if you were here. I didn't see a car in the driveway."

"At the shop. Needs a new muffler." Rusher yawned. "I took it in this morning after I woke up."

"You've heard the news?"

"About Kovak?" He ran a hand through his short dark hair, making it stand in tufts. "Yeah I heard it. They told me at the station when I called in. Quite a shock. Poor guy."

He stepped back. "Guess you'd better come in," he said ungraciously. "I'll make some coffee."

He led the way to a sunny kitchen and stood there blinking. "First time I've overslept in eight years."

"Faulty alarm clock?" Pete asked.

Rusher poured water into the coffee maker. "Shouldn't be, we just bought the darn thing. Everything's junk nowadays, even all the name brands seem to be rip offs from China. We should have just kept the old one, though that was likely from China too."

Pete thought if that hadn't already been a rant on *Your Turn,* it soon would be.

Rusher pressed buttons, sat down.

"Your wife didn't wake you?" Pete asked.

"Arlene's away for for a couple of days helping our daughter move to Guelph for a summer course. Normally she would have woken me when she got up at least."

"An unfortunate combination of circumstances."

"Not really. The station intern was thrilled to get the chance to sub for me. So thought I might as well take the rest of the day off. Like I said, a first for me."

"You just spent the morning at home then? Anyone to confirm that?"

"There's my stepson, I guess," Rusher said, as the smell of coffee filled the room. "He must have been around but we didn't see each other. I'm usually gone before he wakes up."

He rubbed his neck. "Teens, you know. And he would have just got himself off to school. He wouldn't expect to see me in the morning anyway."

"Wouldn't he have been surprised to see your car in the driveway?"

"I doubt it. Like I said, teens live in their own world. They don't pay much attention to the rest of us."

Rusher sat up then, seemed at last to be waking to the drift of the conversation.

"Why all these questions, Jakes? In fact why are you here?"

"There are a few unresolved issues about Andy Kovak's death. We're just filling in some blanks."

"Unresolved issues? I thought Andy had a heart attack like that Leduc guy."

"That would have been a bit too much of a coincidence don't you think."

Rusher shrugged. "Just bad luck. They were both in the age category. It's hell for all us guys after forty – you'll find that out someday too, Jakes."

He straightened, thoughts of coffee-making suspended for the moment, and said more shrewdly. "You didn't answer *my* question."

"Kovak was the victim of a hit and run." Pete said. "Someone ran him down on the trail this morning."

"No kidding!," Rusher sat down, seemingly absorbing the news. Could be feigned though, Pete thought. A radio announcer was almost an actor.

One of the toughest jobs of being a policeman, he thought, is figuring out if a person is telling the truth. It didn't help that most people were nervous or at least rattled by a police presence, further muddying perceptions.

Rusher looked up, and said sourly, "So that's why you're here. Geez man, what are you driving at? Because of the Marathon rivalry thing that's been going on? Because I said I'll bury you Kovak? That was just hype, man. Publicity for the Marathon."

"You seemed to mean every word the other night at the Gala. You're lucky Andy Kovak didn't press charges."

Rusher reddened. "Yeah well ..."

"We understand that you once had a relationship with Debra Toller."

Rusher shrugged impatiently. "Yeah about a thousand years ago."

"We also heard that you were teed off because Kovak didn't give your stepson as much ice time as some of the other kids."

"You think I ran him over because he didn't give Scott enough ice time?"

"Specifically he kept Scott off the ice when the scouts were here in February. Now Scott has to wait till next year to try to qualify."

Rusher stared. Again, it looked like genuine amazement. Hard to tell.

"Like I said, a few unresolved issues. So if you wouldn't mind telling me your whereabouts early this morning."

"I slept in, woke up and called the station."

"What time was that?"

"A little after eight-thirty. The alarm may not work on my clock but it still tells the time."

The station call could be easily checked. If he'd run Andy Kovak down on the Island at six, that left ample time to get back to Bonville before the call.

"When did you take the car in," Pete asked. "Did you have an appointment?"

"I was at the car wash and noticed that the tailpipe was loose."

"You suddenly decided you needed a car wash?"

Rushton sighed. "No, but after I called the station, I hardly knew what to do with myself. I didn't feel like going back to bed, so I went for a little drive."

He saw Pete's sceptical look. "Truth is, I've got a lot on my mind. Arlene's pretty fed up with me, says I've been letting this

Marathon stuff get to me too much. That's why she's away in fact. Said I have to straighten myself out."

Pete said nothing, waited.

"Anyway, I just drove around for a bit. Got a bagel at the drive-through, then stopped at the car wash, where I noticed the tailpipe was rattling. I figured I might as well take the car into the muffler place. They said they'd try and fit it in and that I could pick it up later. I took a taxi back here."

"You see," he challenged, "no time in there to run over Andy Kovak."

He looked over at Pete. "So what happens next?"

Pete shoved his chair back and got up. "Thanks for the report on your movements. We'll need to have our technicians go over your car. Where's this garage you mentioned?"

Rusher waved a hand, said sullenly. "Do whatever you have to do."

He looked up as a thought struck him. "What's going to happen with the Marathon. It's forty-eight hours away, all the teams are ready. What about Kovak's team? What a mess."

His voice sharpened with anger now and disbelief. "You're not here to arrest me *now* for gods sake. This is all so ridiculous." He looked dazedly around the room, at the familiar objects.

"I've got to make that run. Impound my car, whatever, but let me run in the race. My kids, my team, I can't disappoint them all. What harm can it do – where would I run off to? You can run along beside me if you want."

Two things happened then.

The front door opened and a young voice sounded in the hall.

"Dad – are you home? You won't believe what's happened ….."

Just as the young man entered the kitchen, Pete's cell phone rang.

He excused himself, leaving the two in the kitchen. He didn't envy Rusher the conversation.

It was the chief on the phone.

"Good that you called," Pete said. "Rusher doesn't have much of an explanation about where he was this morning. Says he was asleep but has no verification. Says his wife is away for a bit but if you ask me, the woman has left him. And get this, he took his car to the car wash this morning *and* to the muffler shop....."

Halstead broke in. "Never mind that right now. I think we may have found our runaway vehicle. Samson the Mover just called in to report a stolen truck. His driver is missing too."

The coronor's office was on the same street as the hospital. Like so many city thoroughfares these days, this was a busy four-lane stretch of highway, lined by strip malls and office blocks, with nary a blade of grass or a tree leaf in sight. The chief was waiting outside the building, sitting on a bench in the shade of an awning. As Pete drew up, Halstead stood and put his thumb out in the classic hitchhiker's pose.

"Quite the day we're having," he commented as he slid into the seat. "What did you tell Rusher?"

"His step-son had just come in. I told Rusher we'd get in touch with him later. He kept asking me if he'd still be able to run in the Marathon."

Halstead shook his head. "He's got a real mania about that run."

"Yeah, well it looks as if he's about to lose his wife over it."

"I wouldn't blame the woman."

Pete pulled the cruiser out into traffic. "What did Chris have to say?"

"He confirmed that Andy was hit by a fast-moving vehicle."

"A big vehicle?"

"Looks like," Halstead spoke curtly. "A car would have hit him lower down. Instead, he got smacked from head to pelvis. There was lots of damage but the initial strike probably killed him. At least he didn't take too long dying on the road."

The two men were silent for a long moment, contemplating the lanes of traffic.

"A truck then," Pete said.

Halstead nodded. "A truck."

*   *   *

Gerry must have been keeping an eye out for them because the cruiser had barely come to a crunching stop in the driveway gravel when he strode out to meet them.

His big face was still red with fury. He spared no time for greetings but pointed to the empty laneway. "That's where the truck usually sits."

The spot did seem mockingly empty.

"You let your employee take the truck for the night?" Halstead asked.

Samson nodded. "Nothing strange about that. If the move was out his way, Rick would take the truck to his place to save time in the morning. Never any problem before." He spat, "Now he does this, the little bastard."

Halstead raised a calming hand. "Simmer down, Gerry. Tell us how you found out."

Samson ground the story out. "It was all arranged. Rick was supposed to make a run up to Owen Sound today. The folks who were moving left two days ago in their car with the kids and the dog. They planned to visit some relatives in Toronto on the way for a couple of nights, but had left everything packed and ready to go at the house here."

He looked about to blow again. "I gave that weasel the key to get in. Only the bastard never got there !"

Halstead was patient. "Tell it slow, Gerry. What happened next?"

"I got a call from the family. They wanted to remind Rick that he could pick up the key to the new place from a neighbour, but they couldn't contact him on the phone. They wondered what was going on, if the move had gone alright. So I drove over to the house myself, looked in the windows and saw that nothing had been picked up. I could hardly believe it."

He shook his head vehemently, as if that would help make the point.

"All the crates and boxes were still piled up there in the living room. I just can't figure it out. He won't get far - what the hell does he want with a big, empty truck?"

Pete's glance met Halstead's.

I can think of one good use for a big, empty truck. Such as transporting stolen goods.

"Do the Farrons still live out on Island Road 4?" Halstead asked. "I think I arrested a Farron a few years back, for assault."

"This is his brother," Samson said. "People told me not to hire anybody from that family but stupid me, I thought I'd give the guy a chance."

Pete took out his notebook. "We'll need some details from you about the vehicle."

"You know my truck," Samson said tiredly. "Big, blue, a 26 footer. Your basic mover's truck."

"We'll need dimensions, load capacity, registration number to send out to the OPP on the highway."

Samson nodded. "I've got those details inside."

"Thanks, Gerry. We'll be along in a minute."

"Damn." Halstead swore. "This is one for the books. Clark Bernard will never let me forget this, for sure. I went to that investigation conference in Cobourg and insisted to him there was no way that equipment gang could be sniffing around the Island. Meanwhile this guy has been operating right under our noses. And then he tops it all off by killing Andy Kovak."

"Damn !" he said again, hitting out an innocent sapling.

"The hit and run might not be connected at all," Pete pointed out. "Could be a coincidence. I'm not sure Don Rusher is in the clear. He's been coasting way too near the edge lately."

"A coincidence?" Halstead asked. "I don't think so. Our perp was coming along Road 2 in a helluva hurry, left the scene, didn't even call 911. Those are not the actions of a law abiding citizen. This person was fleeing something and making a dash for the causeway."

"Rusher was hardly law-abiding either," Pete pointed out. "Not if he'd just committed a hit and run murder. He had the opportunity this morning, he knew where Andy was running. He could have planned the whole oversleeping story."

Halstead considered. "O.K. right now though, we'd better go in and get a description of Rick Farron. We know he's a thief at least."

Samson had a picture on the wall of himself and the truck. None of his employee, however. "You can try his mother," he suggested. "Mothers always have pictures."

He asked again, "Why would Farron want to steal a truck? He can hardly take it out for Sunday drives."

Pete explained. "We think your truck is being used to transport stolen goods."

"Damn! Like I needed to hear that."

"Do you know the truck tire size offhand, Mr. Samson? And do you have a picture of the tread?."

"There should be a picture of the tread surface in the catalogue," Samson said. "I think the tire size is thirty-five inches. But why do you need that?"

Pete turned to Halstead who nodded. "There's a possibility the truck was involved in a hit and run accident."

Pete filled the trucker in.

Samson groaned. "What else am I gonna hear?"

"The main question at the moment is where the heck is Rick Farron?"

Samson spat again. "Wherever he is, he's driving $90,000 worth of my truck."

*   *   *

"So it was Rick," Jory said. "Boy do I feel dumb. I knew the guy didn't like cops but I thought he was playing it pretty straight. Working at a job, helping his mother. Now look at the trouble he's in."

Pete had picked up Jory, they were going to check out the house where Farron hadn't shown up. The scene was just as Samson had described. A silent, unoccupied house. It was easy to look in the windows, as all the curtains had been taken down. Were no doubt folded and packed neatly away in a big cardboard crate, marked 'curtains'. And there were the other boxes, packed with kitchen utensils, clothing, toys and all the various paraphenalia of family living.

At least the family's possessions hadn't been left waiting out on the lawn, Pete thought. They would experience some inconvenience, but the stuff would arrive at some point.

Next stop was the Farron household, to question Rick's mother. Jory kept saying, "I should have seen it. I'm the one who knows the guy."

"No point in going over that," Pete said. "We're human, we can't know everything. So fill me in on the family history."

Jory was eager to help. "You know about Rick of course, you booked him for that D.U.I. last summer. He's never forgiven you by the way, or any other officer. I didn't really know Tony his brother. I mean Rick is older than me and Tony was even older, about your age I guess."

Ancient, you mean. Pete tried not to wince.

"I never heard there was a dad around the place, it was always just the three of them. Brenda and the boys. Tony spent more time in Bonville than on the Island. Then he got in that bar fight over there and got sent away. He was lucky the guy didn't die or he'd have been sent away for a lot longer."

"Ouch," Pete said. "Not exactly a great home situation."

He drove around orange pylons marking a parked hydro truck. Two men in fluorescent safety vests were wrestling with a wire high overhead.

"What about the mother?" he asked, "the woman we're going to see."

Jory nodded. "That's Brenda. She worked at the nursing home for a long time. My mom used to visit my grandmother at the home and she said that everybody liked Brenda. But a few months ago, she hurt her back lifting a patient and she hasn't been able to work since."

"That's tough," Pete said.

"I think she must be applying for disability but that can take a long time."

Pete checked the clock on the dashboard. Nearly six p.m., almost twelve hours since the incident.

They had arrived at the Farron house. There was no big blue truck in this driveway either, he noted. He pulled the cruiser off the road. There was someone on the porch watching as he and Jory approached. A woman, about fifty with grey-streaked red hair, holding a lottery card in her hand, one of those scratch and win tickets. She wore jeans and a faded t-shirt that read *Why worry?* She looked worried though, wary at least. Obviously had seen official visitors before.

Pete tipped his hat politely, introducing himself and Jory.

She nodded at Jory. "You're Peg Stutke's lad."

"Yes ma'am."

"Wondering if your son Rick is around," Pete asked.

She shook her head.

"Do you know where we might find him?"

"He's away," she said. "On a moving job. I don't know exactly where but he said he'd be away overnight. You could ask Mr. Samson, his boss."

To believe her or not? Brenda Farron could be genuinely unaware of Rick's change of plans. On the other hand she could just be a good liar.

He looked around, assessing the situation. To the back of the house, there was a small outbuilding, that certainly wouldn't hold anything the size of a moving truck. Still they should search it for stolen items.

"Do you mind if we have a look in there?" he asked.

She shrugged. "I suppose I could wait till you get a warrant but what's the point? You won't find anything but the lawnmower and a bag of grass seed. I'll be inside, if you want me."

Things were pretty much as she had said. No fancy new ATV. And there was no place to hide anything else. Outside, Pete knelt at the tracks on the flattened grass.

"The truck was here last night, at least."

He started over to the house.

Jory looked uncomfortable. "Do we have to search there, too? She's not going to like that."

"Not without a warrant." Pete said. "I don't think we need to anyway. I saw some equipment catalogues on the porch table. Pretty well tells the story."

Brenda Farron watched them drive away, a cat in in her arms, her mouth clamped in a tight line. Pete wondered whether even a lottery win would cheer her up.

Jory slunk down in his seat. "That was rough – she knew my grandma !"

"It will be a whole lot rougher when you have to arrest her son."

"Gee thanks." Jory looked glumly out the window.

"Wait a minute !" he turned abruptly to face Pete. "I'm being dumb again. We forgot to ask Gerry Samson whether Bobby Jardine would have been helping Rick load up the truck this morning."

"Jardine?" Pete asked.

"Bobby Jardine. He helps Rick on the moving jobs."

"That big fellow who hangs around the Grill sometime? Would he go with Farron on a long run to Owen Sound?"

"I don't know. But Rick would need him to load up the stuff." Jory looked worried. "The poor guy, he wouldn't be mixed up in anything like this. Or if he was, he wouldn't know what's going on."

"Better find out," Pete said. "Phone Samson."

Jory made the call. "Gerry says Bobby was definitely hired for the day. And Bobby hasn't called in to find out where Rick is."

He frowned. "But then Bobby wouldn't likely do that. He'd just figure he'd screwed things up somehow, got the date wrong or the wrong time."

"So, if he didn't go with Farron, where would we find him? He might be able to tell us something about Farron's whereabouts or plans."

Jory looked doubtful. "Bobby wanders around a lot. I guess we could ask at his parents' place."

Pete nodded, "We'll pick up the chief on the way."

35

The sun was still high at seven as they drove into the Jardine driveway. Two days from summer solstice, the longest day of the year.

"No, we haven't seen Bobby since supper last night," Marg Jardine said.

"Would it be usual for him to stay away for the night? Pete asked. "Maybe at a friend's place in the village?"

Marg looked doubtful. "Bobby knows lots of people and they know him. But he doesn't have any real buddies."

She brightened. "But maybe he stayed with Rick Farron, the fellow he works with. They might have had a moving job today and wanted to get an early start."

That's for sure.

Aloud, Pete asked. "Does Bobby have a cell phone?"

"No, but you could call Mr. Samson or Rick Farron."

Bert Jardine twitched impatiently. "Why all the fuss? He's likely out fishing this afternoon. He hangs around at the marina and some folks take him along to help. Just as well, he's no help to us here."

"Have you been up the lane yet today?" Pete asked.

"No," Jardine said. "We've been planting over in the west field. Too wet, damn it to cut. That's the farmer's life for sure. You go in hock to the bank to get new equipment, you get the hay all nice and ready for cutting and it has to go and rain. The lad has just gone up to check whether it's dry enough to start tomorrow. Here he comes now."

Tyler Jardine rocketed into the yard, stopping the four wheeler in a swirl of gravel.

"Tyler!" Marg remonstrated. "Be careful, you're like to run us down."

The lad paid no attention, "You should see the field up there, Dad. It's all tore up by something."

Jardine senior was galvanized. "What about my new tractor – any damage?"

"It's gone !"

"What do you mean, gone?"

"The tractor's not there, Dad."

Bert looked bewildered, as if he was the victim of some kind of magic trick.

"What the hell's going on around here lately, Chief?" Bert demanded. "You're the police."

Marg grabbed Tyler's sleeve. "Where's Bobby, Tyler. Have you seen him today?"

Halstead looked at the family. Might as well answer them all at once.

He outlined the situation, and the police suspicions – now almost confirmed – involving Bobby. The three faces looked even more mystified. As the words sank in, Marg registered shock, her husband disbelief, and Pete was pretty sure that Tyler was suppressing a grin.

Marg was the first to speak, fastening on the immediate worry. "But where is our son?"

She clutched at her husband's arm, said pleadingly to Halstead. "You must be wrong. Bobby would never want to do such a thing to us. I'm sure he doesn't understand. It's all that Rick Farron's fault …."

Bert brushed her off impatiently.

"Right now I'm going back to the field. See what damage that oaf has done."

"We'll follow you," Halstead said.

"Come with me in the pick-up. The ruts in the lane are pretty bad. Might take out the bottom of your cruiser. Tyler can follow on the bike."

The deep ruts in the lane were still muddy but drying up fast. That was good news for the marathon organizers at least, Halstead thought. The ride was bumpy as Jardine had warned and as the truck emerged from the treed tunnel of the lane, the sun gilded the windshield almost blinding those in the front seat.

The chewed up swath of earth though, was an ugly mess. Jardine in his sturdy knee-high rubber boots, didn't hesitate but got out immediately. The officers followed, mud or not.

"Damn and double damn !" Jardine swore. His shout startled a flock of crows roosting in the poplars. They rose, complaining into the dusk.

Pete made the obvious observation. "A vehicle was here, all right. A big truck. Looks as if Farron was moving up from ATV thefts to bigger things."

Halstead shook his head, marvelling. "They loaded that tractor right in the truck."

"Must have had some special ramp to support that weight," Pete said. "Farron must have been planning something like this for awhile."

"Wouldn't it have been noisy Bert?" Halstead asked.

"Field's too far from the house," Jardine said sourly. "And there was thunder for awhile too."

Tyler arrived then and walked with his father to inspect the damage to the hay on the rim of the field.

Halstead pictured the scene of the theft. "So they drive here in the dark. From the mess here in the field, looks like they didn't have an easy time of it. Got caught in the rain. When was that, do you figure? I woke up some time after it started."

"Nevra was scared of the thunder and woke us up around two a.m. I don't think it lasted much more than an hour or so."

"Long enough to muddy up this field here, though. Especially under that heavy vehicle. I wonder how long they struggled with trying to load the tractor."

"Till nearly six a.m. unfortunately."

"Just when Andy Kovak is running happily along the road. The rain has stopped, the world is bright and green, the birds are singing. The perfect morning for a run."

Pete finished the picture. "Then we've got Farron, frustrated and way off his schedule, bombing down the lane, and pulling out onto the road. Lousy, lousy timing for Andy."

Halstead shook his head. "And Farron keeps on going, dammit. There's no getting around that."

"Yep," Pete said. "He's in big trouble for sure. And it looks like Bobby Jardine is in trouble right along with him."

Halstead nodded grimly. "The OPP should be picking them up sometime soon. That truck won't be easy to hide."

*　　*　　*

But it seemed that Samson's moving truck and its two passengers had vanished. Or at least the search net hadn't found them by eleven o'clock that night. Halstead was at the station, staying in touch with Clark Bernard. No patrol had reported sighting or stopping a big blue truck loaded with stolen goods. There had been a bit of excitement around nine o'clock near Cornwall, but the suspect truck was carrying a load of live chickens.

Pete brought the chief a sandwich from the Island Grill.

"The Kovak's Krusher's team is still up on the blackboard. Gus says they're going to run in Andy's honour."

Halstead chomped dispiritedly at his sandwich. "Last I heard, Rusher's team will likely be the winner in pledges. I doubt that Don Rusher will feel too good about it now, though."

They'd spent the time piecing the story together, had gone over it many times.

"They had a couple hours start, dammit," Halstead said. "Could get a hundred miles away, even in that rig."

"Any farther though, on the highway and they'll be caught." Pete said. "We had the APB out fast." Descriptions of Farron and Jardine had gone out as well, linking the thefts to the hit and run.

"They might be off the highway, holed up somewhere. Or maybe they've already met up with the gang, been sent to a hide out, some barn or warehouse.

Like the ones we've been hearing about."

"Maybe, but they'll have to do something with that rig sometime and it's hardly inconspicuous."

"They might sell that too," Halstead said with tired humour. "Seems there's a market for everything nowadays."

He yawned. "You'd better go home, Ali will be waiting up and we all have a busy day tomorrow. Have to meet with the Marathon Committee and they'll be in a state. They'll want to know whether they have to cancel the run."

"Oh man - is it up to us?"

"We're the ones conducting an investigation. Jory set up the detour today at least."

They said goodnight. It had been a long, sad, frustrating day.

Right now Halstead needed about eight hours sleep. Or at least a portion thereof.

36

Friday morning dawned dry as a bone. Rick Farron pocketed his smart phone after checking the news.

Wouldn't you know it. I had to go after that tractor in practically the only couple of hours of rain in the whole damn month. Coulda been a nice, clean, easy job instead of being drowned in friggin mud the whole time. Coulda got away without complications. Just my luck there has to be a nutso old marathon runner out on the road at five in the morning. And then he has to croak. The truck probably didn't even hurt the guy much, he just had a heart attack like the other one. They shouldn't even let anybody over thirty enter these runs.

He looked with disgust at Bobby, playing pretend with the controls on the tractor. He'd climbed up into the truck to get at it. Vroom, Vroom.

Must be nice, the guy's so dumb he doesn't even realize the trouble we're in.

He still thinks we're going to drive the friggin' truck off the Island.

That we're going to make big bucks when we sell this stuff and he's gonna impress his dad. Yeah right.

Like he has any idea how we're going to get this truck off the causeway now, with the cops looking for us.

Sure wish I did.

The only good news is that they're still looking for us out there and we're still in here. But then that's the bad news too.

What's the dummy want now?

Bobby Jardine hopped down from the truck and asked plaintively.

"When are we gonna get some food, Rick? I'm real hungy."

The sandwiches and pop that Rick's mom had packed for what was supposed to be an overnight journey, hadn't lasted long. They'd finished the food up yesterday except for a couple of chocolate bars.

For water, there was a carton of bottled water that Rick had laid in on an earlier trip. It was lukewarm of course but would do. "Stop complaining," Rick said. "You had a chocolate bar for breakfast."

"But what about lunch? Are we gonna go soon --then we can go to a store."

"Go back and play with the tractor and forget about your frigging stomach. We're not going anywhere for awhile."

Bobby started back to the truck, then stopped, a worried expression on his round face.

"I had a nightmare last night, Rick."

"So, what am I, your mommy?"

"It was about the guy we hit. He was alive and all covered with blood and he was calling me. It was scary."

"I told you the guy we hit was OK." Rick said. "I read it on my phone. Don't you believe the news?"

Luckily the dummy never listens to it.

At least Jardine had helped to get the rim fixed and the tire back on. A rough job but hopefully it would hold. Now if he'd just stay out of my hair and give me time to think up a plan.

The thing is to stop freaking out. The cops don't know we're here. Just have to stay calm and wait till all the panic dies down. A couple more nights and everything will be back to normal on the causeway. And we can get across with nobody noticing.

*   *   *

The mood in the Committee Room was sombre. Both Mayors had come to the hastily convened meeting, as well as all the members of the Marathon organizing executive. Excepting Debra Toller, of course. Halstead appreciated Charlene Bond's calm, practical-minded presence in the face of this emergency.

It was now some twenty-four hours since Andy Kovak's body had been discovered on the trail. In another twenty-four hours, there would be several hundred runners and spectators arriving at the causeway park on Middle Island. Others had already arrived and were staying in local accommodations, such as Steph's Retreat. All expecting to participate in a well-organized Marathon.

A decision had to be made.

Charlene took the bull by the horns. "Of course the run must go ahead. Imagine the uproar and confusion if we had to send all these people home. Accommodations have been booked, and plans in the works for months."

There were some objections. Understandably. One accident was bad enough and now this tragedy. Predictably, Carol voiced her omen warning again.

Even sunny Joyce seemed daunted. "This is more than an omen," she protested. "Now we're just tempting trouble. How can we guarantee the safety of our participants? Of our volunteers?"

Charlene turned to Halstead. Over to you.

"There are many risks running an event like this," he agreed. Adding pointedly, "I think we all realize that by now. It takes a lot of experience."

So maybe we should scrap any thoughts of doing this ever again !

He looked around the table at the anxious faces, awaiting his verdict.

"However, like you, I don't relish the idea of trying to cancel the Marathon. It would be a whole new logistical nightmare. The perpetrators of the recent incident are well off the Island and tomorrow, the route will be supervised by your volunteers.

Officer Jakes will run and scout out the entire course in the morning, before the Marathon begins. With any luck, there won't be any incidents more serious than some bug bites."

Armed with the approval of the two mayors, Charlene and the 'Yes' supporters prevailed in the resultant vote. The committee members agreed to the necessary rerouting around the site of the incident.

Barry looked harassed. "Of course there won't be any way to change the maps, they're already packed away in the runners' kits."

"We'll send a crew out this afternoon to put up new direction arrows and signs," Charlene said. "Then we'll inform everyone of the change with our opening announcements tomorrow morning."

"Of course the runners don't have to know why," she added hastily. "If necessary we can just say there's been some damage on the trail."

The members settled down to confirming details.

The portable toilets had been delivered to various locations. Joyce and Carol had arrangements in place for efficiently signing in the entrants and supervising pick-up of the runner kits. Another volunteer crew would spend the afternoon setting up the station sites. These would consist of a folding camp chair or two, a table, coolers of ice for the water bottles, first aid kit, cell phone. And an orange plastic flag, to make the station clearly visible.

Charlene clapped her hands briskly, calling for attention. "Time to go about our tasks, crew. We've got a big day ahead of us tomorrow."

"Wow," Joyce said, voicing the thoughts of many, "we've done a lot. Are we really going to pull this caper off?"

They looked a bit dazedly at each other.

Carol popped up from her chair, optimistic at last. "Maybe we should have a group hug!" she proposed excitedly.

"Save that for tomorrow night," Barry said drily. "When we've actually got through it."

After the meeting, Halstead spoke briefly with Officer Miller.

"Whew ! Lucky they didn't get that group hug thing going," Miller said. "I was getting nervous."

Halstead shuddered. "I was thinking I'd have to pull rank."

They talked briefly about the hunt for the truck. There were no new reports from the police patrols regarding its whereabouts.

Miller shook his head. "They must be holed up on some sideroad. There are hundreds of spots, could be anywhere between Cobourg and Montreal."

"They'll have to get out on the highway some time," Halstead said. "If you want to sell stuff, you have to get the goods to the buyer."

Back at the station, he found Jane on the phone. She handed it to him.

"Chris Pelly," she mouthed.

Halstead took the phone into his office, and listened intently for a few minutes. He switched off and turned soberly to Pete.

"That was an interesting call. Chris says the lab analysis shows a paint smear on Andy's shoe is from a recent model SUV. And get this, after a closer look, they feel that he suffered two types of injuries overall. In fact that he was hit *twice,* by two different vehicles, within a relatively short time frame."

Pete winced. "As if it could get any worse. Poor Andy!"

Halstead nodded, thinking the same. "So, going on your theory, you think that paint comes from Rusher's car?"

"Easy enough to find out. I *knew* that guy was hiding something."

He stopped. "So which vehicle hit him first, can Chris tell?"

Halstead spread his hands. "They're still working on it. But he's pretty sure the truck finished him off."

He grimaced. "There are several injuries that would have killed him, take your pick. In any event, the drivers can fight it out in court. They're all guilty in my book. They all left Andy to die."

"What now?" Pete asked.

"We make a trip to Bonville and confiscate Mr. Rusher's souvenir hat. That's as close as that guy's going to get to this marathon."

37

As on the previous visit, Rusher opened the door to his house himself. He took a mock step backwards, raising his arms in a warding off gesture.

"Two officers this time. I guess I've been promoted."

He didn't get a laugh from his audience.

"We'd like to talk to you for a few minutes," Halstead said. "It's kind of personal, so if you'd rather come to the station…"

Rusher dropped his arms, shrugged. "Scott's staying with a friend, so there's no one here but me these days. Come on in."

He led the way into the kitchen. "The living room is a bit of a mess since I've been batching it," he explained.

The kitchen wasn't as tidy as last time either, Pete noticed. The sink was full of dirty mugs and there was an empty pizza box on the table. Rusher tossed it carelessly to the counter.

"Have a seat." He didn't offer coffee. He looked as if he hadn't slept well, and his eyes were bloodshot, though Pete knew he'd managed to do *Your Turn* that morning.

"So what's up?" he said when they were all seated. "Last I heard, you guys haven't caught that truck driver yet who ran down Andy Kovak."

Talk about taking the bull by the horns ! Pete thought. Rusher still had plenty of nerve. Sitting there, bluffing ignorance, when he must know damn well why they'd come.

Halstead nodded. "That's just the story for the public so far. Truth is, there's a bit more to the hit and run incident."

"Really?" Rusher kept his voice steady, but his body had tensed. "Sounds interesting. Or am I just considered a member of the public?"

"Oh I think you can likely tell *us*, all about it," Halstead said. "Seeing as how you were there at the time. Your car was, anyway."

"And how do you figure that?"

Halstead sighed. "You've seen those forensics guys on TV. You should know that no car wash or mechanic's shop can ever get rid of every trace. An autobody shop maybe, but guess you didn't have time for that. There's a couple of paint smears on Andy's shoe that's a match for your SUV model. I'm sure when our technicians go over the car, they'll have no difficulty finding the scratch. Add to that your odd behaviour yesterday morning and the fact that that no one can verify your statements as to how you spent your time, and it makes a pretty damning picture."

He paused. "Care to comment?"

But Rusher had sunk into himself, deflating slightly like a waning balloon. Pete had seen it before with other suspects. The surrender to the inevitable.

When he spoke, his words came out in a hoarse whisper.

"I never got over hating him. I thought I had but it was always lurking there underneath. No matter how well my life was going – meeting and marrying Arlene, bringing up the kids, becoming manager of the station, then part-owner. My show is known by everyone in the city, for God' sake. I've been approached for syndication you know. The big leagues ….."

He broke off. Neither officer spoke.

"I was brought up to be competititive. We were three boys and my father set us against each other all the time. You didn't want to be the loser. When I started dating Debra, I was definitely the winner. My brother's girl friends couldn't hold a candle to her. We were that high school couple that all the kids wanted to be. And she was going to marry me – I was on top of the world."

Then Kovak came to town. And that was that. All over, all gone."

His chuckle was bitter. "Until recently of course. Now another woman tells me she's going to leave me because I've been fighting too much with Kovak. Pretty ironic. Why couldn't the bastard just have lived somewhere else where I didn't have to see or hear about him every goddamn day of the week ....."

He filled in the details gradually on the drive over to the Detention Centre and later when they taped his statement. His voice was now a lifeless monotone, nothing left of the hectoring host of *Your Turn.*

"Of course I didn't oversleep that morning at all. I woke up at five, just as I always do. I have a good work ethic, I can thank my father for that at least. I would never miss a show if I could help it. But then I saw Arlene's e-mail.

She said that she was going to stay in Guelph for awhile. That she was going to stay at her sister's till she found a job and an apartment. She was sorry to send such news in an e-mail but that I couldn't be too surprised. She said she couldn't talk to me in person, that she'd tried but I always got too angry. That she was afraid of me."

He paused to repeat this seemingly unbelievable fact. "She was *afraid* of me. As if I was some kind of monster. That was what I'd become."

"I couldn't just sit there, staring at the computer screen. I had to *do* something. So I thought I'd drive over to the trail where I could run, just to get rid of some of my feelings."

"When I was crossing the causeway I saw another car in front of me. Andy Kovak's, couldn't mistake that old Chevy of his. We were the only ones on the road at that hour. Something in my head just exploded. Here was the guy who'd lost me two women, right in front of me. I dropped back and followed him to the lay-by by the trail. I don't know what was in my head, it just felt like a boiling red cloud in there."

"I gave Andy time to park and get going. I watched him start out. Next thing I knew he was lying on the road in front of my car. I didn't know how it had happened, but I didn't seem surprised. I was going to get out to see how he was – at least I like to think I wanted to do that. But then I heard that truck come barreling down the lane like a train engine. I panicked and left."

"When I heard that the guys in the truck were being blamed for what happened, it just seemed as unreal as everything else. I think with enough time, I would probably have convinced myself that was what really happened."

Silence. The words had stopped.

Halstead switched off the tape and signalled to the waiting guard to take Rusher away.

"A jury might consider Rushton's story a mitigating factor for the others," Pete said. "Why Farron didn't see Andy on the road. He was already down."

Halstead was adamant. "Like I said before, to me, they're all equally guilty. They all left Andy to die. Now I just want to get the other two put away before they do harm to anybody else."

*   *   *

Ali had invited Miranda and Emily over for supper. Miranda brought dessert, freshly-picked strawberries and a squirter container of cream for the fun of it. Later the friends sat enjoying the evening. The fireflies were just coming out, tiny magical lanterns bobbing in the long grass. Nevra darted here and there, chasing them, while Emily followed excitedly, wondering what she was up to. Pete joined the chase too, with a mason jar to try and catch a couple.

Ali was subdued, talking to Miranda. "We began the Marathon project with such high hopes last winter. Everybody's worked so hard. But tonight I can only think of poor Andy and Debra."

Miranda patted her hand, but nodded towards the laughing little girl.

"That's sad, no doubt. Fortunately though, life does have a tendency to go on."

"I can't help but think of Bobby Jardine too. He's in so much trouble ! Do you think the courts will recognize his particular problems?"

Miranda shrugged helplessly. "He's still done wrong. And I hope he knows it. One of the little stories we read was about a person wrestling with her conscience. We talked quite a bit about that."

After their guests had left and Nevra was sound asleep, Ali and Pete lingered in the porch. It was a beautiful night, no clouds, no hint of rain. The moon hung like a hoop earring in the sky.

Ali frowned. "I don't like to think of you out there tomorrow morning, running by yourself. Not after all that's happened."

"That's the best time to run," Pete said. "And I'm not alone. Snapper Turtle Girl will be looking out for me. I think she expects me to come by now. She always ducks back down into the water when I pass."

He grinned. "Besides, this is my last chance to beat Stutke's time."

Five kms up the road at the Retreat, Stephanie Bind made her night check of the premises. It was only ten o'clock but Bud had retired an hour ago and even Livy had gone up to bed. Rosie's Runners were preparing for the early morning start as well and the lights in the cabins had gone out one by one.

Steph looked out at the moonlight on the water. The night was still and undisturbed, save for the occasional soft splashing of a fish rising for insects.

She crossed her fingers. For a peaceful, uneventful morrow.

MARATHON DAY
5:30 a.m.

Bobby Jardine opened his eyes. There was a fluttering in the rafters over his head. A movement of pigeons against the patch of blue sky. Darting swallows too, there were several mud nests in the barn. He could hear the young ones frantically peeping for food.

For a time, he just lay there watching the birds. He didn't feel like getting up at all, which was strange. Usually he liked mornings. He liked to get up, have breakfast, and think about the day ahead. His walk in the village, who he might see, like Gus and the folks at the Grill. What he might do, maybe work for Mr. Samson ….

OK there was the bad spot, move away from there.

Only he couldn't.

He moved his head a little bit, reluctantly looked.

But there was the truck, sitting there like a big blue monster, ruining the morning. Ruining the whole day.

He looked back up at the patch of sky. Is this what jail would be like, he wondered. At least there might be some food in jail. A nice big bowl of chili maybe. And bread and butter to mop it up with.

He'd finished the last chocolate bar yesterday afternoon. Hadn't had anything since, except for some wild strawberries he'd found growing out behind the barn. And that was almost worse than nothing, just left his stomach growling.

Now the long, empty day stretched ahead. While all the rest of the Island folks were going to be having fun at the Marathon, like a great big party. He bet there'd be food at the end too, everybody sitting at the picnic tables in the park. Filling their paper plates with hot dogs and potato salad and pickles and chips and ice cream.

He wished he was in the run, he bet he could have done pretty good. Maybe not as good as Jory Stutke, but pretty good still.

Instead he was stuck here in this old barn with Rick and the truck. No fun at all. Rick said they weren't going anywhere till tomorrow. At least when they finally did get up on the 401, maybe Rick would stop at one of those highway places where they had all the fast food joints. They made a pretty good chili. He could almost taste it now.

*   *   *

5:45 a.m.

"Daddy, wake up." Nevra tugged at the blankets. "It's running day."

6:15 a.m.

Halstead warily opened one eye. Heard only cheerful bird-song. No pattering of rain on the tree leaves. Had he half-hoped for more rain? No, it was going to be a fine day, he could tell already. The morning air was soft, fresh and sweet. A perfect day in June. A fine day for the run.

Steph was still asleep. He rose, might as well get some points for making the coffee. There were stirrings from the guest cottages. One Rosie's Runner was already out doing tai chi on the lawn. Soon they'd all be out, stretching and chattering with excitement. The scene would be repeated all over the Island, now that the big day was finally here.

But first there was coffee.

6:30 a.m.

Jory Stutke woke from a dream about Livy. That kiss in Turner's Lane. But the day awaited ! He leapt up and headed for the shower.

7:45 a.m.

The park by the causeway was a hub of activity, as volunteers were assigned to their tasks. Gus had set up an outside coffee station and left Tammy to manage it.

A crew had set up the speaker's platform the day before and were now erecting the finish line portal. This was a big plastic, blow up archway, ordered specially for the occasion. There was a foot pump to fill it with air and the arch filled up quickly. It fell down a few times though, to the laughter of the people struggling to anchor it. Finally they tied it to a couple of heavy picnic tables.

Ali was worried that Carol would talk of omens again but even she seemed thrilled with the beautiful weather. The day was predicted to continue sunny but with a high of only seventy degrees. Perfect for running.

"I knew all along, everything would work out," she said.

No one commented.

9:00 am.

All the trail volunteers set out for their various tasks. Some were manning the kilometer stations, others were entrusted with the task of assisting the marathon participants with any problems and generally seeing that things ran smoothly.

The ambulance was in attendance, parked by the causeway.

Pete Jakes had already arrived back, reporting on a clean, safe route and had gone home for a shower.

10:00 a.m.

The Marathon participants had started to arrive and the park was rapidly filling up. It made a bright, cheerful scene, all the runners in colourful shorts and the marathon t-shirt and cap. Many families were running together with their children. Others were couples who looked as if they'd come straight out of a feature in runner's magazines, with their own chip timers and waist belts for water bottles.

People excitedly greeted friends and team members, donned their number bibs and warmed up by running on the spot. Ali spotted Andy Kovak's team, who were dedicating their run to respecting his memory. The CKAS radio team was also present, she knew, though of course without their leader.

Even Charlene looked a bit excited as she ascended the decorated stage to make the final pre-race announcements. Like the rest of the organizers and crew, she was wearing the marathon t-shirt and cap. Also a lanyard with a name card identifying a member of the committee, and a special issue whistle, which she blew now for quiet.

"I know you're all raring to go," she assured the crowd, "but we must take a moment to thank the people who have worked tirelessly to make this wonderful event happen. Some of them are here with me now, many others are already out at their stations, waiting to cheer you on. Others have been preparing refreshments for all of you when you're done the run. Let's have a round of applause."

Both Mayors, also clad in shorts, sneakers and caps, raised their arms in victory salutes. It had been decided that they wouldn't give speeches till the end ceremony.

Barry Bram addressed the crowd next, with information of the last-minute change in the course. Making no mention of the real reason why.

"The detour will be well marked, and there will be volunteers to guide you." He pointed to the fluorescent yellow X on his own vest. "They'll be dressed like me."

"The average finish time for the half marathon is about two hours, for the shorter course a bit more than an hour. But please just move at your own pace and enjoy the day. Those walking with children or pushing strollers, please start in the back of the running pack, so as not to get hurt. If marathoners are unable to reach the finish line by 3 p.m., they will be pulled from the run for their own safety, as the course will no longer be supervised.

"There will be well-marked first aid stations and toilets along the route. Also water supplies and energy snacks at the kilometer stations. A special message to friends and family who want to cheer and encourage runners. Please stay well back from the finishing line archway, your entrants will hear you I'm sure."

"A reminder that this is not a race. Everyone is here for some exercise, a good time and to raise money for our district hospital. You are all winners already, in our books."

He finished to a swell of enthusiastic clapping and cheers rose from the audience.

Charlotte returned with some final comments.

"You all have your number bibs by now. There will be ribbons for the top five in each run but all finishers will receive a certificate of participation. Please join us for the picnic at the end of the run. Showers are available at the school. Bring your own towel."

She raised her arms.

"Good luck, drink lots of water, have fun !"

"Please remember we're all winners in this run, the hospital most of all."

11:00 a.m.

The flagholder, a grade two student at the Island school, had the honour of dropping the starting flag – with her father's help. To the supportive shouts from the audience, the runners, walkers, and stroller pushers were away.

39

Rick paced restlessly in the barn. He was sick of the place, this hanging around was really getting on his nerves. And it didn't help that Jardine asked every five minutes when they were going to leave. At least he was busy playing out in the truck for awhile, so Rick could check the news on his phone again. See if the cops were still looking for Samson's truck along the highway.

He skipped past the national headlines, paused briefly to read that the Jays had won their game the night before. They were doing O.K, but it was early in the season. It would be nice to be able to go to a game. Soon, he hoped. He had instructions where to drive the truck, but there was this slight problem, he hadn't been able to get off the friggin island for the last two days.

Finally, the local news from the Bonville station website. Full of the Marathon stuff of course, biggest friggin deal to hit the Island ever.

Then came the item he was waiting for.

"Police are still searching for the suspect vehicle involved in the hit and run fatality that occurred Thursday morning on Middle Island. The vehicle is a large blue moving truck with an Ontario license plate, stolen from local businessman, Gerry Samson. The public are urgently requested to report any information on the truck's whereabouts. Do not approach the vehicle, the driver and passenger are considered dangerous."

Rick sank to a hay bale and switched the phone off with nerveless hands.

Great, now we're dangerous. That practically gives the cops the OK to shoot us This mess just keeps on getting worse. Cop cars will be all over that highway and they won't be giving up. We won't get more than ten miles in the truck.

Wonder what Tony will think of me, when he hears this? Or Ma, with two sons on the wrong side of the law. Can't think about that stuff now though, just got to think about getting out of here.

But how the hell to get off the Island? The causeway will be crawling with cops too, because of the Marathon.

Bobby came into the barn. He just stood there like a big piece of wall, squinting in the dimness.

"Yeah, what do you want?" Rick snarled.

"I been listening to the radio in the truck, cause I wanted some music."

"Yeah, so?"

"I heard the news. You lied to me, you told me that guy we hit was O.K. But his wife was just on the radio and she said he died. We killed him. *You* killed him, you were driving the truck"

Rick shrugged. "I didn't kill anybody. It was an accident."

"Maybe he didn't die right away. We shoulda tried to help him."

"You're the one who went out to check. You left him too."

"You made me," Bobby said sullenly. "You said we had to hurry."

"Yeah, well none of that matters. The cops will be looking for us even harder now. We gotta get outta here and keep on going. Going real far."

"What about my exam? What about my friends?"

"What friends have you got?"

"Like Gus at the Grill." He didn't want to mention Miranda, Rick would likely only make fun of him.

"Better forget them you dope. We're never coming back to the Island. Don't you get it? The cops know we took the tractor, your Dad will know too. Isn't that what you wanted?"

Bobby just stood numbly, absorbing this. "I don't know anymore. You're making it all confused, mixing everything up. Where are we gonna go, where are we gonna live?"

"Maybe you'll understand this, dummy. If you stay here on the Island, the cops will get you and put you in jail. And not just for stealing a truck, now they'll get you for killing a guy too. Got that?"

"So, what do we do now?" Bobby asked dazedly.

Rick looked outside at the truck and scowled. "We'll stick with the plan and make a run for it tomorrow night. The cops won't be expecting that, they don't even know we're here. They still think we're hiding somewhere out there on the highway."

Bobby shook his head. "No."

"What d'ya mean, No? You got a better plan?"

Bobby turned and started to walk out of the barn.

"Where do you think you're going?" Rick asked incredulously.

"I'm not staying here," Bobby said. "I don't want to work with you anymore. You're a bad dude. A real bad dude."

"So? You think I'm bad because I stole stuff, because I hit a guy with the truck. Let me tell you something, buddy. It won't make any difference with the police. To them, you're just as bad. We're *accomplices*, you know what that means. It means if we're caught by the police, we're both guilty and we both go to jail."

"I know what it means. I was wrong, stealing isn't fun, it's just plain mean. I don't want to hurt anybody else. I never meant to hurt anybody except maybe my Dad. And now that doesn't feel good anyway. Maybe I don't care if the police get me. I'm sick of this barn and I'm sick of you. At least in jail I might get a meal once in awhile. I could study there too and write that exam I shoulda wrote."

"Are you crazy? You're even dumber than I thought."

Bobby had left the barn now and was headed for the lane.

Rick followed, hollering. "Where do you think you're going, a-hole?"

Bobby didn't look back. "I'm going to see Jory Stutke. He's a policeman and I'm going to tell him what I did. Don't worry, I won't say nothin about you. I'm no rat. You can do whatever you want."

"It's not that easy, dummy. They know you've been working these jobs with me. They're going to ask you questions. Where the stuff is, where I am, what's the plan? I'm not going to let you do that. I need time to get away."

He grabbed up an old pitchfork and launched a blow across Bobby's back. Bobby staggered briefly, then righted himself and turned with a roar of anger.

Farron blanched but kept feinting with the pitchfork. Bobby grabbed the handle and the rotten wood crumbled into useless fragments. He clipped Rick hard against his head, felling him into the dirt.

"And don't call me dummy anymore. Nobody's going to call me dummy anymore. And I changed my mind. I am gonna tell the police about you, too. I'm gonna tell them you were driving the truck."

Farron wasn't listening. He was out cold.

Bobby drove the ATV down the truck ramp and roared off down the lane.

A part from a pair of bluejays who had finally stopped squawking at her presence, Livy was alone at her station. She'd long ago set up cups and water jug on her table and now sat quietly on her camp chair, under the surrounding dark firs that lined this section of the trail. She thought that she might look like a photograph in an avant garde picture exhibit, especially with the incongruous blue and white portable potty in the background. *Woman in the Woods with toilet.*

No runners had reached this checkpoint yet. The day was getting warm. She poured water over a napkin and dabbed her neck, glad of the ice. Though that wouldn't last much longer. She had lots to think about, chiefly the job she'd recently applied for, and how the interview went. Some of the questions made her think twice. She was fine when talking about the education, skills and strengths required for the job.

But then there was the question asking where she saw herself in five years. What a horrible question ! She hoped there was more spontaneity to life than that.

Nevertheless, you had to come up with something. Even a year ago, she would have answered the question glibly enough. She wanted to travel, expand her horizons, work at something useful and interesting. This job with an international aid agency would offer all those opportunities.

So what was the difference now?

Of course she wouldn't be staying here. The Island was a place you came back to when you'd seen and been everywhere else. Although the place did have its attractions. And like an embodiment of her thought, here he came.

Jory Stutke. Ahead of the pack, by himself. Not another runner in sight.

Looking good, in his running gear and with that big "shucks I'm a country boy" smile of his.

"Can't stop," he waved, pointing to his watch.

"I know," she said, and blew him a kiss.

* * *

Rick woke, groaned, and lay there still stunned in the dirt.

He stared with loathing at the truck. The end of his dreams, his plans.

Self-preservation and the survival instinct started to kick in though. He couldn't stay here, not when Jardine was running like a big crybaby to spill everything to the cops. Painfully, he hauled himself up.

He wobbled as he stood, his head throbbing.

* * *

Once down the lane, Bobby pressed the throttle on the ATV and the machine leaped forward like a hungry beast onto the trail.

At last, he was driving it at last ! What he'd been dreaming about for days.

Only it wasn't as much fun as he thought. The fun was all spoiled.

He should have felt free as a bird. But he wasn't, he wasn't free at all.

Boy he'd really screwed up this time. And he couldn't blame it all on Rick.

It was like that story he'd read with Miranda about the inside voice that told you about what was right and what was wrong. The voice he hadn't listened to.

Well, he was listening to it now.

He slowed, there was someone up ahead. Looked like Mrs. Jakes, Miranda's friend.

*   *   *

The relay runs had been going well. Ali was stationed at the turning post but was in touch by phone with parent volunteers at all the key relay handover points. Reports were that both teams would soon be coming into sight. Tiffany's *Island Contenders* were running ahead of Trevor's *Victory Laps.*

Tiffany, hovering anxiously beside Ali, had her own phone glued to her ear.

Here came the runners now. Penny Colman, running with the baton in hand, the *Victory Lap* boy about twenty feet behind.

"Come on Penny !" Tiffany urged, her own hand outstretched and ready to grab for the baton.

Just then disaster ! Penny tripped and went sprawling on the track, the precious baton spiralling away. Tiffany reacted first, darting to catch the stick, while Ali ran to help the girl. Penny lay moaning on the track. She was sitting up, but clutching her leg.

"Penny !" Ali knelt beside her. "Are you alright?"

"Oh Mrs. Jakes," the girl cried. "I think I broke my ankle."

There was a cry from Tiffany too. "Mrs. Jakes – here comes the *Victory Lap.* I've got to get going !"

Ali looked at the two young, distressed faces.

"Go !" she said to Tiffany. "Good luck."

She turned her attention back to Penny. "Let's see if you can get up."

But the girl whimpered, as soon as she tried to put some weight on her foot. Ali sighed. She supposed it had been too much to hope for, that the day would go off without a hitch.

"We'll call your mother."

The Colmans came, made clucking sounds over their daughter and carried her off to their car. Alone again at her station, Ali helped herself to a bottle of water, then looked up at the sound of a vehicle coming along the trail.

An ATV. She frowned. No motorized taffic was permitted on Marathon Day. Too much of a hazard. She stepped out to warn the rider away – no helmet either, another infraction -- then recognized him.

"Bobby !"

He stopped the machine.

Her first reaction was to smile – she was glad to see him. Then she remembered all that had happened.

"Bobby, where have you been ! Everybody's looking for you. Your parents, Miranda ….. *the police,*" she stopped, confused.

She waited for him to say something. She saw now that he was unshaven, that his jeans and shirt were mud-stained. He seemed overwhelmed at seeing her.

"I feel bad about Miranda," he said finally. "Did she get in trouble for me?"

Ali nodded. "A little."

She looked at the ATV. "Where are you going?"

"I'm gonna talk to the police. Tell them about the stealing and stuff."

She nodded calmly. "That's a good idea Bobby. A really good idea. Where is your friend Rick now?"

"He's not my friend. He's a bad dude. I hit him."

Ali took out her phone. "I'm going to call Chief Halstead and tell him we're coming in. Then he can meet us in the village."

Bobby drew back. "I'm not so sure anymore. I don't want to go to jail. Will I go to jail?"

She couldn't lie to him. "You'll go to jail for sure if you run away. But if you talk to the chief, he could help you."

He thought about this. She could see the doubt and fear mounting.

"I'll go with you. Would that be OK?"

She hopped on the seat behind him before he could object.

41

Charlene looked at her watch. She and other members of the Marathon Committee were waiting at the finish line. Some of the 10 km runners would be starting to come in soon.

"Here comes somebody now," Carol said excitedly. She jumped up from her camp chair and ran over to the finish line. Barry joined her on the other side of the arch, stopwatch at the ready.

"It's Jory Stutke," he said. "Will you look at that. He's even beaten the runners on the shorter route."

And indeed he had, there was no one in sight behind him. Stutke had a clear field. As he made his final sprint into the park, he raised his arms in a victory salute. The waiting crowd broke into a cheer. Jory dashed through the arch as Carol dropped the flag and Barry stopped the watch. Then, though bent almost double to get his breath, he turned to Barry with the all-important question.

Barry smiled and held up the watch. "1:32:06. Congratulations! That's close to Olympic timing."

"Hot damn!" Jory whooped. Pete Jakes had been clocked this morning at 1:38:03. He did a little dance around Carol. She made a face, "You'd better have a shower."

This was a rudimentary arrangement, basically the park garden hoses. Jory simply held the sprayer over his head and played the water over his neck and shoulders. He took a drink too.

Then he joined the others at the arch. "I want to see Miller come in. See his face when he sees I'm already here."

"Here comes somebody else," Carol said.

But as the runner came closer, they saw that it was Corrine, the gym teacher. They cheered her on. She was grinning as she passed through the arch with a time of 1:48:02 and did a big high five with Jory.

Miller was next, with a time of 1:51:06. and a satisfactory grimace when he'd seen Jory and Corrine waiting at the arch.

"Not bad for an old feller," Jory said charitably.

Others would be trickling in over the next couple of hours. Jory's moment of triumph was done for now though and it was time to get back in uniform. At least he'd get to crow to Jakes.

He could hardly believe the crowd when he arrived at the causeway. Spectators were pouring into the park, adding to the throng of relatives and friends of the runners. He'd never seen so much activity on the Island. A harried looking man wearing shorts and a safety vest, stood by a yellow sawhorse traffic barrier. He looked up in relief at seeing Jory.

"It's crazy here – I don't know where all these folks think they're going to park."

"Where's Pete Jakes?" Jory asked.

The man looked around distractedly. "I saw him a couple of minutes ago."

Jory found his fellow officer directing a group of a half-dozen volunteers in an attempt to organize parking.

"Hey Stutke," Pete said. "It's good to see you ready to do some work. Give us a hand over here."

Jory picked up the other end of a barrier.

"So go on," Pete said. "What was your time. I know you're busting to tell me."

Jory shrugged. "It was pretty good."

Pete waited.

"1:32:06."

Pete nodded ruefully. "Pretty damn good, you mean. Congratulations, I should have put some money on it." They lifted the barrier into place. "How were things out on the trail?"

"It was good. Folks looked happy."

"I talked to Ali a little while ago. The kids were doing fine on the relay run."

"Where's the chief?"

"Having lunch at the Grill. Wish I was there too, it's getting pretty hot out here."

Jory stood up and wiped his brow. He wouldn't mind another swipe with that hose right now.

He tensed suddenly. "Jakes, what the heck is that?"

*   *   *

Rick Farron hung on desperately to the truck steering wheel. His head was aching as if a pile driver was banging in there. His vision was blurred, the scene confusing.

Holy crap, where did all these people come from?

And all these cars! Can't even find the road.

Why does my head feel like this?

Why is the truck shimmying? Can't control the thing!

*   *   *

Pete looked up. People were scattering frenziedly off the road, there were outraged shouts. A big truck, seemingly out of control, was wobbling crazily and careering toward the newly-erected barriers at the side of the causeway.

He couldn't see the driver's face, only a pale oval shape through the windshield. He flashed a look to Jory and the two of them stepped out from opposite sides of the roadway, holding up their hands. STOP.

The truck veered widely to the left, Pete only barely managed to leap out of the way. It careered off the road completely then and struck the big lamp post at the entrance to the causeway. Had stopped this time, for sure.

Pete and Jory ran up to the truck. Somehow the chief had appeared too, with another officer behind him.

"That's Gerry Samson's truck !"

Pete was the first to look in through the shattered windshield. The door on the driver's side had sustained a terrific dent and wouldn't open.

"It's Rick Farron," he called back to the others.

"How is he?" Halstead asked.

Farron hadn't been wearing a seatbelt, and the force of the crash had slammed him against the window. There was blood running down his face.

"Farron !" Pete called through the open driver's window. "Can you hear me?"

The man shifted slightly in the seat. He moved his hand up to his face and groaned.

"He's dazed but conscious," Pete called back to the others. "Likely in shock."

"Here's the ambulance people," somebody said.

"Move out please," the paramedics said. "Coming through."

Pete helped to pull Farron across the truck seat to the passenger door. He moaned as they lifted him onto the stretcher.

"Wait a minute," Halstead halted the medics. "Ask him where Jardine is," he told Pete.

Pete leaned down, "Where's Jardine, Rick? Where's Bobby?"

"Up the trail," Farron managed to say. "Took the ATV."

"Where on the trail?" Pete pressed.

But Farron had passed out.

"That's enough," the medic said. "We've got an injured man here."

They watched the little procession move towards the ambulance. There were other watchers too, by-standers with shocked faces. Halstead spotted Charlene in the group and signalled to her.

"I hope the diversion is over and we can go on with our run," she said brusquely. "Luckily it all happened quickly and the incoming runners had no idea what was going on. Barry and Carol kept on taking times, right on through."

Lucky indeed that none of the watchers had been hit.

"I'll just make an announcement that there's been a traffic mishap," she added. "Keep it simple."

Halsted nodded. That was simple alright. "Add too, that no one will be able to leave over the causeway for a bit."

Charlene headed purposefully back to the park.

"That woman could organize world war III and not be fazed," Halstead said.

He turned to matters at hand. "We'd better go after Jardine. He's not too bright and he'll be desperate."

Pete shook his head. "Where do you think he's headed?"

"That machine can go on any terrain," Jory said. "He could go up any number of lanes or tracks. We might better use ATV's ourselves to find him."

He sounded excited at the prospect.

Halstead looked around frustratedly. "We've got to get this darn marathon over with first. There's still runners all over the trails and crossroads."

He checked his watch. "How much longer?"

"Another hour anyway," Pete said.

Halstead nodded. "So we wait. If we go now, we're just going to alarm a lot of people."

Belatedly, he noticed a message on his phone. Must have come while he was busy with the numerous calls of the chaotic past half-hour.

He listened, then gestured to Jakes and Stutke.

"It's a message from Jane. Ali called the station a few moments ago. Said that Bobby Jardine is coming into the village on an ATV and it sounded as if she was coming with him."

"Coming with him?" Pete frowned. "Is that safe? You just said that Jardine is desperate."

He turned to Jory. "You know the guy, what do you think? Can he handle this situation or is he likely to drive himself and Ali away somewhere. Or maybe even into a tree to end it all?"

"He'll be OK," Jory said. "Bobby wouldn't hurt anybody. Not usually anyway," he added less certainly.

Pete took out his own phone and dialled. But Ali wasn't answering.

"Where were they when she called?" he asked Halstead.

"Coming up on Km 4."

"I'm driving up there," Pete ran for the car, Jory following.

"I'm coming too."

Ali hung on tightly to Bobby's waist. The ATV was bouncing over the rough track. At every bounce she felt she was about to be thrown off. The thought occurred to her that her decision might have been a little rash. Or maybe just downright crazy. She really didn't know Bobby Jardine well at all. Then abruptly, the vehicle stopped outright ....

* * *

Pete pounded along the trail, vaguely aware of Stutke somewhere behind. He didn't even remember whether he'd shut the car doors.

They passed some startled runners, who scurried hastily to the sides of the track.

He ran faster, imagining the scene ahead, the overturned vehicle, wheels spinning in the gravel. Ali .....

He was passing the Km 3 post, when he came upon the ATV just ahead.

Not overturned, but stopped. With no riders.

Desperately Pete rounded a curve in the track and suddenly, there they were.

"Ali !" he called.

She turned in surprise.

She was fine, unharmed. They'd run out of gas.

"You beat me," Jory gasped as he came up.

"Sheer adrenalin," Pete said. "Just sheer adrenalin."

Stutke and Bobby Jardine headed for the cruiser. Jory had a tight hold of the big man's arm but Bobby went peacefully, offering no resistance. He'd paid no attention to the ATV, just looked sorrowfully back at Ali.

"I guess you have to take him in," she said to Pete.

He kissed her forehead. "Only you would say that like it was a bad thing, my sweet. After the guy was an accomplice in several robberies – in one case his own parents – and was party to a hit and run."

She sighed. "He was coming in voluntarily, he was going to tell the Chief everything."

"That's something in his favour," Pete agreed. "But a very little something, considering all the charges there will be against him and Farron. It will all be up to the courts now, honey."

She looked over at the ATV, now silent and stranded uselessly on the track. "I could kick the darn thing, all the grief it's caused. All for nothing."

"It's not the machine that caused the trouble. It's people wanting it."

He looked around, "Are you OK here for a bit? I'll send Jory back for you."

"I'm fine." she said. "There are still runners coming along. I won't be alone."

"Sure?" he asked doubtfully. "It's been quite a day."

"I'm sure. I think I'll just walk though. I could use some thinking time." She smiled, "I could use a comb too, I feel pretty windblown."

He kissed her again. "It suits you."

The ride to the village was silent. Bobby, handcuffed and slumped behind the wire mesh barrier of the back seat, his gaze cast down, seemed almost catatonic, unreachable.

On reaching the village, Jory looked over at Pete. *Where to?*

Pete had already contacted Halstead.

"The detention centre," he said. "We'll get Bobby checked in there."

A towing vehicle was in the last stages of winching Samson's truck off the shoulder of the causeway. Bobby roused then. He groaned at the sight and slunk further down in the seat, holding his cuffed hands before his face. He didn't ask what had happened to Rick.

*   *   *

Despite all the activity going on around them, Charlene and the others had managed to keep some order in concluding the run. The causeway action had been a little to one side of the Marathon route, though hard to ignore. There had been sirens, the sickening thud of the truck going into the pole, police racing to the scene.

However, though intense and dramatic, the events had all actually happened within about a half hour. Most of the incoming runners were so intent on reaching the finish line that they didn't even notice the disruption. They were full of excited chatter about the run and how it went, as friends and family carried them off for the celebratory picnic.

The chief difficulty was going to happen when people wanted to leave. There were still flashing orange lights and police tape across the road.

"We'll cope," Charlene said. "The tow truck has already come and gone and I'm sure the police will clear a lane pretty soon."

They left some volunteers to keep watch for the stragglers who were still coming in, while she and Barry prepared for the award presentations and the closing ceremony.

It was a jubilant crowd that greeted the announcement that though the final tally wasn't yet in, it seemed their combined efforts had actually raised more than the goal for the hospital equipment fund. A representative from the hospital presented Mayors Sheehey and Byers with an embossed thank-you plaque for their respective communities.

Gradually people packed up and drove away, leaving an exhausted crew of volunteers.

"There's still some sandwiches and lemonade left," Carol said brightly.

Charlene groaned. "To heck with lemonade, where do you find a real drink on this Island?"

43

Halstead switched off the telephone. He'd been talking to Clark Bernard in Cobourg. Pete had heard some of the conversation but Halstead did a recap anyway.

"Clark's pretty pleased. The names and information that we got from Rick Farron are some good leads."

"Not arrests?"

"Not yet. They'd rather go slow and get some of the big guys too."

That made sense. Pete bet there'd be some undercover work going on too.

Yesterday, Farron had been totally subdued in his hospital bed. He looked thin and exhausted in the blue gown, a bandage wound tight around the wound on his forehead and his right arm in a cast. Soon he would be transferred to the detention centre to await his hearing.

There had been a lawyer present, but Farron didn't object to the questioning about the thefts. He answered Halstead's questions coherently, if despondently. He had no surnames for his contacts and even the first names were likely phony. But he provided good physical descriptions of the two men he'd met, plus the planned meeting place on the outskirts of Montreal, and what they would be driving.

He didn't even ask whether the information would affect his sentencing, though the lawyer made the point it had been given voluntarily. Farron grew defensive though, when Halstead brought the conversation around to the night of the hit and run.

"It was an accident," he kept insisting. "It was dark, what was the guy doing out on the road in the middle of the night?"

"Yet you didn't stop, or call for help."

There was no answer to that.

"So, it's all good on our end?" Pete said now. "The Marathon was a great success, the hospital got a whack of money, the thieves are caught and the equipment returned to the rightful owners."

Halstead sighed. "This part rarely feels good."

Pete knew what he meant.

Andy Kovak dead and two Island lads off to jail. Not so good at all.

*   *   *

The volunteers had certainly done a terrific clean-up job in the park. A maintenance crew had even already repaired the pole that had been damaged in Rick Farron's desperate dash to escape.

"It's as if it never happened," Livy said, "The Marathon, the crowds, the picnic."

And indeed the park was quiet once again, a cool green space, where the tree leaves rustled softly in a gentle breeze from the Bay. Just a lovely Island summer morning.

"It happened all right," Jory laughed. "I've got my Marathon ribbon to prove it. Mom has already put it in her scrapbook."

"Tomorrow the world," she teased. "I see endorsement contracts for sneakers and sports gear."

"Yep, they'll be rolling in." He leaned back on the bench, his hand resting lightly on her bare shoulder. "I noticed the Storms and

Owen boys in the clean-up crew. Starting their community service for the summer."

"I hope they learned their lesson," she said. "And that their parents won't be visiting them in jail some day. Not like poor Brenda Farron, now she's got two sons there."

Jory nodded. "My Dad and I will be going to help her with the outside chores."

"That's nice of you."

He shrugged. "Neighbours."

He shook his head. "I can't believe they were stowing the stuff in that old barn on Turner's Lane. If we'd walked just a bit farther that day ....."

She blushed. "We were otherwise occupied."

He grinned and moved to repeat the experience but she turned and the kiss just landed on her soft cheek. She looked pensively over the park, where two grey squirrels gambolled around a tree truck.

"July is just beginning," she said. "But in a strange way, I feel as if summer is already over."

He winced. "Guess that means you're going to take that job in Ottawa?"

"They've offered me the position." Her face lit up, "It's an interesting job."

He knew how she felt, he'd had the same excitement after he'd resolved not to be a farmer.

"I could come home on weekends, some times." she finished up.

They'd be in the same country at least. He should be glad for that. And there was nothing to stop him from travelling up to Ottawa for the occasional weekend either.

This time his kiss found its proper designation.

Eventually though, they returned to their respective vehicles. Jory had a Monday run out to the various marinas to check boating reports and Livy was replenishing supplies for the Retreat.

"I saw Samson's moving truck was in at Byer's garage for repairs," Jory said. "I guess he'll be looking for some new helpers."

Livy looked sad. "Poor Bobby Jardine, he loved that job. But what's going to happen to him now?""

*   *   *

It was a refrain heard throughout the Island. "What's going to happen to Bobby Jardine?"

At the Island Grill, Gus had washed off the blackboard and replaced the marathon stats with the Daily Specials. *Tomato Rice Soup and Meatloaf.*

The weekend crowds had receded but there was still a brisk trade in the diner and the summer influx was just beginning. Gary Plug once again held court.

"I heard Bert Jardine hasn't even been over to see him. He just said good riddance to bad rubbish."

"It doesn't look good for the fellow, that's for darn sure."

Something new to bet on. How many years the thieves would get.

*   *   *

Jane Carell burst angrily into the station, tossed the mail onto the front counter and carried straight on in to Halstead's office door.

"Honestly, some folks never have a good word to say about anybody. To hear them tell it, Marg Jardine is at fault for not teaching her son about right and wrong. Poor Marg, after she's always done her best for that boy !"

Halstead put down his pen. "Have you looked at Bobby Jardine, lately? He's no boy Jane, he's nearly thirty."

She ruefully acknowledged this, but added. "He's a good fellow though, chief. And he did try to help at the last minute. He was going to turn himself in."

"That may be a point in his favour. I don't know if it will help much though."

"What do you think the sentences will be?"

He shook his head. "The thefts are one thing. But the hit and run? Could be penetentiary time."

She knew what that meant. If the sentence was more than two years, a prisoner was sent away from the Detention Centre to the provincial lock-up.

"What about Bobby's …. intellectual challenges, I guess you'd say. Isn't there some consideration given for that?"

"Nobody forced him to participate in the thefts. He certainly showed lack of judgement, and that he was easily led into crime. But he said himself he was trying to get back at Bert."

"And no wonder," she defended. "The way that Bert treated him over the years. Maybe Bert should be charged."

"You've got a point there. Lousy parents should be held accountable and have to share the blame. Brenda Farron has always been a hard-working woman. If she'd had some help from the boys' father, they might not have turned out so badly."

*   *   *

"You're quiet," Ali commented.

Miranda had barely said a word the whole trip over to Bonville.

"I'm trying to think what to say to Bobby. I'm supposed to be supportive but I'd really like to box his ears."

"That's such a neat expression," Ali laughed. "But what does it actually mean?"

"A smart slap on both sides of the head."

"Ouch !"

Still, she thought, Bobby would have preferred that to whatever punishment he was likely to get. It wasn't even clear yet whether there would be a chance for bail. People said his father would never pay bail but that his friends would raise the money.

Ali drove into the parking lot. Beside her, Miranda drew in a sharp breath at sight of the Detention Centre, the cluster of bleak concrete buildings, the chain-link fence, topped with strands of barbed wire.

"What a dreadful place ! Hardly an encouragement for rehabilitation."

"I'm not sure that's the main purpose," Ali said wryly.

The plan was for Ali to leave Miranda for an hour.

She asked a bit anxiously, "Are you going to be alright? Wouldn't you like me to come in with you at least, just to see you get sent to the right place."

"I'll be fine, thank you. Don't fuss. I'm expected, you know. The authorities said that I could talk to Bobby about continuing his studies."

"Here at the Detention Centre? You mean you would come here regularly?"

"Whatever is necessary."

Purse and briefcase in hand, back straight, Miranda left the car. At the entranceway to the building she stopped to speak to a woman who seemed to be hesitating about going in.

"You must be Brenda Farron.," Miranda said. "I think you knew my friend Alma Court. She was a resident at the Maple Lane nursing home a few years ago. She always spoke very highly of you."

The two women went into the building together.

* * *

Island Marathon raises $50,000 plus for Hospital Scanner
(The Record)

"So?" Steph asked. "Ready to do this all again next year? You could get in training now."

"Bite your tongue," Halstead growled. "Not funny."

"Charlene will be pleased with the story," Steph said. The photo showed the hospital director receiving a cheque from a smiling Charlene and Barry.

She put the newspaper back down among the breakfast things on the table. "Even you have to admit that was a pretty impressive amount we raised."

He reached for the marmalade. "It was a $50,000 headache, I'm glad it's over."

She laughed and patted his had. "Poor Bud !"

He looked warily out towards the guest cabins. "When are those romance writers coming in today? Have I got time to get out to the boat?"

She smiled conspiratorally. "They're delayed, not coming till tomorrow. I thought if you could use a mate on the *Loon* today, I could come with you."

He pretended to consider. Finally grudged. "That could be nice."

She grinned. "I've already packed the lunch."

*   *   *

On the other side of the Island, a canoe bobbed lazily along the shore.

Ali stayed her paddle and trailed her fingers in the cool, clear water. Powder puff clouds gambolled in a perfect July sky.

"I wonder if azure is a Turkish word," she mused.

"Of course it is," Pete said. "And there's no Google out here on the water to prove us wrong."

No phones, no television, nothing but their own voices.

Pete wasn't really paddling much either. They were only round the bend from Ralph and Edna Peterson's dock, where they had rented a cottage for the weekend. Just the two of them, this trip. Nevra was staying with her school friend.

Edna sold eggs, bacon and canned beans in the Marina shop, and they'd packed a box of fancy chocolates with their pyjamas. So that took care of the luxury dinner whenever they got back.

It was quite funny really. After all Ali's research into exotic anniversary plans, they had ended up on the other side of the Island from home. Actually, they were going to take a trip in the fall. Maybe. But for now, this peaceful time together at the shore, seemed all the bliss needed.

It was a bit tricky pouring wine even in a slow moving canoe, but they were working on it. A startled kingfisher darted into the safety of the low-slung willow branches. Nearby, a prettily marked turtle sat sunning on a warm rock.

'They're supposed to bring luck," Pete said.

"Really? In Turkey we have charms against the evil eye. But I guess this is some ancient Canadian lore."

"It's Pete Jakes lore," he grinned. "Newly minted for our occasion."

The turtle hadn't moved. Ali looked into its wise and knowledgeable eyes.

"To luck," she said. "And love."

Epilogue

The big female snapper is content. She's completed her task, for this year anyway.

She's laid her eggs.

Now with her great effort accomplished, she can sink back into the soothing green waters of the swamp.

The pounding footsteps on the trail have ceased, the frogs are back on the lilypads, the dragonflies stitch a fresh pattern in the summer air.

All's right with the world once more.

Printed in the United States
By Bookmasters